The Girl in the Ragged Shawl

Cathy Sharp is happily married and lives with her husband in a small Cambridgeshire village. They like visiting Spain together and enjoy the benefits of sunshine and pleasant walks, while at home they love their garden and visiting the Norfolk seaside.

Cathy loves writing because it gives pleasure to others, she finds writing an extension of herself and it gives her great satisfaction. Cathy says, 'There is nothing like seeing your book in print, because so much loving care has been given to bringing that book into being.'

D0958823

Also by Cathy Sharp

The Orphans of Halfpenny Street
The Little Runaways
Christmas for the Halfpenny Orphans
The Boy with the Latch Key
An Orphan's Courage

The Girl in the Ragged Shawl

CATHY SHARP

HarperCollins*Publishers*

This novel is entirely a work of fiction.
The names, characters and incidents portrayed in it are
the work of the author's imagination. Any resemblance to
actual persons, living or dead, events or localities is
entirely coincidental.

HarperCollins*Publishers*
The News Building,
1 London Bridge Street,
London SE1 9GF

A Paperback Original 2018
1

www.harpercollins.co.uk

Copyright © HarperCollins*Publishers* 2018

Cathy Sharp asserts the moral right to
be identified as the author of this work

A catalogue record for this book
is available from the British Library

ISBN: 978-0-00-828665-1

Set in Sabon LT Std 11.5/14.5 pt by
Palimpsest Book Production Limited, Falkirk, Stirlingshire

Printed and bound in Great Britain by
Printed and bound by CPI Group (UK) Ltd, Croydon CR0 4YY

All rights reserved. No part of this publication may be
reproduced, stored in a retrieval system, or transmitted,
in any form or by any means, electronic, mechanical,
photocopying, recording or otherwise, without the prior
permission of the publishers.

This book is sold subject to the condition that it shall not,
by way of trade or otherwise, be lent, re-sold, hired out or
otherwise circulated without the publisher's prior consent
in any form of binding or cover other than that in which it
is published and without a similar condition including this
condition being imposed on the subsequent purchaser.

MIX
Paper from
responsible sources

FSC **FSC™ C007454**
www.fsc.org

This book is produced from independently certified FSC™ paper
to ensure responsible forest management.

For more information visit: www.harpercollins.co.uk/green

CHAPTER 1

Eliza curled into a ball, crossing her arms over her stomach as the ache became a gnawing pain of hunger and she bit her lip to stop herself moaning. It was three days since she'd eaten anything, and she'd drunk only a few sips of water that Ruth had risked a beating to bring her just after she was shut up in here. Since then no one had come near. She was so cold that her fingers felt numb and her teeth were chattering. She believed she might die, locked in this dark cellar because of the mistress's spite. She'd been beaten and thrown in this terrible place without a blanket or a mattress to lie on, all because she had told Mistress Simpkins that she was a liar.

'You wicked, evil child!' the incensed mistress of the workhouse had yelled at her. 'How dare you say such a thing to me? How dare you speak to your betters in such a tone?'

'You told us a lie.' Eliza had stuck to her guns, despite her fear. 'Tommy Hills died because you beat him for falling over when he was working but he was ill and – and it was your fault, because you withheld his rations,'

1

she ended defiantly, staring proudly at the woman who ran the female side of the workhouse. Tommy was not in Mistress Simpkins' ward, but she'd given him the task of clearing a pile of heavy wood intended for repairs to the roof. He'd suffered with a malady of the lungs and he'd been coughing and gasping for breath when he staggered and fell, dropping an armful of the logs in front of the mistress. In a rage, Joan Simpkins had beaten the lad with the cane she carried at all times, striking him across his shoulders and arms until he'd collapsed into a heap on the ground at her feet.

Eliza had tried to help him and so had Ruth, but they'd been told to go about their business and the mistress had had one of the men carry him to the infirmary, where he'd died in the night. An infection of the lungs, so the mistress had told them, but the inmates all knew who was to blame. Only Eliza was foolish enough to say it out loud and now she was being punished for her audacity.

'You are both disorderly and refractory,' Mistress Simpkins said in a cold voice, 'and you know the punishment for breaking the rules, girl. You will be put on short rations and removed to a place of solitude until you are suitably penitent.'

Eliza had stared at her defiantly, refusing to be cowed by the woman's cruel threats and for that she received several hard blows across her face. She had been seized by the arm and dragged into the dismal punishment room and there she had been stripped by other women and forced to wear the filthy garb of one judged disorderly, after which she had been brought here to this dark place and thrust into it.

'You are disobedient, a wicked evil girl,' the mistress had told her. 'It would serve you right if I just left you there and forgot you.'

She couldn't do that! Ruth had told Eliza that the harsh rules of the workhouse allowed for the punishment she'd just been given, but surely the mistress could not leave her here to die? Yet Mistress Simpkins was a law unto herself. It was lawful for her to hire the inmates out for work because she was allowed to recover the costs of keeping them in the workhouse from any employer – and sometimes she charged far more than she was owed, which made it impossible for many to leave in order to take up work unless the employer was willing to pay. Ruth had told her that it was mostly men who came to the workhouse, wanting workers they could beat and work almost to death.

'An honest employer can take a child or a young woman from a poor family and treat that person fairly,' Ruth had told her. 'But a man who means to work his servant to the bone, giving them poor food and expecting them to work all hours, comes here where no questions are asked. If a child or a woman dies after being beaten, who will bother about them if they are from the workhouse? An honest father might inquire after his daughter if she died suddenly – but who will ask for you or me?'

Eliza had shaken her head, because she had no answer. The only person who cared for her was Ruth. In the workhouse there were several other children who had no one, but some remembered their parents, many of whom had died of fevers or starvation, for there was little help for the destitute anywhere. Eliza, however, had been brought here as a babe and knew no one but

Ruth and the other inmates. Ruth said it could be worse on the streets, though Eliza could not credit it. For some reason the mistress had taken against her and the other orphans stayed clear of Eliza lest her wrath fall on them.

Even those children who had a mother and father seldom saw them. Families were segregated, the men separated from their wives and children, and the women were not allowed to see their children, except at the discretion of the master or mistress on Sundays when they attended the church. It was forbidden to speak to your husband or wife except during the permitted times and breaking that rule could lead to severe punishment.

Some workhouses had their own chapel, but the roof of the chapel here had fallen in during a storm last winter and as yet sufficient money had not been found to repair it and so the favoured inmates were allowed to walk to church at the end of the road on a Sunday morning. On their return, the families were allowed time together until after the evening meal, when they were once again locked into their separate wings. All the inmates should have been permitted access to a place of worship, but if they chose, the mistress or master could withhold the privilege, and they did – as with schooling, which was meant to be provided for the children. Here there was no resident schoolmaster and lessons were given by the rector, who came three mornings a week, but children were sometimes prevented from attending as a form of punishment. Eliza was more often than not put to work in the laundry when she should have been at her lessons.

'You have no need of learning,' Mistress Simpkins

had told her more than once. 'A wicked girl like you deserves no such privilege.'

The lessons provided did not include reading or writing, and for the girls were more likely to be sewing, spinning and weaving, and for the boys, carpentry, masonry, or anything that would be useful in the kind of work they would be expected to do in their future lives. The rector told them beautiful stories of the Christ Child and sometimes he would write things on a blackboard with chalk, explaining that the squiggles he made were writing and that the stories he told them were all written in a book. Eliza was curious about the letters and had asked what they meant, but he'd looked at her sadly and shaken his head, because only a few of the boys were ever given a chance to learn those letters. Eliza had been taught to mend and to weave a little, but she'd hoped that one day she might be taught what the symbols meant inside the book he called the Bible and resented that she was refused that knowledge. The most she'd been taught were the letters of her name so that she could sign the register, though many inmates simply made their mark.

Eliza's rebellion had built in recent weeks, but left here alone, she was afraid that she might never see Ruth again. Ruth had taken her precious shawl, because Eliza feared the mistress would snatch it and she would never see it again. It had once been a beautiful thing, made of soft ivory wool and edged with satin ribbon and lace but the lace had frayed long ago, because Eliza kept it with her always, even when she was in her bed. It was her only link with the past; Ruth had told her that she had been brought into the workhouse, wrapped in that shawl, and ragged as it was, she could do with it around her shoulders now, even though she knew the mistress would have taken it from her when she was stripped.

It was so cold lying on the stone floor, and very dark in the cellar beneath the workhouse. A tiny chink of light came from an iron grating above her head, but it wasn't enough to show her more than the shapes of wooden crates and old, broken furniture that had been stored in here. Eliza had tried to find something to sit or rest on, but there were only bits of chairs and broken chests that would one day be used as firewood. Rats scuttled in and out of the rubbish, and one had run over her feet, making her scream, but she was no longer afraid of them: she was too numbed by hunger and cold to feel fear.

Eliza rubbed at her face, but she wasn't crying. Tears only made you weak and they didn't help; she'd learned that long ago. Her first memories were of Ruth talking to her and feeding her bread and milk slops sweetened with a little honey that her dearest friend had got from somewhere. She knew that it was a miracle she'd survived in this terrible place for all of her twelve years, for she'd been brought into the workhouse as a baby of a few weeks and in a few more weeks she would be thirteen. Ruth had told her the story so many times.

'You be the child of a fine lady, my Eliza,' she'd whispered as they sat huddled together on cold nights, trying to instil warmth into each other, for there were never any fires in the dormitories in which the inmates slept. Only in the kitchen was there a good fire to be found and that was used to fuel the big black iron range that Cook used to heat their food. 'That shawl be of the finest wool and lace. The mistress didn't notice, for you be wrapped in a coarse blanket and the shawl be beneath it. She give you to me to care for because she did not want to be bothered with a child that never stopped cryin' and I hid the shawl until you be older for had she seen it she would've taken it.'

'It belongs to me,' Eliza said and clutched the shawl to her. There was no fear Mistress Simpkins would sell it now, for it was worn thin and the lace almost gone, but she might still have taken it from spite.

'Aye, but if she'd seen it then she would have taken it and I doubt not she'd have sold it,' Ruth said and touched her hand when she saw Eliza's anger. 'She would sell the clothes off her back if it wouldn't shame her to go naked. But she don't know all . . .' Ruth touched the side of her nose. 'Ruth be up to her tricks and mistress don't know all.'

'What do you mean, Ruth?' Eliza asked.

'I did find somethin', my lovely,' Ruth said, 'and I hid it away where none shall find it – for 'tis yours, Eliza, and one day you shall have it, but not till we be safe away from here, for she would have it off you if she spied it.'

'What is it?' Eliza was curious, but Ruth only shook her head and told her she must wait. Eliza sometimes wondered if Ruth had just made it up to amuse her and take her mind from the hunger and cold, because even when Eliza wasn't punished by being sent to bed without supper she was always hungry.

Despite the rules that said inmates should be properly fed, Eliza and most of the women could not remember being given sufficient food, unless an important visitor

7

was due. Thin soup of some kind was provided in the middle of the day and sometimes they were given a sliver of cheese at night, but a bowl of porridge or gruel and a small piece of bread twice a day was hardly enough to keep her strength up for the tasks she was made to perform. Only on Sunday, which was a rest day, did the women and children sup on a watery stew with more vegetables than meat, or when the Board of Governors paid a visit, though the men were given stew most days because they needed meat and could not work unless they were fed properly. Their work might be anything from chopping wood or repairing the building, to breaking stones into small pieces, or picking oakum, which was used to help repair the holds of ships, though, of late, the master had acquired good work for the stronger men making rope. The women, though, were mostly given domestic chores, scrubbing, washing and sorting rags that brought in a few pennies for their mistress. They washed and ironed the clothes for the inmates; some of the more skilled women did weaving or spinning, and one woman did the most beautiful sewing, which earned money for the mistress, but some were just too sick to work much and they were either lying in beds in the infirmary wing until they died or sitting hunched up wherever they could find shelter from the cold.

Mistress Simpkins seemed to pick on Eliza more often than anyone else. She was made to scrub floors and empty the slops from the women's dormitories every morning, and any dirty or unpleasant job that needed to be done was given to Eliza. Sometimes, she wondered why the mistress hated her, but Ruth told her to keep her head down and do whatever she was told.

'I've been sold twice to different masters; they call it hiring but selling is what it is,' she'd told Eliza. 'The first one beat me and starved me and then he died and his wife sent me back here; the second one fed me, but he wanted more than a servant and I didn't like the stink of him so I ran away. I lived on the streets for a few weeks but then I was caught beggin' and the beak sent me back here to the spike; since then no one has asked for me.'

'Why do you not leave?' Eliza asked innocently. 'Could you not ask to be signed out, as the men do?' It was easy enough to give the three hours' notice, which was necessary for the lengthy forms that had to be signed, but to leave without permission was deemed a crime, and if you wore the clothes provided for you by the workhouse it was theft, for they belonged to the master and must be paid for.

'A man may take his family out if he has work to go to, and in the spring and summer there be work aplenty for those with a strong back,' Ruth said, 'but for a woman 'tis not easy to find work unless it be offered afore she leaves, and the fine ladies think twice of taking a servant from the workhouse, for they think us be lazy good-for-nothings. I be not beautiful, my lovely. Not many men look twice at me, and since you came I've been content to bide my time here – but they will look at you when you're older. We must get away from here before that happens, Eliza. Mistress might have sold you afore this if she be willin' but she refused – and I worry what she plans to do with you, my lovely.'

'What do you mean?' Eliza had asked, but Ruth would only shake her head and mutter something she could not understand but knew concerned her friend.

Eliza closed her eyes. How long had she been in this cellar? Far longer than the rules allowed, she was sure. Her fingers and toes were turning numb with the cold. Her eyelids were feeling heavy and she was so tired. Surely, she should have been released before this? She felt as if she were drifting away, being dragged down in the dark cold waters of a deep cavern and it was almost too much trouble to breathe. Perhaps she was dying – and surely death must be easier than living with this pain . . .

'Eliza! Oh, be you not dead, my lovely.' Ruth's voice seemed to come from a long way off. 'I swear that I will kill that evil witch if you be dead, my sweet babe, for as innocent as a babe you are and she a hell-born monster.'

Eliza's mouth felt so dry and she tried to moisten her lips and ask for water but the words wouldn't come. She felt Ruth's rough-skinned but gentle hands stroking her forehead and her eyelids flickered. Her lips moved as she tried to speak but failed.

'Sip a little of this, my lovely,' Ruth said, and Eliza felt the sweetness of cool water on her lips and in her mouth. A trickle went down her throat and she made a little choking noise. 'She 'ad no right to keep you shut up there that long. Now sip this for me . . .'

'Not too much,' a man's voice said, and Eliza thought she knew it but she couldn't be sure. Surely the master wouldn't be here in the women's side. He never bothered with the women and children, leaving all that to his sister. 'I thank you for coming to me, Miss Jones. I cannot afford to have another child die so soon. Mr Stoneham is still demanding answers about the lad who—'

'Eliza was punished for speaking out, sir. She believed it was because the mistress beat Tommy that he died.'

'Well, well, no more is to be said of that, do you hear? My sister is a good warden and I won't hear her slandered – but she should not have left the girl for so long in the cellar. One day shut up is the rule and two on short rations. I fear that she might have died had you not begged me to save her – and I have done so. You must be grateful to me and not speak ill of my sister to the doctor when he comes. The girl hid in the cellar and the door slammed on her. We have been looking for her – do you understand me?'

'Yes, sir,' Ruth agreed eagerly. 'May I heat some milk and honey for her, sir – and then some nourishing broth?'

'Yes, yes, tell Cook to give you whatever necessary, but in return you will give the story I have prepared – do you agree?'

'Yes, sir, I do. Thank you for what you did, sir.'

'Well, well, I am not a bad man,' Master Simpkins said and cleared his throat. 'My wife was an angel and she ministered to those in her charge – as you will recall, Ruth. You were but a child when she took ill of a fever and died. Was she not an angel?'

'Yes, sir, 'tis so. The late mistress was a good woman and I do wish she was still with us.'

'Well, well, it is what we all wish. My sister is not the woman my wife was – but she does her duty by you all. Now, I have work to do. Remember, if you are

11

questioned by the doctor – or Mr Arthur Stoneham, in particular – you must tell them that the girl ran away and locked herself in the cellar. You do understand me?'

'Yes, sir, I understand, and thank you for helping me.'

Eliza vaguely heard their conversation and then the sound of a door closing. 'Where am I?' she asked, her voice cracked and hoarse. 'Can I have some more water please?'

'You're in the infirmary and I be told to look after you. The master said I am not to leave you until you're better, my lovely. I will bring you some warm milk sweetened with honey and you must drink it, a little at a time, for it will make you strong again. When your throat's better you shall have bread and milk and Cook says she shall save you a little of the stew from the master's dinner, for she always cooks too much.'

'Kind . . .' Eliza murmured and drifted away into sleep.

She did not know how long she lay without stirring, but then she became aware of a man bending over her, touching her, and she cried out in fear.

'Now then, child, there's nought to fear.' The doctor's voice calmed her, for she had seen him tend other sick inmates. 'There's no real harm done. It's fortunate your friend found you or you might have died in your hiding place.'

'No . . .' Eliza tried to deny the lie, but her words did not reach her lips. 'She shut me in there . . .'

'What is she saying?' a voice Eliza did not recognise asked. 'She seems distressed.'

'It is just the ordeal she has suffered,' the doctor said. 'There is nothing to worry about, Mr Stoneham, I do assure you. Bed rest, nourishing food and the care of this good woman here and all will be well.' The doctor turned to Ruth. 'Remember, keep her warm, feed her – and a bath would not come amiss. I think it must be a long time since this young lady was properly bathed; her hair is crawling with lice and this dirt on her skin did not get there in three days. It is a sin not to clean yourself and the girl must be told this. So make sure she is bathed and has clean clothes – can you do that?'

'Yes, if the mistress permits,' Ruth said.

'You must do exactly as the doctor tells you,' Mistress Simpkins said in a soft caressing voice that Eliza did not recognise. The sound of it made her whimper and try to deny her lies, but her moans just made the doctor laugh.

'These children do not like soap and water, Mistress Simpkins, but cleanliness is next to godliness – and I think she must learn to keep herself clean and to pray. I do hope you take your inmates to church every Sunday while your chapel is out of order?'

'Of course, sir. I am not sure it makes any impression on them, for many of them are base and idle, but we try our utmost to keep them clean in body and mind.'

'Our good queen sets us all an example by her conduct,' the doctor said in a pious tone and the mistress agreed, for since the attack on Queen Victoria's life some years earlier the people had taken her firmly to their hearts. 'We must all attempt to live godly lives.'

A tear ran down Eliza's cheek, because being dirty was one of the punishments heaped on her for dis-obedience. She had not been allowed to wash for weeks because she was deemed to be unworthy of the privilege.

Feeling a gentle but firm hand on hers, Eliza tried to look at the man bending over her, but her eyes wouldn't focus properly.

'Things will improve, I promise,' he said in a soft whisper that only she was meant to hear. 'Have faith, child.'

Eliza's fingers fluttered, trying to communicate her need, but he'd removed his hand and he and the doctor were leaving. She closed her eyes and waited until she heard the sound of the mistress's footsteps returning.

'If ever you dare to tell Mr Stoneham or the doctor that I shut you in the cellar I shall kill you!' she hissed

Eliza opened her eyes and stared at her. The mistress met her look for a moment and then walked away. Eliza believed her threat, because children often died of fever or near starvation in this fearful place and one more would not be noticed. The mistress stood in place of a matron, which every workhouse was meant to have, but she cared little for the health of her inmates and anyone who was sick was left to rot in the infirmary unless Ruth or one of the other women cared for them.

'Eliza, are you awake at last?' Ruth's face was bending over. 'Can you drink a little milk now, my lovely?'

'Yes please.' Eliza felt herself raised against the hard pillows and a cup was held to her mouth. 'She will punish us, Ruth. Just as soon as she thinks it safe, she will punish us again.'

CHAPTER 2

'I swear there is something badly wrong at the work-house in Whitechapel,' Arthur Stoneham said to his companion as they lingered over the good dinner of roast beef and several removes Arthur's housekeeper had served them. 'I saw a child there today and she was barely alive. The tale was that she'd fallen down the stairs of the cellar when hiding to avoid doing her work – but those bruises looked to me very like she'd been beaten, and the idea of her having locked herself in the cellar is ludicrous.'

'What do you mean to do about it?' Toby Rattan asked. The younger son of Lord Rosenburg, Toby tended to spend his days in idle pursuits, gambling on the horses and cards, riding and indulging his love of good wine and beautiful women. He yawned behind his hand, for at times Arthur could be a dull dog, unlike the bold adventurer he'd been when the pair was first on the town in 1867 when they were both nineteen years of age. Something had happened about that time and it had sobered Arthur, making him more serious, though Toby had never known what had taken that devil-may-care look from his friend's eyes, but their friendship had held for more years than he could recall since then, despite the change in Arthur's manner.

'I am trying to change things, but it is very slow, for although some of the board are well-meaning men they believe the poor to be undeserving,' Arthur said and laughed as he saw Toby's expression. 'You did not dine with me this evening to hear about such dull stuff as this, I'll wager.'

'If only you *would* wager,' Toby said and smiled oddly, because he was inordinately fond of his friend, even though he did consider him slow company when he got on his high horse about the state of the poor. 'Actually, I agree with you, my dear fellow. If it would not bore me to death I would sit on the Board of Governors with you and help you get rid of that wretched woman.'

'Ah, dear Toby, as if I would ask you to sacrifice so much,' Arthur said and arched his left eyebrow mockingly. Toby was as fair as Arthur was dark and the two men were of a similar build and well-matched in form and looks, turning heads whenever they entered a room together. Toby grinned, for his sense of humour matched Arthur's. 'Fear not, all I would ask of you is that you donate a small portion of your obscene fortune to helping me repair and reform the workhouse.'

'In what way?' Toby smiled affectionately, because he admired his friend's unswerving purpose in trying to rescue unfortunates from poverty and worse. 'Are you going to install gas lighting or new drains?'

'Firstly, they need a new roof, and I have already installed some new water pipes, but there was an outbreak of cholera in that area recently and I fear

16

more needs to be done in the area as a whole,' Arthur said and laughed as Toby's lazy attitude fell away and he sat forward, suddenly intent. 'Gas lighting is going a little too far for the moment, but I was hoping for both money and your help with changing opinions. For most the workhouse is a place of correction—'

'Was that not its true purpose?' Toby interrupted.

'In 1834, because the demands of the destitute were so heavy on some parishes, the law was changed so that the poor could not claim on the parish unless they entered the workhouse,' Arthur informed him, though he doubted his friend was ignorant of the law. 'However, it was meant as a place of refuge where men, women and children would be cared for in return for work. The rules are strict, because they have to be – but I think Mistress Simpkins is not the only one who abuses them.'

'In what way?'

'I am fairly certain that they interpret the laws, using them for their own benefit. That girl had been in the cellar for three days, when the legal punishment in solitary confinement is one day, and she was lucky to be alive. Only a week or so back a boy died in mysterious circumstances in that same house and I believe the conditions to be much the same in many other workhouses.'

'You do not hold to the opinion that the poor are shiftless and undeserving?' Toby murmured one eyebrow lifting. 'Most would say they have to prove their worth.'

'Money is a privilege, not a right,' Arthur said. 'If I had a lazy servant to whom I paid good wages I would dismiss him – but I spoke to some of the men in that place and

I believe that they are ready to work and care for their families. When they do have a situation, the wages are so poor that they can save nothing for the times when there is no work and so are forced into the workhouse through no fault of their own.'

'You are a reformer, my friend,' Toby chided. 'You should take my father's seat in the House of Lords.'

'I leave the law-making to men like your father, Toby, but I would ask you to beg him to add his voice to those who seek reform. It is time the poor were treated with respect and given help in a way that does not rob them of their pride. Men should not be forced to take their families into the workhouse – and women should not be forced to prostitution to keep from starving. I also have it in mind to set up a place of refuge for such women.'

'You know I am in agreement with that.'

'Yes, I know – but I need help with these reforms at the workhouse.'

'You have my promise,' Toby said. 'And if you need money for your reforms I will offer you five thousand immediately.'

'I was sure I could count on you,' Arthur murmured. 'What I need most is your support. The more voices raised against those dens of iniquity the better, Toby, and I speak now of the whorehouses, not the spike, as the unfortunates within its walls call the workhouse. I would wish to have all brothels closed down, but every time I try to raise the subject I am told that such women are more at risk on the streets. At least in the brothels they are protected from violence and their health is monitored, so they tell me – and I fear it may be true, poor wretches.'

18

'It is the children certain men abduct and initiate into their disgusting ways that disturbs me,' Toby said, all pretence of being a fop gone now that Arthur had raised a subject that angered him. Toby enjoyed a dalliance with a beautiful woman as much as the next man, but he chose married or widowed women from his own class, women who were bored with their lives and enjoyed the company of a younger man. Visiting whores at houses of ill repute was something he had not done since he'd seen for himself the terrible consequences such places inflicted on the women forced to serve them. 'If a woman chooses to support herself in this way it is her prerogative, but to force mere children! I told you of my groom's twelve-year-old daughter who was snatched from her own lane, not two yards from her home?'

'Yes, you did. When she was eventually found two years later, she had syphilis and was deranged. I know how that angered you, Toby.' It was sadly but one case of many. Victorian society was outwardly God-fearing and often pious to the extreme, but it hid a cesspool of depravity and injustice that no decent man could tolerate.

'Had I found the person that snatched poor Mary, I should have killed him,' Toby vowed.

'Exactly so.' Arthur smiled at him. 'I knew you were of the same mind, my dear friend. In our society the whore is thought of as the lowest of the low, but who brought her to that state? Men – and a State that cares nothing that a woman may be starving and forced to sell herself to feed her children.'

'Yes, true enough, we are all culpable, but the ladies

of the night do have a choice in many cases – the children sold into these places do not, Arthur. It is the children we must protect.'

Arthur reached forward to fill his wine glass. 'We are in agreement. Thank you, Toby. I shall put your name at the top of my list – and I know of one or two influential ladies who will add theirs, but it is men we need, because for the most part they have the money and the power.'

'I shall ask my father and brother to add their names. They will not do more, though of course I can usually extract a few thousand from my father for a good cause.' Toby smiled, because he knew that his father indulged him. 'I find the ladies are more vociferous when it comes to demanding change.'

Arthur raised his glass. 'To your good health, Toby. Now tell me, have you visited the theatre of late?'

Arthur looked at himself in the dressing mirror as he prepared for bed. It was three in the morning and Toby had just departed to visit a certain widow of whom he was fond, and she of him. Their arrangement had lasted more than a year and Arthur thought it might endure for some time because the pair were suited in many ways, and Toby was too restless to marry.

He envied his friend in having found a lady so much to his liking. Arthur had thought of marriage once or twice but at the last he had drawn back, perhaps because he was still haunted by that time . . . No, damn it! He would not let himself remember that which shamed him even now. It was gone, finished, and he had become a better man, and yet he had not married because of his secret. He could never wed a young and beautiful girl, for he would soil her with his touch, and as yet he had not found a woman of more mature years of whom he might grow fond. Perhaps it was his punishment that he could not find love in his heart.

He had good friends, several of whom were married ladies that he might have taken to bed had he so wished, but he lived, for the most part, a celibate life. Yet he enjoyed many things – sharing a lavish dinner with his friends was a favourite pastime, as was visiting Drury Lane and the other theatres that abounded in London. On occasion he had even visited a hall of music, where singers and comedians entertained while drinks were served. He found it amusing and it helped him to see much of the underlife that ran so deep in Victorian society. It was seeing the plight of women thrown out of the whorehouse to starve because they were no longer attractive enough to serve the customers that made him feel he must do something to help, at least a few of them.

Mixing with a rougher element at the halls of music brought him in touch with the extreme poverty that the industrialisation of a mainly rural nation had brought to England. It had begun a century before, becoming worse as men who had been tied to the land followed the railways looking for work and then flocked to the larger towns, bringing their women and children with them. The lack of decent housing and living space had become more apparent and the poor laws which had once provided help, with at least a modicum of dignity, had failed miserably to support a burgeoning population. Public houses catered to the need to fill empty lives with gin, which brought temporary ease to those suffering from cold and hunger. It was because the towns and cities had become too crowded that the old laws were no longer sufficient to house and feed those unable to support themselves, so the workhouses had been built. All manner of folk, weak in mind and body were sent there, as well as those who simply could not feed themselves.

Arthur frowned as he climbed into bed and turned down the wick of his oil lamp. He'd long ago had gas lighting installed downstairs but preferred the lamps for his bedroom. His thoughts were still on the workhouse. It had been thought a marvellous idea to take in men, women and children who were living on the streets or in crumbling old ruins in cities and towns; to feed them, clothe them, and give them work, though production of goods made cheaply by the inmates was disapproved of by the regular tradesmen, who felt it harmed their livelihoods. Indeed, it should have been a good solution, but it was being abused. Women like that Simpkins harridan abused their power. Arthur frowned as he closed his eyes. His instincts told him that she had beaten the boy that died and locked that poor girl in the cellar – but was that all she was up to?

CHAPTER 3

Joan Simpkins was in a foul mood. She had sharply reprimanded by her brother, because he'd been warned that if there were more deaths they would be investigated and he could lose his ward-ship of the workhouse.

'You must curb your temper,' he'd told Joan after the latest meeting of the Board of governors. 'I've been informed that we're bein' watched and if they find we're mistreating the inmates we'll be asked to leave.'

Joan felt her temper rise. Nothing annoyed her so much as knowing that those mealy-mouthed men and women, who understood little of what the poor were actually like, taking her to task. The Board consisted of gentlemen, prosperous businessmen, wives of important men, and even a military officer – and what did they know of the stinking, coarse wretches she was forced to deal with every day? Even when water and soap was provided some of them didn't bother to wash, and some thought it dangerous to take off the shirt they'd worn all winter until it was mid-summer – and the women who came to the workhouse bearing an illegitimate child got no sympathy from Joan; they were

23

whores and wanton and deserved to be treated as such. She made them wear a special uniform that proclaimed their sin and, if she had room, segregated them from the others in a special ward and made them scrub floors until they dropped the brat.

Now, she glared at her brother. 'That wretched girl accused me of causing that stupid boy's death. I had to make an example of her. If I hadn't nipped it in the bud there would've been a rebellion. If something like that reached the ears of that interfering man Arthur Stoneham . . .'

'Well, well, I daresay you had your reasons. However, Mr Stoneham has been very generous to us, Joan. He paid for the installation of new water pipes and we've not had a return of the cholera since then. He has granted us money towards some very necessary repairs to the roof and that will give the men work for weeks and us extra money.'

It was all right for her brother, Joan thought resentfully. Robbie was weak and lazy. He always took his cut of any money that came in. The funds for running the workhouses were raised by taxing the wealthy, which caused some dissent, but others saw it as a good thing that vagrants were taken off the streets, and made donations voluntarily. Joan did not share in her brother's perks and was only able to save a few pence on the food and clothing she supplied to the women and children in her ward. If it were not for her other little schemes she would not have a growing hoard of gold coins in her secret place.

Joan hated living in the workhouse. The inmates stank and their hair often crawled with lice when they were

24

admitted. Most of them obeyed the rules to keep themselves clean, but there were always some who were too lazy to bother. It was all very well for Mr Stoneham and the doctor to say the inmates should be given more opportunities to bathe. Heating water cost money and so did the soap she grudgingly gave her wards. She needed to pocket some of the funds she was given for their upkeep, because one day she intended to leave this awful place.

Joan had dreams of living in a nice house with servants to wait on her, and perhaps a little business. Once, she'd hoped she might find a man to marry her, but she was now over thirty and plain. Men never turned their heads when she walked by in the market and she resented pretty women who had everything given to them; like the woman who had brought that rebellious brat in and begged her to keep her safe from harm.

'One day I'll come back and pay you in gold and take her with me,' the woman had promised, her eyes filled with tears.

She'd crossed Joan's hands with four silver florins and placed the squalling brat in her arms. As soon as she'd gone, Joan had given the brat to one of the inmates and told her to look after it. She'd told Ruth that the child had been brought in by a doctor, though she hardly knew why she lied. Perhaps because she liked secrets and she'd believed then that the woman would return and pay to take the girl with her. She'd kept the girl all these years, refusing two offers to buy her, because of the woman's promise, but the years had passed and the girl was nearly thirteen. She was a nuisance and caused more trouble than she was worth. It was time to start thinking what best to do with her . . .

Eliza paused in the act of stirring the large tub of hot water and soda. A load of clothes had been dumped into it earlier and it was Eliza's job to use the wooden dolly stick she'd been given to help release the dirt from clothes that had been worn too long. They smelled of sweat, urine and excrement where the inmates wiped themselves for lack of anything else, and added to the general stench of the workhouse.

It was steamy and hot in the laundry, though the stone floors could be very cold in winter, especially if your feet were bare, and Eliza had been set to work here again once she recovered from her ordeal in the cellar. So far she'd been asked to stir the very hot water and then help one of the other women to transfer the steaming clothes to a tub of cold water for rinsing. Eliza wasn't yet strong enough to turn the mangle they used to take out the excess liquid before the washing was hung to dry on lines high above their heads, which were operated by means of a pulley.

'Watch it, girl,' a cackling laugh announced the approach of Sadie, the oldest inmate of the workhouse. She'd been here so many years she couldn't remember any other life. 'Mistress be in a terrible rage this mornin'.'

Eliza looked at the older woman in apprehension. Sadie was handy with her fists on occasion and Eliza had felt the brunt of her temper more than once. She was the only one that didn't seem to fear the mistress and was seldom picked on by her.

'I've done nothin' wrong, Sadie,' Eliza said. 'Do you know what has upset her?'

'I knows the master took in a boy this mornin' – a gypsy lad he be, dirty and rough-mannered, and mistress be told to have him bathed and feed him. She can't abide gypsies.'

'What exactly is a gypsy? I've heard the word but do not know what it means.'

'They be travellin' folk,' Molly, another inmate, said coming up to them with an armful of dirty washing. 'They ain't always dirty nor yet rough-mannered. I've known some, what be kind and can heal the sick.'

Sadie scowled and spat on the floor. 'You'm be a dirty little whore yerself,' she snarled and walked off.

'Sadie's in her usual cheerful mood.' Molly winked at Eliza. 'Do you want a hand with the rinsing, Eliza love?'

'Would you help me?' Eliza asked hopefully. 'Sadie is supposed to give me a hand lifting the clothes into the tub of cold water, but she gets out of it whenever she can.'

'You're too small and slight for such work, little Eliza,' Molly said and grinned at her. 'And I'm too big.' She laughed and looked at her belly, because she was close to giving birth again. Molly had been to the workhouse three times to give birth since Eliza had been here and each time she'd departed afterwards, leaving the baby in Mistress Simpkins' care. Ruth had told her that the warden sold the babies to couples who had no children of their own.

Since workhouse children who were found new lives were thought to be lucky, no one sanctioned the mistress for disposing of the babies as she chose.

'You might hurt yourself,' Eliza said as Molly took up the wooden tongs. 'If you lift something too heavy it might bring on the birth too soon.'

'What difference?' Molly shrugged. 'If the babe be dead it will be one less soul born to misery and pain.'

Eliza looked up at her. 'Would you not like to keep your child and love it?'

'They wouldn't let me. I should have to leave the whorehouse and I have nowhere else to go and no other way of earning my living,' Molly said and pain flickered in her eyes. 'They own me, Eliza love, body and soul.' She smiled as she saw Eliza was puzzled. 'You don't understand, and I pray to God that you never will.'

'If you are unhappy why don't you go far away?' Eliza asked. 'When I'm older I shall go away, go somewhere there are flowers and trees and fields . . .'

'What do *you* know of such things?' Molly laughed as she started to transfer clothes from the steaming hot tub to the vat of cold water.

'Ruth's father was a tinker and they used to travel the roads. He found work where he could and they lived off the land, foraging for food and workin' for what they could not catch or pick from the hedges.'

'And where did that get them?' Molly said wryly. 'He took ill one winter and was forced to bring them into the workhouse. Ruth Jones has watched all her family die, one by one, and now what does she have to look forward to? It be a life of toil in the workhouse unless she be given work outside – and when men come looking for a servant we all know what they want.' Eliza shook her head and Molly laughed. 'No, you be innocent as a new-born lamb, little one, but that won't last – and

28

when you understand the choice you'll know why I choose the whorehouse.'

Eliza did not answer. She did not consider that Molly was free, for Ruth had told her the whorehouse was no better than the workhouse, even though the food was more plentiful and at least Molly had decent clothes and was able to wash when she wanted.

'You, girl – come here!'

Eliza jumped because she'd had not noticed the mistress approaching. She left the rinsing to Molly and went to stand in front of the mistress, but instead of hanging her head as most of the inmates did, she looked her in the face and saw for herself that Sadie was right: mistress was in a foul mood.

'There's a boy,' Mistress Simpkins said, looking at Eliza with obvious dislike. 'He's filthy and disobedient and refuses to answer me. Tell Ruth to scrub him with carbolic and give him some clothes. I want him present-able – and in a mood to answer when spoken to; if he refuses he will have no supper. You know that I mean what I say.'

'Yes.' Eliza's eyes met hers. She knew all too well that Mistress Simpkins gained pleasure from punishing those unfortunate enough to arouse her ire. 'I'll find Ruth – what is the boy's name, please?'

'His name is Joe, so I am told, but he refuses to answer to it.' Mistress Simpkins' eyes gleamed. 'You might tell him what happened to you, girl.'

Eliza met her gloating look with one of pride. If it had been Mistress Simpkins' intention to break her by shutting her in the cellar her plan had misfired. The horror she had endured had just made her hate the warden more and she was determined to defy her silently, giving her nothing she could use to administer more unjust punishment.

'Yes,' she said. 'I might . . .'

'You impertinent little bitch!' Mistress Simpkins raised her hand as if she would strike but Molly made a move towards her and something in her manner made the mistress back away. 'Get off and do as I tell you or you will feel the stick on your back.'

Eliza ran off, leaving the clammy heat of the wash-house to dash across the icy yard to the kitchen. She knew that if Molly hadn't been there to witness it, Mistress Simpkins would have struck her. Molly had some status in the workhouse. Eliza didn't know what it was but she thought perhaps the master favoured her.

She found Ruth in the kitchen helping Cook prepare vegetables and told her what the mistress had instructed her to do. Ruth nodded, for she was used to being given such tasks. Mistress Simpkins always passed on the children she could not be bothered with herself, and it was usually Ruth that had the task of caring for them.

'Let's fetch the lad here,' she told Eliza with a smile. 'We'll give him a drop of the master's stew – is that all right with you, Cook?'

'Aye, Ruth lass. Let the boy get some food inside him and he'll feel more like talkin'.' Cook smiled at them. 'I daresay you wouldn't mind a drop of my soup, Eliza love? No need for the mistress to know. She grudges every penny she spends on our food, but she dare not question what I spend on the master's dinners.' She winked at them. 'A little deception does no harm now and then. What say you, Eliza?'

'I don't want you to get into trouble or Ruth . . .'

'Nay, lass, there'll be no trouble. Mistress knows if I left she could not replace me. There's not many would work here for the pittance they pay. So she would have to do the cooking herself or get another inmate to do it and none of them have the first idea how to start so I'm safe enough.'

Eliza smiled and took the bowl of soup Cook offered, drinking it down quickly as if she feared Mistress Simpkins might appear and snatch it from her.

'Lawks a' mercy,' Cook said. 'You'll get hiccups, girl. Off with the pair of yer and let me get on or there'll be no soup for the men.'

Ruth winked at Eliza as they left the kitchen. 'She's not a bad woman, Eliza for all her sharp tongue at times.'

'I like Cook,' Eliza said and smiled, the goodness of the soup giving her a lovely warmth inside. 'Sadie said the new boy was a gypsy – his family travel, like yours, Ruth.'

'My father was a tinker. He mended pots and pans and did odd jobs of any sort, but he wasn't Romany,' Ruth told her. 'The true Romany is special, Eliza. The women often have healin' powers – and the men are handsome and strong, and some of them could charm the birds from the trees.'

'Perhaps Joe is Romany,' Eliza said. She pointed across the wide, cobbled courtyard, swept clean every morning by the older boys no matter the weather. It was bounded by high walls with only one way out: a pair of strong iron gates that were impossible to scale. 'Look, that must be him, standing near the gates.'

'Aye, the poor lad be feelin' shut in,' Ruth said and there was pity in her tone. 'I mind my father standin' like that for many a month afore he grew accustomed to this terrible place.'

'Doesn't he know that he can't leave unless his father comes for him – or unless he's taken by a master?'

'If he knows, he won't admit it in his heart,' Ruth said. 'A lad like that needs to be free to run in the fields and breathe fresh country air.'

'I'll go to him.' Eliza set off at a run, ignoring Ruth's murmured warning to take care. As she approached, the boy turned and looked at her, glaring and angry, his blue eyes smouldering with suppressed rage. 'Are you Joe?' Eliza asked. 'I'm Eliza. I was brought here when I was a babe. It is a terrible place but I'm goin' to leave one day and then I'll go far away, somewhere there are fields and wild flowers in the hedges.'

'You don't know where to find them,' the boy said, and Eliza was startled by the sound of his voice that had a lilting quality. 'You're not Romany.'

'No – are you?' He inclined his head, his eyes focused on her so intently that Eliza's heart jumped. 'I think I should like to live as you did – travellin' from place to place.'

'In the winter it be hard,' he said. 'Ma took sick again this winter and Pa came to Lun'un lookin' for a warm place to stay for her and work – but they said he was a dirty gypsy and a thief and they put him in prison for startin' a fight, which he never did.' His eyes glittered like ice in the sun. 'My Pa never stole in his life nor did harm to any. He be an honest man and good – I hate them and all their kind.'

'So do I,' Eliza said and moved a little closer. 'Master is not too bad as long as you don't disobey him openly – but mistress is spiteful and cruel and she's boss of her brother. I hate her so much. I should like to kill her.' Eliza made a stabbing movement with her hand. 'See, she's fallen down dead.'

A slow smile spread across the newcomer's face. 'I like you, Eliza,' he said. 'Shall we kill her together?'

'Yes, Joe – one day, when we're bigger and stronger,' Eliza said. 'For now we have to do as she says – or pretend to. Let her think she rules, but she can't rule our hearts and minds – she can't break us even if she beats us. If you come with Ruth and me, Cook will give you some of the master's stew. It's good, much better than they give us. Mistress said we shouldn't feed you until you were bathed and changed your clothes, but Cook said you should eat first. Will you come?'

'I'll come for you,' Joe said. 'You're pretty – like my ma. She's beautiful, but the travellin' don't suit her and she be ill in the winter.'

'Where is your ma?' Eliza offered her hand and he took it, his grip strong and possessive. Her eyes opened wide and she seemed to feel something pass between them, a bond that was not spoken or acknowledged but felt by both.

'Bathsheba took her to Ireland,' Joe told her. 'She's Pa's sister and travels with us, though she has her own caravan. They wanted me to go with them but I ran away to be near my pa. When I can I shall visit him in prison and let him know I be waitin' for him.'

'You will need to get away from here,' Eliza said. 'How did they catch you?'

'I went to the prison gates and demanded to see my pa; they tried to send me away but I refused and kept shouting at them. They sent the constable to arrest me and he brought me here because I had no money and nowhere to stay and he said I be a vagrant.'

'They won't let you go unless your pa comes for you or a master takes you,' Eliza said with the wisdom of a child reared in the workhouse. 'You could try to escape. Not many do because it's hard out there, so they tell us. I've never been anywhere . . .' Eliza's eyes filled with tears, for there were times when she ached to be free of this place. Joe reached out to her, smoothing her tears away with his fingers.

'You shouldn't cry. You should just hate them. You're be too pretty to cry, Eliza. Your hair's like spun silk . . . My ma has hair like yours but 'tis darker, not as silver as yours.' He smiled at her and leaned his head closer. 'When I escape I'll take you with me.'

'Oh yes, please let me come with you,' Eliza begged. 'We could go and live in the fields and you can show me where the wild flowers grow.'

Joe nodded and then scowled. 'I be hungry. 'Tis ages since I've eaten more than a crust of bread. I'll wash 'cos I don't like nits in my hair – but I want my own clothes. Can you wash them for me and give them back? If she gets them I'll have to ask her for them before I leave and she wouldn't let me go for I am too young to be alone on the streets – at least that's what they claim.'

'Yes, I can do that for you,' Eliza said, though if she

was caught stealing from the laundry she would be beaten. 'You'll have to wear what you're given for now, but you can hide your things and then when you escape, you can wear them.'

'You're a bright girl,' Joe said and smiled. 'Can you read and write, Eliza?'

'Rector taught us to write our names once and Ruth helped me practice, but I can't read,' Eliza admitted and the smile left her eyes. 'Mistress never lets me take lessons with the vicar now. She says all I need to know is how to address my betters.'

'You're better than her,' Joe said fiercely and once again his eyes glittered like ice, 'and don't you forget it. Ma taught me to read, write and my numbers – and I'll teach you.'

'Yes.' Eliza felt the warmth spread through her. 'We'll be friends, Joe – me and you. Whatever they do, we'll always be friends . . .'

CHAPTER 4

'It is time the rules were reformed,' Arthur said to a group of men as they moved to leave the inn parlour that had been their meeting place. 'Some of them are too harsh – and I believe the wardens should be more strictly regulated.'

'You would relax the rules for the undeserving and regulate the hard-working men and women who enforce them?' one of the board members asked incredulously. 'Have you lost your wits, Stoneham?'

'No, Sir Henry, I think not,' Arthur replied. 'I believe that the rules were set up in good faith but they are open to abuse by the master and the mistress – and I think it is time they were reviewed. Just as I do not believe that a master should be allowed to beat his servant for some small misdemeanour.'

'Good grief! You would turn society on its head,' Sir Henry said, staring at him with eyes that bulged in disbelief. 'You cannot imagine what chaos could ensue, my dear Stoneham. Your compassion does you credit – but they are cunning wretches. You must not believe a word they say. A servant who complains of his master's whip has probably stolen from him – and if dealt with

36

firmly would be sent for a year's hard labour. He is lucky to escape with a beating.'

'Come, sir,' Toby said and raised a lazy eyebrow. 'Are all the poor undeserving wretches?'

'Most – and if not they are usually insolent and impertinent and should be kept in their place or a man will not be able to keep hold of his property. Only those that prove their worth and know their place should be promoted.'

'And what if I had proof that the rules were being abused and vulnerable girls harmed?' Arthur asked.

'Well, in certain circumstances we might have to replace the master and the woman who assists him as matron or whatever.' Sir Henry yawned, obviously bored. 'These meetings are tiresome. I must be off to my club – good-day, gentlemen.' He tipped his hat and went on his way muttering about reformers.

'You see what I am up against,' Arthur said, and his gaze followed the baronet in disgust. 'Any mention of reform and they fear for their property.'

'Sir Henry does not speak for us all,' a deep voice said from behind them and they turned to see another of the governors looking at them with interest. 'I agree that the rules may need updating.'

'Major Cartwright . . .' Arthur nodded. He was not inclined to make an ally of the old soldier and yet it seemed that he might have to take what votes he could get. 'I believe that some of the punishments used on children are too severe.'

'Ah yes, the poor young ones,' the major said but looked odd. 'Well, I am not against reform. You may rely on me if you need my vote – good day, gentlemen.'

Arthur watched him leave. 'Why don't I trust that man?'

'I've met his sort before . . .' Toby shook his head. 'Not sure you are right not to trust him, but he might be an ally if you need one, Arthur.'

'I'm glad you decided to sit in this morning,' Arthur said. 'Now, I propose to treat you to a dinner at my club to make up for all the boring chatter you've been forced to endure.'

'And so I should think,' Toby said and twirled his Malacca cane with its silver knob. 'At least you got the money for the new drains passed so it's not all bad, my friend.'

'Tell me, Molly, is that my brat in there?' Master Simpkins smiled and touched her swollen belly. 'I dare swear I've swived you enough to claim it.'

Molly laughed and reached for the tankard of strong ale on the table beside her, drinking deeply from it and wiping her chin with the back of her hand before kissing him on the mouth and thrusting her tongue inside. He tasted of strong ale and his breath smelled, but she'd known worse and she tolerated him. Robbie could be coarse, and he'd taken her virginity by force when she was a young girl, but she'd more or less forgiven him because she accepted that it was her lot in life. Robbie wasn't the worst of the men she served and these days she used him as much as he used her. He was weak, a creature of lust and greed, and yet he could be generous if he chose. Because of Robbie, Molly was able to come here to have her child and leave again when she chose.

Few knew that he was part owner of the whorehouse where she worked and lived, though he had nothing to do with its daily life, but Molly had discovered it long since. It made her smile to think that his sister was ignorant of what her brother got up to in his quarters.

Oh, Mistress Simpkins had her own dirty little schemes but Molly would bet that Robbie was as ignorant of what his sister was up to as she was of his part-ownership of the brothel. However, whereas Molly could accept Robbie's involvement, she hated his sister and what she did with a deep vengeance. Grown women selling themselves for money and a life of comparative ease was one thing, but condemning children to the brutality of the evil men that used them was quite another. If she'd thought that she could stop Joan Simpkins from selling the children she would have told Robbie, but she knew he would either disbelieve her or be unable to control his sister; Joan was the stronger of the two and though she held her post through him, he seldom interfered with her.

'You're not a bad old sod,' she told him now. 'I can't let yer ride me, Robbie love, 'cos I'm too big – but I'll give yer a treat if yer like.' She moved her hand suggestively to his bulging breeches and smiled. 'You'm be hung like a horse, me darling. It must be painful fer yer with yer breeches so tight . . . let Molly ease yer.'

'Yer the best, Molly. Yer always look after me,' he said and pulled her in for a kiss. 'Get on with it then – and take your time.'

Joan Simpkins paused outside her brother's door listening to the disgusting sounds coming from inside. He and his whores thought she was ignorant of what they did in his rooms, but she'd learned what he was long ago – even before his wife died. To hear him speak

39

of his wife anyone would think he'd adored the woman he called a saint, but if he had loved her it had never stopped him indulging his baser needs with whores.

She frowned and turned away, making her own secret tour of all the wards while her brother was otherwise engaged. He had no idea that she overlooked his side of the workhouse, but she knew all the spyholes and enjoyed watching men, women and children as they moved about their quarters or lay in their beds, believing that no one but their companions knew of what they did in the hours of darkness; their misery satisfied her and eased her own self-pity.

Joan had learned of the baseness of these creatures when she was but a young girl. Spying on them, she saw the furtive couplings between certain types of men, and it pleased her that she knew their secrets – the filthy beasts were no better than animals to her mind. She grudged what comfort their couplings gave them for she thrived on the suffering of others. When gentlemen instructed that these creatures should be treated as human beings she hardly knew how to contain her ire. Men like Mr Stoneham, used to the luxury of clean linen, warm fires, and all the wine and choice foods he desired, had no idea what kind of beasts they dealt with here; ignorant, filthy, base creatures who would do nothing to help themselves unless prodded to it. They rutted like animals and deserved no better treatment.

Joan also knew that some of the men fought off those others and sought their pleasures with the women, sometimes their wives if they could find a way, but often another young woman taken with her consent and, at times, without. The strict rules meant that the men and women were segregated and locked in their own wings to prevent this kind of thing, but they were cunning and some had discovered how to move about the work-house even after the doors were locked at night. When she discovered where their illicit key was hidden she would take great pleasure in punishing the culprits. For the moment it amused her that they believed themselves safe.

Joan had not interfered even when she witnessed the rape of a young girl by her own brother. It had amused her to watch for the girl was nothing but an impertinent upstart – and pretty. She deserved her fate.

Soon afterwards, the girl had come to her and confessed she was with child. Joan had told her she had her just deserts for fornicating and offered her a choice – she might go to an asylum for correction or enter a whorehouse. The girl had chosen the life of a whore, which just showed that Joan was perfectly justified in her opinion of her character.

Molly was a slut and always had been. She was a whore at heart and there was no more to be said, but it irked Joan that she seemed to enjoy her life. Why should she be happy and free to come and go when Joan was tied to her post, not by duty but the need for money? When she left this place it would be for good and she needed a great deal of money to live in comfort – or she would one day find herself once more in a place like this but as an inmate.

Eliza lay snuggled up to Ruth beneath the blanket they shared. Now that she was thirteen she was allowed to sleep on the women's wing instead of being sent to join the other young children at night. Lying close to her friend was the only way to keep warm and Eliza liked being with the woman she called friend, but this night she found it hard to sleep. Joe had told her about his life while he ate his meal in the kitchen and Eliza felt an aching need inside her to see what it was like to be free, to travel wherever she wished.

The only place she'd ever been taken to was the church at the end of Farthing Lane. It was a treat on Sunday and she was given a clean dress on the days she was allowed to go, but that was not often. A group of children and women and a few men went every week, because the Board of Governors insisted that the inmates hear the word of God, but Mistress Simpkins did not allow everyone from her ward to go. A few women and girls were chosen and supervised by Mistress Simpkins and Sadie, and they were dressed cleanly with aprons and little white caps over a grey dress. Eliza sometimes wondered why the men and women did not just walk away on these outings, for neither Sadie nor the mistress could have stopped them, but when she asked Ruth, she'd told her that they simply had nowhere to go.

'Life is hard in here,' she'd said looking sad, 'but it can be terrible cruel on the streets, Eliza. Here we be given food every day; it may not be much and 'tis often hard to stomach, but it is better than no food at all. The men bring their families in when they be close to starvin'. I tried to live on the streets and it's no place for children, my lovely. There are dangers out there that we be protected from in here. The women won't leave without their kids and the men won't leave their families here alone so they stay until work is offered and they can sign themselves out, though many are back in a few months when the work dries up. 'Sides, if they walked off in the uniform they could be taken up fer stealin'.'

Ruth was fast asleep and snoring gently, and Eliza wished she might sleep, but her rebellious nature kept her wakeful. One of these days she was going to run away. She would like it to be with her new friend Joe, but if not she would go alone. Eliza knew her chances of surviving on the streets alone at her age were slight; she had to hold on, to endure the mistress's spite for another year or so. When she was older she could ask for work and might be given it. At the moment she was too young and slight. Most people wanted a strong girl to do all their chores and Eliza might not look strong, even though the years of hardship had toughened her. They would want an older girl or a woman and that was why she was still here after so many years.

Yet perhaps if she and Joe ran away together they could manage. In the country, perhaps, folk were kinder than in town . . .

'I've been lookin' round,' Joe told Eliza the next morning when they met after breakfast. It was a time when the two sides mixed in the dining room and then dispersed, each to their own work. 'I've been put to work with the men making hemp rope. There's a man called Bill and he knows a way to get out, though he says he's not ready to leave yet. I asked him to tell me, but he said if I used it, it would spoil his chances when he goes, but if there is one way there must be others.'

'No talking!' Eliza looked up and saw the mistress watching them. 'Get to your work, girl, or you will feel my stick.'

'Don't you dare hurt her,' Joe said and moved in front of Eliza. 'Lay a finger on her and I'll see you dead – I'll lay a curse on you and you'll die in agony, withered and alone!'

For a moment the colour left Mistress Simpkins' face and Eliza thought she saw fear in her eyes, but then in a moment it had gone.

'I do not believe in your curses, gypsy,' she said and raised her stick bringing it down hard, but Joe was too quick for her and seized it, twisting it from her hand with a flick of his wrist. 'How dare you? I shall see you are flogged for this – and you'll have no food this day.'

Joe stared at her defiantly and then broke the stick over his knee and flung down the pieces. She raised her hand and struck him again about the face but though he flinched he stood firm, his eyes daring her to touch him again.

'Now then, now then,' the master's voice made Eliza spin round for she had not noticed his approach, but Joe and the mistress had not taken their eyes from each other as if neither would give in. 'What has this boy done to upset you, sister?'

'He is a disobedient, dirty gypsy and he needs to be punished. He broke my stick and he dared to threaten he would put a curse on me.'

The master looked at Joe severely. 'Did you do as the mistress claims, boy?'

'Yes, sir, 'tis true. She be goin' to hit Eliza and I told

44

her I'd curse her if she did – so she tried to hit me with her stick and I broke it.'

'Did you indeed?' For a moment it looked as if the master approved of Joe's action but then he frowned. 'Well then, well then, boy – what am I to do with you? This won't do, you know. I cannot allow you to defy the mistress – even though you are in my ward, not hers.' His thick brows met as he looked at his sister as if sending her a challenge.

'He must be flogged and sent to the hole – and no food today, none!' Mistress Simpkins' voice had reached a shrill pitch that made the master frown.

He reached out and took hold of the collar of the worn and much-patched jacket Joe was wearing. 'You come along with me boy,' he said looking angry. 'You have upset the mistress and you must be punished.'

Eliza watched as Joe was dragged off, holding back her tears. She was so angry and yet so frightened for Joe. He'd been rebellious from the start because he was used to living free and he didn't understand how hard life was in the workhouse. Open defiance made the mistress lose her temper and she had been known to beat a child until the blood ran in one of her rages.

'What are you staring at, girl?' the mistress snapped suddenly making Eliza jump. 'Get to your work or you'll find my stick about your shoulders.' A glint of temper showed in her eyes as she looked down at the stick Joe had broken. 'Don't think that will save you. I've another stronger and thicker that that gypsy brat won't break.'

Eliza turned and walked towards the laundry. Her heart was racing wildly and she wanted to run but she made herself walk. She must never show fear, never show weakness. If the mistress once thought she could break you, she would never let up.

Eliza's back felt as if it were breaking when she finished her day's work. She'd filled the vats with hot water from the copper and then stirred ten piles of dirty clothes into the water that had turned a muddy brown colour by the time she'd finished the last. They were only allowed to heat one tub of water a day but they used two tubs of cold water to rinse the clothes, so that when they were mangled for the last time they smelled reasonably fresh and the dirt had gone. Once the washing was hanging high above their heads under the vaulted ceiling, they had to empty all the vats and tip the filthy water into the ditches that ran past the rear of the laundry out into the gutters in the lane and finally into the sewers. It was back-breaking work and all the women were exhausted by the time they were told to take their places for the second meal of the day in the dining-hall.

Ruth was waiting for her and had saved a place for her. Every day Ruth fetched a piece of the coarse brown bread and soup for them both, as well as a cup of water.

That day the soup was vegetable but there was a flavour of something more and Ruth told her that Cook had used the bone left over from the master's ham to flavour their soup and put a little goodness in it.

'You're tired, Eliza,' Ruth said as Eliza swallowed a little of the liquid which tasted better than usual. 'They work you to death in that damned place – and you're not strong enough for such labour.'

'I'm all right,' Eliza said and summoned enough

strength to smile at her. She looked around her but could see no sign of Joe. 'Have you seen or heard what happened to Joe, Ruth?'

'No, my lovely, I be none the wiser than you. 'Tis whispered he was beaten but Jigger told me he was made to sweep up in the rope store. Mebbe the master thought he was better at work than in the hole. Though it seems he has not been sent for his supper.' It was forbidden for the men to speak to the women but there were times when a trustee like Jigger was sent over to their side of the workhouse to do some work and he always passed on messages, even though he risked a beating for disobedience.

'Joe will be so hungry,' Eliza said, because she knew what it felt like to be beaten and sent to bed with no supper, though often Ruth smuggled something to her, even if it was only a crust of bread.

An idea came to Eliza as she ran the last little piece of her bread round her soup plate and swallowed it. She was still hungry even after their meal and she knew Joe's stomach would be aching from the pain of hunger. She looked along the line of women and children. Not one of them had left a crumb of bread. No food was ever wasted on this side of the dining room because there was never enough.

If she wanted to smuggle some food to Joe she would have to go to the kitchen and beg something from Cook. She thought the kindly woman might be sympathetic, because she sometimes gave Ruth bits of leftover food from the master and mistress's table. Master liked his food and did not stint on what he gave Cook to provide for his meals; the mistress contributed nothing for her food but dined with her brother and shared his. Yet even so there was often a piece of soft white bread or a small corner of cheese left over. Cook was fair and would share the extras with the inmates who were currently in her favour. Most people took care never to upset Cook, because the scraps she dispensed could mean the difference between survival and near starvation, particularly on the women's side. The men's food was a little better and they had a nourishing stew three times a week with potatoes and sometimes carrots or turnips in season. So Cook saved her scraps for the women and children.

Eliza made an excuse that she needed to relieve herself and stole away to the kitchens when the inmates were lining up for evening prayers. Every night after supper, the master led them in prayers of thankfulness for what they had been given and gave them a little lecture on the evils of sloth and idleness. Eliza was unnoticed as she slipped out of the hall and ran to the kitchens.

Cook was polishing one of her saucepans when she entered, breathing hard. She looked at the girl through narrowed eyes as Eliza struggled for breath.

'You want something for Joe, don't you?'

'Yes, please, Cook, if you will be so kind as to give me a piece of bread and a little milk.'

'I cannot spare the milk, child, but I have bread – and there's a piece of cheese, and . . .' She hesitated, then went to the pantry and brought out a half-eaten pie, from which she cut a chunky slice. 'This be apple pie, Eliza. I doubt you've ever tasted it, but 'tis tasty and will help moisten his mouth. 'I'll wrap it in a bit of linen and you can hide it inside your tunic. If mistress sees it we'll both be in for it so be careful.'

'Yes, I will thank you. You be so kind to us, Cook.'

'Well, well, 'tis only right,' she muttered beneath her breath. 'It breaks a body's heart to see what that woman makes folk suffer. When I was a lass I worked in the kitchen as the lowest of the low, Eliza, but Cook fed me and she taught me about good food. She would turn in her grave if she saw what I have to put up with here for she believed in good ingredients, and if you tasted her apple pie you would think you'd gone to Heaven.'

Eliza's interest was caught. 'Where did you live when you were a girl, Cook?'

'I don't remember the name of the house,' Cook said with a sigh, 'but I recall 'twas near the sea. I think 'twas on the South Coast, near a place called Bournemouth but I never went there in my life. When Cook retired, mistress made me Cook in her place for I had learned all that I could and she took me with her when the great house was sold and they came to London town. The family had fallen on hard times and it was a much smaller house. The master drank, you see, and lost his fortune. Then he died and mistress was forced to sell up and go to live with her sister. She took her personal maid but the rest of us were let go.'

'Did you come here as an inmate then?'

'No, I worked for an elderly gentleman for some time – but in the end he died too and then I cooked for working men on the docks at a canteen there for it was all I could find. They were rough-tongued but it was well enough, until I fell afoul of a rogue. He persuaded me to run off with him and be his mistress and like a fool I did, and he left me when I became pregnant. That was when I came here until I had the child and it died

49

soon after it was born. I would have left then for I could always find work but the late mistress asked me if I would cook for them; she was a good woman and I stayed for her – and here I be until this day. It be not such a bad place afore the old mistress died – though we did often suffer the cholera and 'twas that killed her. Mr Stoneham told the master it be the old water pipes and he put in fresh and since then 'tis not visited us.'

'I'm so glad you stayed here,' Eliza said, and her eyes stung with tears. 'You and Ruth are all that makes this place bearable.'

'Well then, child, off you go,' Cook said. 'Keep that food safe and take the lad a little water in this cup. You must bring it back to me when you can.'

'Yes, Cook. I shall.' Eliza left with her precious bundle inside her clothes. Cook's kindness had made weepy and she felt tears on her cheek, which she swiped away with the back of her hand. Cook's story was sad but not as bad as many of the men and women who came to the workhouse. She'd had a good life until she allowed a rogue to deceive her.

It was dark when Eliza crept from her bed and moved noiselessly between the rows of sleeping women. To reach the boy's dorms Eliza had to leave the women's wing and cross to the men's side, which she did by climbing through a window that had no bars because it led only to the inner courtyard. The main door of the men's wing was locked, and she was not privy to the key, but it was easy enough to go through the window at the back of the workroom where the men made hemp ropes. This was never locked, because the room needed plenty of fresh air while the men worked, and Eliza was aware of it as were most of the inmates, and she was not the only one to use it that night. When she entered the workroom, she saw one of the men entering through the window. His name was Jamie and he had a wife and son in the workhouse; he'd spoken to her kindly a few times in the past. He put his finger to his lips.

'You will not tell you saw me?' he said, because if he was discovered out of his dorm he would be punished. She shook her head. 'Good girl. Joe's not in his dorm but in the cellar. My boy is sick in the infirmary, and I sneaked out to visit him. Master sent him to bed after the work was done, but he told me that mistress put Joe in the cellar. I thought I would take him this later.' Jamie pulled a piece of bread and a little stone bottle out from under his shirt, which he offered to her 'Water.'

Eliza thanked him but said, 'I shall take the water, but you keep the bread. I have food.' She knew he must have saved the bread from his own ration. She turned back from the window because she knew the way to the cellar well enough.

She returned to the hall and then found her way in the semi-darkness by pressing her hand against the wall until she reached the cellar door. When she reached it she fumbled for the lock and found the key was still there. Mistress left it there so that she could not be blamed if the child died; she'd sworn that Eliza had shut herself in and no doubt she would swear the same of Joe.

Turning the key, Eliza removed it and put it in her pocket. She went inside, leaving the door slightly ajar so that the faint light from a window showed her the steep stairs. Her hand against the wall for there was no rail, Eliza gingerly moved down the steps one by one.

'Joe, are you there?' she called.

'Eliza – is that you?' his voice answered, and she could just see a dark shape. He had been lying on the floor of the cellar but now he was standing and he moved towards her. 'Stand still. I can see in the dark; I'll come to you.'

Eliza did as he told her and the next moment she felt him touch her hands, drawing her in further. She stumbled against something and he steadied her.

'It's a wooden crate I found to sit on,' he said 'and there are sacks. I made a bed of them.'

'I did not find them when I was shut in here with the rats.' She shuddered.

Joe laughed. 'I be not afraid of them. I like to hear them moving about – and they be clever, rats.'

'What do you mean?'

'I'll tell you when I be ready,' Joe said, and then, a new note in his voice. 'Why did you come, Eliza? If mistress finds out, she'll beat you.'

'I don't care. She hits me all the time,' Eliza told him. 'I brought you food, Joe. I didn't want you to go hungry as I did.'

'How did you get in for I know the door was locked?'

'Mistress left the key in the door. I nearly died in here, Joe, and she was afraid if you died she would be blamed so she left the key – and I have it, so she cannot lock us in.'

'You'm be clever like the rats,' Joe said and hugged her. 'And brave. Not everyone would do what you have, little Eliza.'

'You're my friend,' Eliza said. 'I asked Cook and she

52

gave me food – a piece of bread, cheese and a slice of apple pie.'

'A feast fit for a king,' Joe said and there was laughter in his voice. 'Sit here on my box and share it with me, Eliza.'

'I have supped; it is for you.' She pressed the parcel into his hands.

'Nay, we shall share it,' Joe insisted. 'It is a bond between us, Eliza. One day we shall leave here. The rats will show us the way and if you give me the cellar key it will make our escape easier and sooner.'

Joe had broken the cheese as he spoke and gave a piece to Eliza. She put it in her mouth and the taste made the moisture run for she had seldom had anything so good and when Joe gave her a piece of the pie and told her to eat it with the cheese she sighed with pleasure.

'It be like Heaven,' she said. 'Be we both dead, Joe?'

'No, we're alive, and one day we'll be free,' he said and smiled at her. 'You'm be my girl one day, Eliza. No matter if they part us – no matter what happens to us, you mind what I say. We were meant to be together and one day I'll make it happen. I swear it on my heart – now swear on yours that you'll be mine.' Joe took her hand and placed it over her chest. 'Swear, Eliza. Swear to be true . . .'

'I swear it, Joe. I swear it on my heart . . .' Eliza felt the touch of his lips on her cheek and his arm about her. It was at that moment that the door of the cellar was flung open and at the top of the stairs stood the master and the mistress, both holding a candlestick and looking down at them.

'I know you're there, you little slut,' mistress said viciously, though she could not see down into the darkness of the cellar. 'Your master would not believe you so wicked – but I knew you had stolen food to bring that gypsy brat.'

Eliza wanted to protest that she'd been given the food, but if she did that Cook would be in trouble. The food she gave to the women and children did not belong to Cook; it was the property of the master and Cook could be branded a thief. Eliza knew that she must take the blame.

In the darkness of the well of the cellar, she handed the key to Joe, who slipped it inside his tunic. He squeezed her arm and whispered to her and she nodded, for Joe could see clearer than she in the darkness.

'Our time will come, believe,' he whispered as she walked towards the mistress and began to ascend the steps

'You shouldn't have put him here to starve like you did me,' she said boldly as she reached the top of the steps and received a sharp slap across her head.

'Insolent child!' Mistress Simpkins took hold of her arm, her fingers digging into her upper arm so that Eliza almost cried out with the pain. 'I shall tell Cook that you are on short rations again tomorrow.'

'I don't care what you do to me,' Eliza defied her. 'He is my friend.'

'You dirty little slut! What have you been doing with that gypsy?' the mistress demanded and grabbed hold of Eliza's arm as she reached the top of the cellar. Rutting like the beast you are no doubt. 'Give me the key!'

'I do not have it,' Eliza answered boldly. 'The door was unlocked and there was no key.'

'Liar!' The mistress slapped her face. 'The key was there for I left it so.'

'Then someone must have taken it,' Eliza said and held her head high.

For her pains she received another slap and Mistress Simpkins would have continued to beat her but the master intervened.

'Perhaps you mislaid it yourself, sister. Take her back where she belongs. I shall deal with the boy. He is *my* ward. Come up here to me, Joe. I have something to say to you.'

Eliza looked back as she was dragged off by the furious Mistress Simpkins and saw Joe emerge from the cellar. She saw the master give him a cuff round the ear and their eyes met before she was pushed around the corner and out into the courtyard.

'You may wait out here until I'm ready to speak to you and I shall want to know how you managed to get out of your dorm,' the mistress said as they reached her office. She slapped Eliza several times on the arms and head. 'Sit in the corridor and wait – and if you dare to disobey me I'll thrash you until you can neither lie down nor sit.'

Eliza did not answer, nor did she hang her head. It was cold and she was sleepy but if the mistress wished it, she would have to wait all day and go without both her breakfast and perhaps her supper. Yet it had been worth it for the pleasure of sitting with Joe and eating delicious apple pie and cheese, and if Eliza died now she would keep the memory in her heart forever.

CHAPTER 5

Joe was put back to work with the men working on the rope the next day and Eliza met him when they gathered for the mid-day meal. They were not supposed to mingle, and talking at mealtimes was strictly forbidden, but Joe lingered at the serving table and brushed against her as Eliza went up to get a drink of water.

'I'll meet you tonight in the cellar,' he whispered. Eliza looked at him and nodded, because she knew what she risked if she was caught but she wanted to spend time with Joe and it was the only way.

'No talking there,' the master said and glared at them. Joe winked at her before walking off to join the men he'd been working with that day.

'Be careful, Eliza, love,' Ruth said when she sat down next to her. 'If mistress sees you, she'll punish you again.'

Eliza nodded but didn't answer. Her heart was singing because now she knew that she had a true friend other than Ruth and she felt drawn to him in a way she could not explain. Joe had said they were bound to each other and Eliza believed him. Having somewhere they could meet and talk without fear of being seen or heard was worth any risk and she could hardly wait for darkness to fall.

She looked at the men working on breaking stones in the yard as she left the dining hall and walked back to the laundry for another stint of hard work. Each man was hammering at large rocks, which they had to break down into small stones for use in building the new railways that were gradually spreading all over the country. Eliza didn't know what a train looked like but the men who worked on the stones had told Ruth that these stones went between the lines that held the great fire-breathing monsters that ran on them.

Some of the younger boys were sweeping the yard, and two old women sat on stools picking over rags and putting them into baskets. Their clothes were little better than the rags they sorted and their long grey hair straggled about their heads. One was coughing and looked so ill that Eliza thought she ought to be in the infirmary instead of working in the bitter cold.

Entering the laundry, Eliza found Joe's clothes, which she'd hidden once they were dry, and tucked them inside her dress. Her coarse, striped apron hid the bulge and she would give them to Joe that evening so that he could hide them somewhere ready for when he ran away.

'You came then?' Joe greeted her as she crept down the cellar steps that night and he guided her to the upturned crate where they could sit and talk. 'I thought you might not be able – or that you would fear what that old witch would do to you.'

'I hate her – and she will punish me if she finds out,'

Eliza said, 'but I don't care. You're my friend, Joe. I want to be with *you*.'

'I'm going to run away soon,' Joe told her. 'I think there is a way out of the cellar, a tunnel that leads to outside the walls. I stole a piece of candle from my dorm and I'm going to find the entrance and then, when I'm ready, we'll both go – we'll leave this place together and never come back.'

'Oh, Joe!' Eliza gave a little squeal of excitement. 'You promise you'll take me with you when you escape?'

'I promise,' Joe said and caught her hand, pressing it to his chest. 'If they prevent us some way, I won't forget you – and I'll come back for you.'

'I promise I'll never forget you,' Eliza said and sat snuggled up to his shoulder. They had no feast that night, nor in all the nights that followed that week and the next, but the warmth of friendship kept Eliza warm as no blanket ever had in this terrible place. Even her love for Ruth, the woman who had cared for her as a mother, did not make her feel like this. Joe was special, and she knew that nothing could ever make her forget him even if they were parted.

Sitting in the dark, hugging her precious ragged shawl about her, listening to Joe talk about his family and his travels from one country to another, took Eliza to the outside world, opening her mind to the idea that there was a different life – another place where it was possible to be happy and not to live in fear. Now that Joe was her friend, Eliza believed that it would not be long before she was free to leave the workhouse. She would go with Joe and they would find work somewhere while they waited for Joe's father to be released from prison and then she would live with them in their caravan and go to wonderful places that she had never heard of.

'I have a disobedient girl I want schooling,' Joan said to the man who sat in her office drinking ale one morning, some twelve days after the gypsy boy arrived. Her visitor was a gentleman by birth, but his secret trade was not one he would ever wish his family to know of and he and Joan had done business more than once in the past. 'What will you pay me for her? She is fresh and well-looking enough if she's washed and clothed as your clients like.'

'How old is she?' the man asked, eyes narrowed. 'Some interfering fool is making a fuss in the House of Lords about young girls being used for immoral purposes and if she was seen on the premises I might lose everything. Most of the time my clients turn a blind eye, but recently I've heard some of them question a girl's age before they buy her services.'

Joan glared at him. In the past he'd been only too eager to take the younger girls. She knew he liked them himself and often used them first before passing them on to his rich clients. Only if the girl was virgin and very lovely did he keep her fresh for the highest bidder.

'It is all very well for you, but we had an agreement. What am I to do with her? She defies me at every turn and beating her does no good – besides, the last time she nearly died and one of the governors told me if it happened again I should lose my place here.'

'That would be Stoneham, I dare swear?' her visitor said and nodded. He swore and spat on the floor, drawing a frown from Joan. She disliked his coarse manners, and would not have admitted him to her rooms had he not proved both useful and generous in the past. 'He never visits my place nor any other brothel from what I can gather – sanctimonious fool! He has been stirring things in the background and one of his friends spoke in the Lords for half an hour concerning young girls – the white slave trade, he called it. What else is there for little guttersnipes but lying on their backs to earn their keep? Tell me that! They get food, clothes, a warm bed and a few shillings – left to themselves they'd sell their bodies for food and gin and sleep in the gutter, so where's the harm? I swear they're better off in my house. Damn the Honourable Toby Rattan and his friends! Such nonsense gets into the newssheets and it makes the clients edgy. They fear exposure for many of them have reputations to lose.'

'And wives and children they would not wish to know of their guilty pleasures,' Joan said, nodding in understanding. 'I am disappointed, sir. I had hoped you would take her off my hands.' It was inconvenient that he'd had an attack of conscience regarding young girls. Despite putting the girl on short rations and threatening her, Eliza still looked defiant and there was a smile in her eyes that irked Joan.

'You should sell her to a master who would work her until she was too exhausted to defy him.' Her visitor smiled unpleasantly. 'He will use her in whatever way he chooses and no one will question him, for she will be his servant, and bought from the workhouse she has no rights – or none that she knows of. The law has double standards, for if it was known he took advantage of her in my house they would deem it unlawful, but in his own, none will know or care.'

'Yes . . .' She smiled cruelly. 'I could not be blamed if she died at her master's hands. I hired her to him in good faith – in the hope and belief she would have a new and useful life.'

'Exactly.' His eyes met hers in amused agreement. 'Once all this fuss has died down I'll take the girls again.'

'I think I've found the way out,' Joe told Eliza when she joined him that night. She'd managed to find a piece of soft bread in the kitchen, which she shared with him. 'As I thought, it's a tunnel of sorts. Once this cellar had a chute for coal outside the walls of the house. It has become neglected, covered by debris and filled in with earth and filth – but I can dig it out with my hands and a small digging tool I stole from the vegetable garden. Someone had left it lying on the ground and I took it.' Eliza looked at him doubtfully in the darkness. 'Well,' Joe protested, 'he should've taken more care of it!'

Eliza shook her head. Stealing food was punishable by restrictions and being shut up alone, but stealing a valuable tool from the vegetable plot was serious – Joe could be taken to the magistrate and sent to prison, which she'd heard from Ruth was much worse than being here. He might be birched, and he would be made to do hard work, perhaps even harder than he did now.

'You must be careful, Joe.'

He laughed. 'I shan't get caught. I've hidden it with my clothes and the key to the cellar, and, as soon as

61

we're ready we'll steal some food from the kitchen and then we'll escape at night.'

'Yes, I'm ready to go,' Eliza said. 'Can I help you clear away the debris?'

'No, for it would make your clothes filthy. I work on the rope, so no one takes notice of me, but if you got your dress dirty they would be suspicious – and it would hurt your hands.' Joe grinned at her. 'It won't be long, Eliza, I promise. Another week or so and we can leave this accursed place – and I'll put a curse on that old witch too.'

Eliza giggled. It was fun to sit with her friend and plan their escape together. She nursed her secret inside as she went back to the dorm and snuggled up to Ruth, who was fast asleep. Eliza wasn't sure if her friend knew she was meeting Joe, but if she did she wouldn't tell anyone because Ruth would never do anything to hurt her. Eliza longed to escape from this place, but a part of her was reluctant to leave Ruth behind.

'Mistress says you're to wash yerself and put this on.' Sadie thrust a dress at Eliza. It was old and worn but better than the uniform she was wearing, which had been mended so many times it had more patches than Eliza could count and marked her out as being refractory and therefore subject to punishment. 'Be quick about it! She wants yer in her office sharpish or you'll feel her stick.'

'Am I going to church tomorrow? Is that why I've been given a different dress?'

'How should I know?' Sadie's look was cunning and filled with malice. 'Mistress never tells me what she's goin' ter do.' Yet Eliza was sure she did know and was pleased.

Ruth looked at Eliza anxiously when Sadie had gone. 'I wonder what mistress be up to now, my lovely,' she said. ''Tis not Sunday tomorrow but Saturday so it cannot be church.'

'Is she goin' to send me away somewhere?' Eliza felt a spurt of fear. There had been a time when she'd longed for someone to come and take her away, but she was too old to be adopted by a family. They always wanted babies or very small children. So it must mean that she was to be sold as a servant. 'I have to see Joe – I have to tell him . . .'

'If you go to the men's workrooms you'll be in trouble and so will he,' Ruth said. 'No need to be scared, my lovely; it bain't always bad to be taken away by a master and might be better. Some folk find good masters and a new life – better than in here.'

'No! I don't want to leave you and Joe,' Eliza said her eyes stinging with tears she struggled to hold back. 'Joe and me are goin' ter run away together one day and live in the country – and you could come with us, Ruth.'

'Bless you, my lovely,' Ruth said and smiled at her. 'I be too old for a life on the road; I know what it be like to go without food for days and never have a place to lay yer head. You've no idea, Eliza. As a girl of your age I worked makin' chain for two shillin' a week, burned by the heat of the furnace and my shoulders aching fit to break; tiny links we made, and paid by weight not length. My ma worked long hours at it for not much more than I earned, and workhouse be better

63

than that or the open fields when 'tis cold and wet.'

'I long to be free,' Eliza said passionately not listening to her wise counsel. 'And I want to be with Joe.'

'Wash yerself and change yer dress like mistress bid yer,' Ruth said. 'I'll get a message to Joe and mebbe he'll find yer afore mistress gets her claws in yer, my lovely.'

'Ruth, I love you,' Eliza said and flung her arms about her, sobbing against her plump body.

For a few moments Ruth held her close, her hand stroking the silky hair that was the colour of moonlight when it was fresh washed. 'Be brave, my Eliza. If mistress be made up her mind to hire yer out, we cannot stop her. You've lived here all your life and she has clothed and fed you and is entitled to her fee. One day I'll find you again, I promise. Find out the name of the master you be sold to and tell Joe afore you leave. I'll come lookin' fer yer one day – and if I can't, then Joe will know where you be.'

'I don't want to go! I hate her but I want to stay with Joe and you.' Eliza's tears streamed down her face.

Ruth let go and held her away from her. 'Wash yerself well, Eliza, and don't let her see yer tears, for it's that will pleasure her. Remember, you've got friends and one day we'll see each other again.'

Washing herself with the coarse soap and scrubbing her fingers through her hair until her scalp tingled, Eliza wondered about her new master. Would he be like Master Simpkins, who mostly abided by the rules and treated the men better than his sister treated the women in her ward? If he was fair and did not beat her, then Eliza would not mind working for him long enough to repay her bond – though she did not know how many years that would take.

If she could just talk to Joe before she left, make certain he knew that she did not want to leave him and was ready to go away with him when the time was right, she would not mind so very much.

Eliza had not realised what it would feel like to be inspected by the man who had purchased her from the mistress. He was not a tall man, but he was very fat with little piggy eyes that seemed to bore into her, stripping away her clothes and leaving her vulnerable. First of all he walked round her, nodding to himself, and he touched her hair, which had sprung into natural waves now that it had dried after the scrubbing Eliza had administered. Then he stood in front of her and told her to open her mouth; when she did not obey instantly his eyes narrowed and a cold shiver went down her spine: this was not a kind man.

'I said open your mouth. I want to see if you have your teeth and are healthy.'

'She is not a horse,' Mistress Simpkins said and for the first time ever Eliza felt gratitude towards her. 'You can see she is young, strong and clean – do you want her or not? I can sell a girl like this six times over for as much as you offered and perhaps more.'

His mean little eyes narrowed but he nodded and flicked Eliza's ear with his finger. 'I'll take her as she is then – she looks strong enough and my wife needs a servant for she is carryin' her fourth child in as many years and has no strength.'

'Make sure you work her hard,' the mistress said

with a look of menace at Eliza. 'She can be troublesome unless you're firm – so do not feed her too well and beat her if she disobeys you.'

'I've me own ways of taming a wild cat,' the man said and took hold of Eliza's arm firmly. 'I'm Fred Roberts but you call me master and you do as you're told or I'll flay the skin from yer back – do yer understand, girl?'

Eliza inclined her head. She couldn't speak for if she did she would weep and beg the mistress to keep her. Mistakenly, she'd believed that nothing could be worse than her life at the workhouse, but seeing the glitter in the man's eyes told Eliza that she was about to discover how bad things could really be.

Lifting her head proudly, she looked once at the mistress who had sold her and then turned to follow her new master. As they left the office, Joe came hurtling at them, grabbing at Eliza's arm.

'Fred Roberts – tell Ruth,' she whispered giving him a look of appeal. 'I don't want to go!'

'I won't let him take you,' he cried and tried to tow her away but her new master raised his arm and sent Joe flying with one heavy blow. Eliza screamed and bent over him as he lay on the floor. She whispered in his ear before she was yanked to her feet by her hair and forcibly propelled from the workhouse, into the courtyard.

Tears were on Eliza's cheek as she looked back and saw Joe stumble out into the courtyard after them. He raised his hand and placed it over his heart and Eliza did the same, passing the message that only they understood. She did not know if Joe had heard what she whispered as he lay stunned on the ground, but it hardly mattered. She'd been sold to this man and it seemed he owned her, just as if she were a horse or a cow.

Eliza knew nothing of laws or of men who sat in parliament and made speeches about the foul trade in young children sold to brutal masters, of young girls imprisoned in brothels and made to serve men until their bodies were diseased and their minds gone. She did not know that one person had no right to own another, nor that there were rules to protect her. In the workhouse the mistress sold women and children for pieces of silver or gold and there was no one to stop her. For that there would need to be proof – and who would believe the word of a little guttersnipe? The mistress had the right to charge for the clothes any inmate was discharged in, and if she chose to put a high price on them who could challenge her?

Eliza's mind was filled with terror as she was thrust into a cart and told to lie on the straw in the back. Warned that she would be pursued and thrashed until the blood ran if she tried to escape, she was frozen, numbed into obedience. The straw was filthy and smelled of the pig that had been transported from the market.

In her terror, Eliza thought death might be preferable to the unknown future because she was being torn from all she'd known her whole life, from her friends Ruth, Cook, and from Joe, her special friend. The memory of those nights spent whispering together seemed like a golden time, now ripped from her, leaving her bereft. There was a huge black hole of misery inside her as she wept. What was going to happen to her now? Her new master had threatened beatings but somehow it was not the thought of physical pain that caused her to shake – it was the sense of being alone, without Ruth and the other inmates. Now she was alone in a harsh world and she was afraid.

Eliza was taken to a back lane in a dingy area of the city. Everything, the buildings, pavements, windows were blackened by smoke and the gutters were filthy, running with rain filled with debris that had been thrown out. A dog was hunting for scraps and a mangy cat sat on a windowsill and hissed at it. She had no idea of where she was, but she knew that the stench was worse than anything she'd ever come in contact with before. Her master told her that the large building at the end of the lane was a tannery.

'It's where they cure animal hides to make leather and the stink is worse in summer,' he told her. 'You'll get used to it – there are worse smells, believe me. Wait until the fishmonger tips his waste in the gutters. That stinks to high heaven, but the rats soon clear it – and the meat goes bad in the hot weather sometimes, particularly the offal. I sell as much as I can, but some folk won't touch it fer a farthin'.'

The house she was taken to was fronted by a butcher's shop, which was just one room with shutters that opened up to the pavement; she could already smell the blood and a lingering bad odour that turned her stomach and even though she tried hard, she couldn't stop herself retching as he propelled her through the back yard to the kitchen door. The sight of her bringing up her meagre breakfast as she vomited in the yard made him roar with laughter.

Eliza wiped her mouth with the back of her hand and stared at him resentfully. She hated him already, more than she hated Mistress Simpkins, and wished herself back in the workhouse. Ruth had been right when she told her that the workhouse was not so bad. Despite all the suffering she'd endured at the mistress's hands, Eliza would have given anything to be back in the workhouse now.

She was thrust into a large kitchen, his large hand at her back. There were thick grey stone flags on the floor and two long tables, one at either end. One was being used for baking by a stout woman dressed in a grey gown covered by a white apron, streaked with stains of the food she had prepared over many days; she was sprinkling flour liberally everywhere and it had spilled on the filthy floor. The other table was clearly a thick wooden chopping board and an array of knives and hatchets were in readiness. She could see that it was wet and had been scrubbed recently, but it was scored and there were deep marks where the hatchet had made ruts and these ruts still held bits of bone and blood, which smelled foul; Eliza's stomach turned again, though this time she had nothing left to bring up.

'See to her, Mags,' her master said to the woman and gave Eliza a slap on her backside. 'I've wasted enough time. Give her a slap if she's any trouble. I'd best see what that fool of a boy of mine is up to or I'll lose all me profits, and watch what you're doin' with that flour!' He grabbed Eliza's arm and shoved her forward so violently she almost fell at the feet of the woman he'd called Mags.

He went through a door, which Eliza realised must

lead into the shop, and she caught a glimpse of carcasses hanging up on thick iron hooks and a heavy wooden counter. The smell of blood and meat was so strong that she felt her stomach heave and ran to the stone sink under the window, hanging over it as she retched. but nothing came up.

'It got me that way too, fer a start,' the woman named Mags said mockingly. 'You'll get used to it in time, girl. It ain't pleasant workin' 'ere 'specially in summer, but at least there's a roof over our heads and enough food. Master gives me meat to make pies and stews, and 'tis always fresh for he won't eat the stuff what's gone off – though there's many that will take it a bit on the turn if it's cheap.'

'I don't think I'll ever want to eat meat again,' Eliza groaned and Mags laughed, her double chins waggling.

'Aye, I felt that way at the start, but you get over it. My pie has tasty gravy and you should eat what yer can, for if he sees yer waste good food he'll be angry.'

'I don't care if he beats me. I wish I was dead.'

'Now then, girl, 'tis foolish to talk that way.' Mags looked at her thoughtfully. 'You're no good to me while you're still pukin' so I'll give you a glass of my lemon barley water and a currant bun. That should ease your stomach and then we'll get you settled.'

Eliza nodded, because at least this woman didn't frighten her. She was like some of the older women in the workhouse, capable, with a weathered face that told of long-suffering, and dark hair streaked with grey that she wore pulled back into a knot at the back of her head, covered with a white cap that had seen better days. Her tone was harsh and there was no kindness in her, but thus far she had refrained from hitting her.

'Where am I to sleep?' Eliza asked looking about her.

'You'll sleep with me in the attic when we've finished for the day,' Mags said. 'Master, his son and the mistress have the only bedrooms on the upper floor, 'cos she won't sleep with 'im. She says he stinks of meat and so he 'as his own room, though he goes to her when he's a mind to it whether she will or no – three children that poor woman's had, not counting the one she's carryin', and only one lad lived. God knows how many miscarriages she's had in-between. You'd think he'd let her rest now, but he's always at her like a ruttin' ram.'

'What do you mean?' Eliza asked, though at the back of her mind she thought she knew. Men and women were strictly segregated in the workhouse, but the rules were broken sometimes and occasionally a man managed to sneak into their dorm. Eliza had once asked what was going on beneath humped blankets and Ruth had told her it was all for a bit of comfort and nothing to worry about, but Mistress Simpkins had spoken to her and Joe of rutting and made it sound bad and dirty, and Mags had the same tone in her voice. 'Do you mean what men and women do for comfort?'

'Lawks, but she's an innocent,' Mags said and shook her head. 'You watch out the master don't catch you in a dark corner or you might find out – and you won't like it, girl.'

'I'm called Eliza.'

'Are you now?' Mags nodded. 'Well, if you answer to it, it will do.' She put a glass of a whitish liquid in front of Eliza and a bun.

71

Eliza sniffed at the glass. It smelled sharp and she sipped it, feeling the cool taste on her tongue. 'This is nice,' she said. 'Thank you, Mags.'

'It should stop you feelin' sick for a bit,' Mags said shrugging her broad shoulder. 'Eat yer bun, because I want yer to start work as soon as yer've done. The bedrooms want turnin' out and that means polishin' as well as sweepin' – and then there's this floor to be scrubbed. I suppose yer know how to scrub and clean?'

'Yes, I can scrub. Mistress didn't give us polish but I can learn.'

'If yer willin' ter work 'ard yer'll be all right 'ere,' Mags said. 'I'll just put me pie in the oven and then I'll take yer upstairs. You had best meet mistress fer a start. She may want her pot emptied and that will be one of yer jobs, Eliza. Yer'll be workin' from mornin' 'till night and 'er upstairs will 'ave yer on the run all day if she gets the chance.'

CHAPTER 6

'How is your latest project coming along?' Toby asked Arthur when they dined together at Toby's club one evening in May. He was in a mellow mood. The weather had improved of late, he had spent a pleasant day riding in Richmond Park, and he had recently bought a horse he intended to race at Newmarket. 'Have you made progress with your drive to reform that workhouse?'

'Very little,' Arthur admitted ruefully. 'Master Simpkins promises everything but delivers little – however, I think him weak rather than truly evil. His sister is another matter. I just do not trust that woman. I have been talking with some of the other members of the Board about her conduct, but unfortunately they seem to think her exemplary in her behaviour.'

'How can that be?'

'I fear that most of my fellow members believe that those unfortunates in the workhouse deserve their fate. They tell me the rules are strict because they need to be, and I cannot deny it – but I can smell the rottenness, Toby. I know things are wrong in that place, but until I have proof that she has broken the rules I can do nothing. I have no power to dismiss her without proof.'

'Then pay the workhouse an impromptu visit on some pretext.'

'Yes. I have been thinking of setting up a home for fallen women—' He saw the wicked smile in his friend's face and laughed. 'No, not that kind of home, you idiot – a place where those who are destitute may go to rest, rather than the workhouse.'

'You will find few to support you, though I might know of someone . . .' Toby shook his head and smiled oddly. 'You will have to wait and see.'

'I wait with bated breath,' Arthur murmured sardonically.

Toby summoned a waiter to bring more wine, mulling over what his friend had said. He sipped the rich red wine that perfectly complemented their roast beef and nodded.

'You mean to inquire at the workhouse for someone to work in this home? I'll wager it will not be easy to find a woman who has not been corrupted in that hellhole.'

'No one said any of it was easy,' Arthur replied and smiled. He was thoughtful as he toyed with the delicate stem of his glass. 'I've been wondering how that girl fares – the one I told you of before. I asked Master Simpkins and he told me that she was perfectly well, but I have not been able to put her from my mind.'

'She cannot run your hostel for you, surely?'

'No, not at all, but there was a woman who looked after her. A woman called Ruth who seemed to care for the child. If she is still there I might question her, consider if she would be suitable.'

'Yes, perhaps.' Toby nodded and studied his wine. 'I am pushing for my father to bring forward that Bill in the Lords, to raise the age of consent – and I've got them talking in the clubs about setting up a commission to look into the problem of child prostitution, but these things take time, Arthur. There is already a movement afoot to help women who have been abandoned by their fathers, husbands and their community for some small misdemeanour and forced into prostitution, but these same worthy gentleman do not wish to admit that children are being abused. Some of those who should support the movement against it are throwing obstacles in the way and I fear I know what is behind their reluctance.'

'I daresay they are culprits themselves in some cases.'

'Yes, though it disgusts me I must admit you are right.' Toby frowned. 'Sometimes I despair of this society we live in, the hypocrisy and lies – but I am doing my best to educate them where I can.'

'Yes, you've done wonders stirring up the press.' Arthur smiled at him and raised a delicate wineglass in salute. 'Tell me more of your plans, my friend. My house is a small matter compared to what you attempt. We must stir the conscience of the nation. Child labour must be abolished, at least until the age of fourteen. Only last week I heard of a six-year-old child being forced up chimneys to clean them.'

'Good grief, I thought that had been outlawed in 1840,' Toby said, frowning.

'Yes, so did I, and the Chimney Sweepers Regulation Act of 1864 made the punishments for using children under the age of twenty-one more severe – but it still happens, as do so many other terrible crimes against young children. It is a disgrace in a civilised country like ours.'

'You know I agree. Has the culprit been punished?'

'He has been fined ten pounds, reprimanded and threatened with imprisonment should it occur again.' Arthur frowned. 'But that is only one case – and the trouble is that poverty often makes the parents agree to give their children to a master who may ill-treat them. When they have too many children to feed and clothe it must seem the least of many evils – indeed, their only option.'

'Furnish me with the details and I will speak to others who think as we do,' Toby promised. 'Now then, Arthur. My father has a musical evening next week – and I insist that you attend to bear me company for unless you do I may die of boredom.'

Arthur laughed and inclined his head. 'Yes, I shall come for I would not have you despair of me, Toby. Your father is a good man and he has been generous to the cause.'

'Also, there is someone I would like you to meet.'

'Ah, I see – male or female?'

'A lady,' Toby said and arched one mobile brow. 'A very beautiful lady, Arthur, but not, I must tell you, in the first flush of youth. I understand she suffered a tragedy in her family some years ago and has been caring for her father until his death – a worthy woman, but also good company.'

'Am I to take it that you have intentions or is it that you hope to interest me in the fair sex?'

Toby laughed and shook his head. 'Neither, for she

is not my type and I know it would be useless to present her to you as a wife – but as someone who might take an interest in your work, perhaps.'

'You have succeeded in arousing my interest,' Arthur said arching an eyebrow. 'And now, my friend, a hand or two of whist before we call it a night?'

Eliza tumbled into bed beside Mags and was soon fast asleep. She'd been working from the moment she entered the butcher's house until it was finally time for bed. First of all his wife had had her running errands for more than an hour and when she finally exhausted all her requests, Mags set her to scrubbing the cold stone floor.

It was hard work, for it had not been done in weeks and Eliza had to empty and fill four buckets with hot water. As soon as she mopped one bit of the floor the water turned a reddish brown and went greasy, the smell making her stomach turn. Every time she went out into the yard to tip the hot water down the drain she retched, though little came up for she'd been offered nothing to eat after the bun and cool drink. It was only when all her work was finished that she was told to come to the table. Mags had set the table for supper and there was a large ham-and-egg pie she'd made earlier, boiled potatoes and a dish of pickles to go with it. Mags gave Eliza a piece of moist crust and some egg and potatoes but did not place any meat on her plate.

Eliza took her place shyly down at the end of the table. Master sat at the end and his son Pike at his right hand; next to him was a thin man with sparse grey hair that hung from a bald patch on his pate and was lank with grease. He was the outside man and Eliza had seen him scrubbing the yard with a heavy broom to get rid of the blood from the slaughtered animals.

A pig had been killed right in front of the kitchen window that afternoon and its squeals of fright and pain had made Eliza bite her lip hard to hold back the tears. When she'd looked out at the man gutting the dead pig, she'd seen him grin at her evilly and felt her stomach clench with fear, but Mags told her to take no notice of him.

'Jake is mean and likes his work, but he's afeared of the master,' Mags told her. 'He wouldn't dare lay a hand on you or me, don't you worry. I'd soon hit him wiv me rollin' pin and master would thrash 'im.'

Eliza had nodded but she didn't like the way Jake looked at her across the supper table and was glad he wasn't sitting next to her. When she cleared the dishes into the scullery later, after everyone had finished eating, he came up behind her suddenly and grabbed her.

'What's yer name, little brat?' he sneered. 'Give us a kiss then. . .'

Eliza whirled on him, holding the carving knife she'd been about to wash in the hot water and coarse soap. 'If you come near me like that again I'll stick this in your guts like you did that pig!' she said fiercely and had the satisfaction of seeing him turn pale.

'I'll tell the master of you,' Jake threatened.

'You do that,' Mags said from behind him. 'Yer know what yer'll get so you'd best stay clear. If he doesn't thrash yer, I shall!'

Jake snarled and spat on the floor but slouched out of the scullery.

'He grabbed me from behind,' Eliza said, more indignant than upset. 'Dirty old man.'

'Aye, he is that and yer've made an enemy of him so yer 'ad best steer clear of 'im, girl.'

'I shall,' Eliza vowed and turned back to her work. The hot water stung her hands, which were already red and sore from scrubbing the floor. She made a note to wipe them thoroughly when she'd finished, because they would become very sore if she did not take care of them.

'I'll give yer a little drop of pig grease to rub into yer hands,' Mags said. 'It will stop them cracking between the fingers.'

Eliza wrinkled her nose, because the thought of it had turned her stomach again. After she'd washed and dried all the dishes, Eliza was told she could go to bed and Mags gave her a pewter chamber-stick with a lighted candle.

'I'll be up shortly,' she told her. Use the pot under the bed if you need it – you can empty it in the morning.'

Eliza nodded, for it was a job she'd often been given in the workhouse and she was accustomed to carrying slops to the ditch, though she would not have wanted to visit it at night, for if she'd slipped into it she might never have got out of the foul murk.

The bed was cold in the tiny room under the eaves where she and Mags were to sleep. Eliza missed Ruth's warm body beside her and the companionable snuffles of the other women in the workhouse. Her eyes were wet with tears as she turned over in the bed, which was actually softer and smelled better than the mattress she'd lain on in the workhouse. She was asleep when Mags came to bed and eased her over to one side and she did not stir.

Ruth lay sleepless in her bed, missing the warmth of Eliza next to her and wondering where her friend was and how she was faring. She hadn't realised how much she would miss the girl and her hatred for Mistress Simpkins increased. It made her realise that she was wasting her life here in this awful place and she determined to get out of it somehow.

Hearing one of the older women cry out, Ruth got up and took the lantern to investigate. Meggie Stevens was staring up at her oddly, one side of her face twisted and her mouth open, dribble running over her cheek.

'There, lass, it's all right,' Ruth said and stroked her cheek. She'd seen the elderly taken like this before and knew it was the result of a hard life. Meggie should have been sitting by a warm fire to see out her days, not picking over rags in the cold all day.

'Help m-me . . .' The thin hands clawed at Ruth's hands as Meggie's mouth worked and no sound came out, but Ruth could not call help for Meggie until the morning and by then it would likely be too late. All she could do was to sit with her and soothe her as best she might.

Watching the life fade from Meggie's eyes, Ruth was determined that she would leave here somehow. She would not stay here until she died, alone and sick, in this friendless place.

All she could hope was that her beloved Eliza was in a good place.

Eliza wasn't sure what she'd done to make her master so angry. It was just three weeks after she'd arrived that he seemed to turn against her. Up until that morning, he'd hardly noticed her, merely warning her to get on with her work if she saw her standing idle in the kitchen for a moment. He might clout her ear in passing or shout at her, but he shouted at everyone. She'd been tending his wife, helping her to wash and change her linen and was carrying her pot out to the midden when Fred Roberts grabbed her arm, causing her to slop some of the urine over his boots.

'Now see what you've done, you clumsy wench,' he muttered, clearly furious. 'Look where yer goin', girl!' He brought his hand back and clouted her at the side of the head, making her senses swim. Even as she struggled against her tears, he hit her again.

Eliza knew she must apologise, even though it wasn't her fault. 'I'm sorry, sir. Shall I wipe your boots?' She held her tears back, turning away to look for a cloth.

'I've been helpin' to kill a bullock,' he grunted. 'I can't wear these in the shop. I'll take them orf in the scullery and make sure you give them a good clean.'

'Yes, sir.' Eliza looked at the boots and saw that they were covered in blood and excrement from the beast that had been killed that morning. She gulped, trying to keep down the vomit that rose up her throat; even after three weeks of working in the stink of blood and stale fat, her stomach still rebelled at the thought of the animals being slaughtered in the yard or the sheds.

'Don't look at me as if I'm something out of the midden,' Fred said and gave her another cuff round the ear. He glared at her menacingly. 'Get orf and do yer work or I'll really thrash yer. I can't afford ter keep yer eatin' yer head orf and not earnin' yer bread.'

Eliza turned her head away and hurried off to tip

her pail into the stinking ditch. It was nearly filled to the top and the smell got worse every day; it would have to be emptied by the night-soil wagon soon or it would overflow into the yard. She wasn't sure whether the midden stank worse or the tannery at the end of the lane.

Feeling the sour taste of vomit in her throat, Eliza retched, wiped her mouth and hurried back to the house. She had to scour the pot before she took it back to the bedroom, because Mistress Roberts was fussy about smells and would send her to do it again if it did not smell sweet. After that, Eliza must clean those filthy boots, scrub the floor and then help Mags with the washing, because it was a Monday and the housekeeper washed all the sheets once every two weeks in the summer, and once every two months in the winter.

'If I leave it any longer the fleas will bite us to death,' Mags said. 'If I had a decent back yard I'd wash once a week, but there's nowhere to hang washing, except in the kitchen and I hate steam all over the place.'

'We had a big laundry and we hung the washing from lines high above our heads.' Eliza described the workhouse laundry to Mags who nodded and looked envious. 'Mistress told us to wash the men's clothes one week and the women's the next, but the water turned brown afore half of it was done and we had to rinse it forever.'

'Aye, you would with that lot,' Mags agreed. 'Mistress needs her sheets changed twice a week. We 'ave to do hers separate, 'cos she won't have them wiv his stuff.'

'She told me to do all her personal things careful and gave me some of her special soap so I could wash her nightgowns and undergarments in the sink rather than the copper.' Eliza looked at her. 'Does she never get up? She can get out of bed easy when she wants.'

'Aye, but if he knew that he'd have her flat on her back, so it's best to let him think she's ill, Eliza.'

'Yes . . .' Eliza had begun to understand what Mags meant. She'd heard grunting noises coming from the big walk-in pantry when the master followed Mags in there and she'd hovered outside, not daring to go in. When he left, Eliza went to the pantry and found Mags settling her flannel petticoats.

'Did master hurt you?'

'Nay, not hurt exactly,' Mags said. 'I don't like it, but 'tis easier to put up with it than refuse him . . .' Mags had fixed her with a warning stare. 'Don't let him catch you in a dark place, girl. He'll hurt you far more than he does me.'

Eliza had thanked her and did her best to avoid Roberts as much as she could. Mags wasn't kind to her, but she wasn't cruel either. At their evening meal Eliza sat next to Mags and as far away from both Jake and the master as she could. Yet Fred Roberts was still angry with her.

He stared at her hard each time he saw her that day. Eliza was frightened and wondered what would come next, but the next morning she woke to the sound of screaming from the floor below.

'That's the mistress givin' birth,' Mags said. 'I'll go down to her. Can you go to the kitchen and boil some kettles of water for me, Eliza?'

'Yes, Mags. Do you want me to bring one up – and a bowl?'

'Aye, that would save me legs,' Mags said and smiled suddenly. 'Don't you be worried, girl. Mistress always screams as if she's dyin'. He'll send fer the doctor and like as not she'll come through it.'

Eliza nodded, crossing her fingers behind her back. She ran downstairs to fill the kettles with water and put them on the huge, blackleaded stove. Mags had made the fire in the stove up before she went to bed and all Eliza needed to do was give it a stir with the poker. She ran upstairs with a bowl and some cold water in a jug while the kettles were heating, and then took up two kettles of steaming hot water.

'You'd best put more on,' Mags told her and emptied one of the kettles into the bowl. 'This could go on for hours.'

The screaming went on and on all through the night. A doctor arrived and spent some time in the bedroom with Mrs Roberts and then came downstairs shaking his head. He asked Eliza for water and a bowl to wash his hands, frowning at her as though she were at fault even though she hurried to obey. She was a workhouse girl and as such could not be expected to behave properly unless instructed.

'She's in a bad way, girl. You must pray to God your mistress lives for unless He is merciful, you will soon have no mistress.'

Eliza's throat tightened. Her mistress had never been unkind or said a harsh word, even though she kept her running up and down the stairs on errands. Eliza did not like to think of the mistress in such agony.

84

At seven in the morning the master came down and demanded his breakfast as usual. He glared at her but made no attempt to strike her as she went about her work. Eliza made bacon, fried egg and a thick slice of fried bread and he ate every scrap and drank his tea, and then he went into the shop and closed the heavy door behind him, just as if it were an ordinary day.

Eliza carried a tray of tea and bread and butter with a dish of strawberry jam up to the mistress's bedchamber. She smiled and sipped a mouthful of tea, but Mags ate two rounds of the thick bread with butter and jam and drank two cups of tea to keep her strength up.

'You'll have to keep things goin' downstairs,' she said. 'There's fresh bread made yesterday and a big pork-and-ham pie the master can have with his pickles. Get yourself somethin' to eat, girl, and then scrub the floor and clean the front parlour.'

Eliza wondered why Mags had told her to clean a room that was never used, but later that morning she heard terrible screaming, moaning, weeping and then silence. An hour or so later Mags came down red-eyed and looking exhausted.

'Well, she's out of it, the poor woman. She's dead and the babe with her . . .' She wiped her eyes and sniffed. 'He's killed her this time.'

'The poor mistress,' Eliza said and rubbed her eyes. 'What will happen now, Mags?'

'Once the funeral is over we'll see. He'll certainly have his brothers and their wives here for tea afterwards but it's not for us to speculate on what the master will do next . . .'

Eliza got on with washing dishes and then finished polishing the parlour until it shone. She wondered if she would be needed now that the mistress was dead. Her back ached and her hands were sore. She felt so tired that all she wanted to do was sit down for a bit. A lot of her work had been running up and downstairs after the sick woman, but now she was dead and her babe stillborn. It might be that Master Roberts would let her go – return her to the workhouse. Eliza hoped he might, because although Mags was all right, despite her sharp tongue, she would rather be back with Ruth and Joe.

For the first few days in this house she'd thought of her friends and prayed they might come for her, but nothing had happened and she knew they could not rescue her. However, if her master returned her to the workhouse she would see them again.

Sighing, Eliza sat down in one of the parlour chairs; it was hard to the back being stuffed with horsehair and straight-backed, but she was so tired she fell asleep in seconds. It seemed as if she'd only just shut her eyes when she felt herself being roughly shaken.

'Is this what I pay you for?' her master grunted furiously and she felt his heavy fist connect with her face, splitting her lip. 'There's my wife lyin' dead upstairs and you sittin' 'ere takin' yer ease – I've a mind to send yer back where yer came from, workhouse brat!'

His big fists sent her sprawling on the floor, where she lay dazed for a moment until he kicked at her and told her to get to the kitchen where she belonged.

Tears burned behind Eliza's eyes as she walked into the kitchen. She'd hardly stopped working since she got here and now her face stung where he'd punched her. In that moment she felt as if she wanted to run away. It was worse here than in the workhouse, just as Ruth had told her.

CHAPTER 7

'Good day, Mistress Simpkins,' Arthur said politely that morning at the beginning of May. It was a beautiful spring morning and the trees in the parks were in leaf, some with bright blossom dressing them in their all finery. Having come from his own beautiful garden, he was aware of how dismal the harsh grey walls and high windows of the workhouse really were. Many of the inmates would never catch sight of a tree in full bloom or hear the sound of birdsong. 'I thought I might like to speak with some of your female inmates – if you will permit me.'

'You wish to speak to the inmates, Mr Stoneham? I fail to see the necessity for it. They are all well cared for under the terms of our agreement.'

'I am sure of it, madam,' Arthur said, though he was not certain at all that her wards *were* properly treated. 'It is not an official inspection, I assure you. I wish to speak to some of the women about work I hope to provide in the future.'

'Work?' Her brows went up. 'What possible work could you have for such women?'

'I may have a job to offer the right person – perhaps more than one.'

'Are you looking for a housekeeper?' For a moment her eyes brightened eagerly but he shook his head.

'The position is not in my home, madam, but in a house I am setting up to care for women in need.'

'I see.' The interest died from her eyes immediately. She gave him a grudging look. 'Well, I cannot stop you from speaking to any of the women if you wish, though I do not believe you will find anyone suitable.'

'What about the woman called Ruth? She was caring for that girl – the one who had been locked in the cellar and almost died. She seemed a decent woman.'

'She is a surly creature.' Mistress Simpkins scowled at him. 'Since the girl was taken by her new master she has behaved sullenly and shirks her work. She has caused me a great deal of trouble.'

'The girl recovered, then?' Arthur looked at her with interest.

'Yes, of course. There was nothing much wrong with her except temper. She is a difficult girl and I was unable to control her and so I let her go to a master. He has a wife and a housekeeper and she will be quite safe there – and since he is a butcher and known for his generosity she will be well fed.' Mistress Simpkins sniffed. 'Too well for the likes of her.'

'What is the name of the butcher who hired her services, madam? I should like to make sure that the child is not being ill-treated.'

'I disremember for the moment,' Mistress Simpkins said and then saw the dangerous look in his eyes. 'If you call at my office before you leave I daresay you may find it in my record books.'

'Which you are required to keep,' Arthur said, eyes narrowed. 'No, you need not accompany me, madam. I know my way well enough.'

She opened her mouth to protest and then shut it again. Most of the women were at their work in the laundry or the sewing rooms, where some hemmed sacking and others did more skilled work, for which their mistress received some shillings. Only a few men were taking the air and their morning exercise, the others hard at work making rope or maintaining the building. If the men had complaints she would not be the one in trouble for they were in their master's ward. She frowned as Mr Stoneham left her office. She had made no entry of Eliza's master's name, but she could invent one and by the time he got around to visiting the man she could think of some excuse why Eliza was not there.

Ruth was in the kitchen when the gentleman entered. She knew him at once for he was one of the Board of Governors and she'd noticed him supping at the high table with the master and mistress on rare occasions. A man as attractive and vital as Mr Arthur Stoneham would attract the attention of any woman, even if she was not much interested in men. She looked at him warily. Some visitors asked questions about the mistress and the way the workhouse was run but it was best not to answer, because retribution for any awkward remark would be swift and sharp. Mistress Simpkins punished any that dare speak out against her.

'It smells good in here,' Arthur said and sniffed the air appreciatively. 'What are you cooking between you?'

'I'm making pastry for the rabbit pie for master's dinner,' Ruth said, 'and Cook is making a stew for the men.'

'And what do the women have – a stew similar to the men?'

'No, sir,' Cook spoke up. 'I'm not given meat for the women and children, except on a Sunday or special occasions. I can only flavour their soup with a bone from the beef or the lamb that master has for supper. The women have vegetables made into a thick soup with flour and a hunk of bread.'

'I see . . .' Arthur frowned. 'I must look into that, for your mistress should have sufficient monies to feed you all properly.'

Cook didn't answer, just sniffed hard. His brows went up and he nodded, because he understood what she dared not say.

'I do the best I can with what I have, sir.'

'Yes, I'm sure you do, Cook – or what is your name, pray?'

''Tis such a long time since I be called anythin' but Cook . . .but I think it is Mary, sir. Mary Janes – and I did come from somewhere on the south coast but I disremember where exactly – 'tis too long since, sir.' She smiled at him, revealing yellowed teeth. 'I believe 'twas near a place called Bournemouth though I never visited that town.'

'And have you always been a cook?'

'Yes, always,' Cook smiled. 'I learned from a clever mistress when I was very young and I have cooked for gentry.'

'What brought you here, Mary?'

'Misfortune, sir.' Cook gave a little cackle of laughter. ''Twas a rogue that brought me down, sir – like many a good woman.'

'Ah yes, I believe you're right.' Arthur looked solemn and turned to Ruth. 'And you, mistress?'

'I was brought in by my father, sir. He died and all my family with him. Twice since then I was sold to a master but . . .' she faltered as his brows lowered.

'You were sold, Ruth?' His gaze intensified, as if he could not credit what he heard. 'Are you certain it was not simply the dues owed to your mistress for your clothes?'

'Yes, sir, perhaps . . .' Ruth looked uncertain. 'The man told me he'd bought me, that I belonged to him and had no rights.'

'Your master sold you to him – or Mistress Simpkins?'

'The mistress, sir,' Ruth said and bit her lip. 'You will not tell her I said so, for she would be very angry.'

'I daresay she would,' he agreed. 'I shall say nothing yet but perhaps one day . . .' He hesitated, then, 'I am looking for two women I can trust to run a home for me. I am thinking of perhaps setting up a home for ladies that have fallen on hard times, often through no fault of their own – and yet sometimes it is wilful mischance that brings them down . . .'

Ruth and Cook looked at one another, their eyes opening in wonder as they hesitated. 'Do you mean us, sir?' Ruth asked at last. 'Would it be paid work, sir?'

'Certainly, you would be paid. Not a great deal, but you would have your food, bed, your uniforms – and two pounds a month, which is what my own cook is paid.' He looked at Cook. There was something about the way she faced him honestly that made him feel he could trust her, and Ruth had impressed him from the start. 'I would also need to trust you with the budget for everyone's food and I am sure I could rely on you to buy good quality meat and vegetables for our ladies.'

'Yes, sir, that you can,' Cook told him. 'How soon can we come, sir?'

'As yet I have not found a suitable house, but if I should . . .?'

'Will you think of us, sir? I'd come today if I could.'

'I think Mistress Simpkins would have a right to be angry if you left without notice. We must give her time to find another cook.' He looked expectantly at Ruth. 'What do you say Mistress Ruth? If I should find my property, will you be my housekeeper and care for these poor women?'

'Nothin' would please me more, sir,' Ruth said, 'but I promised Eliza I would try to find her when I left this place.'

'Eliza is the young girl I saw you tending?' Arthur said and nodded thoughtfully. 'Would it content you to know that I am intent on finding the child myself? I think she may have taken work with a butcher.'

'Nay, sir. Eliza was given no choice. She wept to leave her friends here and was frightened – she was sold to him, just as if she were one of the animals he butchers.'

'This is a serious accusation, Ruth. As mistress of the workhouse, Joan Simpkins is entitled to charge a small fee for the expense of keeping Eliza – but it must be the girl's choice whether she takes employment. If she were sold to this man she would be a prisoner, unable to leave if she was unhappy.'

''Tis the same for us all,' Ruth said and Cook nodded fiercely. 'When I was sold the second time, my master thought he owned me body and soul and sought to use me for evil purposes, so I ran away, but I could not find work and was caught begging for food. I was sold twice, but once I was sent back because the mistress did not favour me.'

'You would swear to this on oath?'

'Yes, sir, but who would believe me? I am less than nothing – a wretch from the workhouse with a grudge against my mistress. The master would support her and his word counts for more than mine but if he knew it all . . .' Ruth saw Mr Stoneham's eyes narrow and shook her head. 'I dare not say, sir. I might possibly be believed if I could prove money changed hands when I was sold – but the other . . . it is only whispered of and I dare not speak it aloud.'

Arthur nodded his understanding. 'You are uneasy here. Mistress Simpkins has power over you and you fear her. When you are safe in your own room in my house you may find yourself able to tell me.'

'I'll tell you what has gone on here when we're clear of this place,' Cook said and looked at Ruth. 'We owe it to him, lass. He's a good man but even good men can't stop these things unless they know what's goin' on – and as soon as I think there's a place for me I'm leavin'.'

'Yes.' Ruth raised her head. ''Tis not me I fear for, sir, but Eliza and the other young girls – they're the ones most at risk.'

Arthur's eyes narrowed as he realised what she must mean. 'My God, if I thought . . . but there must be proof. Keep all that I've said to you close. In time I shall return and fetch you both and now I shall set my agents to searching for the child Eliza.'

'Oh please, sir. If I knew that Eliza was safe I should be happy to leave this place for good.'

Arthur nodded and, promising that he would speak to them again when he had more news, went away to question some of the men he'd seen breaking stones in the yard. It was hard, back-breaking work, but no worse than most men would expect to do outside the work-house. The men working on the stones seemed content enough; they answered him fairly in a respectful manner and though Arthur probed none seemed ready to condemn the master of the workhouse.

This reluctance confirmed what Arthur had imagined was the case here. Master Simpkins was a weak man. He probably took his cut of any profit made on the men's work and no doubt would not refuse a bribe if it were offered – but it was his sister who was resented – and it was she who kept this place in order if Arthur was not mistaken. Arthur had no doubt that once he dug deep enough there would be enough dirt to have the woman dismissed, but the inmates were all afraid of her and would not speak out while forced to remain inside these walls.

Taking his leave, Arthur's mind turned to the new order. Mr Disraeli had lost the recent general election and Mr Gladstone had taken his place. The Queen's speech made at this time had spoken of Empire and weighty matters, but there was no mistaking her sadness at losing the Prime Minister who had brought her out of her heavy mourning. Prince Albert had, in 1861, died suddenly of what was believed to be typhoid fever and she'd thrown herself into a state of extreme despair. Her dress was, and Arthur suspected would always be, the severest black, for she sincerely mourned her lost husband, but at last the Queen-Empress had decided to speak out on national affairs again.

It was shocking that when such a good and pious queen sat on the throne of England, and after all the good work Prince Albert had done to bring about a state of decency in high places, establishments like this should still exist.

Arthur set his mouth firmly. He would get to the bottom of the situation here and he would see that wretched woman, Miss Joan Simpkins, get her comeuppance! He would visit the man who had either hired or bought that girl from the workhouse. It was the first step on a long journey – and he wanted to know how the girl fared with her new master. Something about her had touched him and he would be very angry if he found that she was being mistreated.

CHAPTER 8

Eliza felt the oppressive misery in the house. Fred's son crept about like a mouse, red-eyed and silent. His mother had been an invalid much of his young life, but she'd always had a kind word and a peppermint sweet for her son, and now he was just another slave, to be shouted at and beaten by his father like the other servants.

Eliza saw him sitting miserably in what had once been his mother's chair by the fire in the kitchen on the Sunday after they'd buried her, though it was two years since Mistress Roberts had come down to the kitchen to sit, so Mags had told her. The funeral had been held and family had come and gone to mourn the poor lady, who was now in her grave. Pike's father had gone out drinking with friends and was intent on a card game to raise his spirits, so Mags said.

'What's to become of that wretched lad now, I don't know,' Mags said and wiped her eyes on her apron. She too had red eyes, because in her way she'd loved her mistress and tried all she could to save her. 'Here, take him one of my currant buns, girl, and a glass of warm milk sweetened with honey – but don't linger. There's work fer you to do and the Lord help yer if yer neglect it the mood the master's in.'

Eliza took the bun and milk as she was bid and Pike looked at her, his eyes so tear-laden that they threatened to spill over. 'Mags sent these for you,' Eliza said. 'The milk is sweet and the cake tastes good.'

'You have the milk,' he said and gave her a half-smile. 'I'll eat the cake, but I'm not sure I can keep it down. Every time I think of Ma lying there dead, the baby lifeless and blood all over her legs – and him out in the yard killing a pig not three hours later – it turns my stomach'

'I kept bein' sick for weeks, after I came here,' Eliza said. 'It's this place and the smell.'

'You should run away while you can,' Pike said suddenly. 'It's what I'm goin' ter do as soon as—' He went quiet as the back door to the yard opened and his father lurched in, clearly the worse for drink.

'What're you doin' sittin' 'ere, runt?' Fred Roberts muttered. 'There's been enough messin' about over that useless bitch upstairs this week – get through in the shop and clean up ready fer termorrer.' His mean eyes turned on Eliza. 'Get to your task, workhouse brat, or I'll flay the skin from yer back.'

Eliza moved away from him, her heart thumping but his son drew his attention from her.

'My mother is dead havin' the child you forced on her!' Pike stood up to his father for the first time ever in Eliza's hearing. 'You're a rotten bully and I hate yer.'

Before he finished speaking the butcher slashed at him with his great fist, felling him to the kitchen floor, where he lay stunned and bleeding. Seeing his son lying there with blood on him seemed to enrage Fred Roberts even more and he started to kick at the boy's stomach with the toe of his boot.

'Leave him be!' Eliza darted at him, throwing hot milk into his face and making him splutter. He gave a roar of rage and swung at her, but she dodged out of the way and he lurched unsteadily on his feet; in that moment, his son pulled at his ankle and jerked him off balance, Fred crashed down and hit his head on the edge of a heavy joint stool. 'Is he dead?' Eliza's frightened voice brought Mags to investigate.

'Nay, his head's as thick as a block of wood,' Mags said scornfully. 'He'll sleep it off for a while – but I shouldn't want to be you tomorrow, lad – or you, girl. If he remembers what either of you did he'll thrash the pair of you.'

'I'm goin' now.' Pike was on his feet. 'If I were you, Eliza, I'd do the same – or he'll thrash yer.'

Mags laid a restraining hand on Eliza's arm as Pike rushed from the room and they could hear him in the parlour, pulling open drawers and making a racket.

'Let him get on wiv it, girl,' Mags said. 'Master will like forget what you did and if he catches that boy he'll kill him – not that I blame him for runnin' off.'

They heard the sound of footsteps pounding up the stairs and again drawers were pulled out, things knocked over and thrown about, and then the butcher's son came down, carrying a big bundle done up in a shawl.

'I've taken some of my mother's bits and *his* money,' Pike said. 'You tell 'im what I did, Mags. Don't let him blame you or the girl. I'm goin', and if I die of starvation when the money has gone I'll never come back.'

In another instant he was out of the kitchen door and running across the yard. Eliza went out and watched him go. A part of her wished she'd gone with him, but he wasn't Joe, he wasn't her friend. Eliza had hardly exchanged one word with the butcher's son until this morning. It had taken his mother's terrible death and his father's behaviour to make him leave. She went back to the kitchen. The butcher was still lying on the ground, twitching and snorting a little in his drunken stupor.

'Should we wake him?' Eliza asked. 'Won't he take harm lyin' there on the cold floor like that?'

'What do you care?' Mags asked and looked at him with barely disguised disgust. 'He's no better than the beasts he slaughters – and that poor woman's in her grave because of him. If the lad hadn't already taken his till money I might have done the same – but I reckon he's got a pot of gold somewhere. One of these days I'll know where he hides it and then I'll take it and go.'

'Where would you go?' Eliza looked at her in wonder.

'I'd have me a nice little cottage and I'd bake pies and cakes for the market – maybe I'd bottle fruit in summer. It would be a good life, Eliza.' Mags grinned. 'I've put up with that pig for a long while, girl. I reckon I deserve something for all me trouble – I'm pretty sure his money pot is in his bedchamber, and I intend to find it. When I do I'll be off – and now you'd best clean the Mistress's chamber thorough, because I intend to sleep there tonight, and you can 'ave my bed for yerself.'

'You'll sleep in mistress's bed?'

'Aye,' Mags grinned at her. 'You need not look like that – it were 'im as told me to do it, and I knows why.

'E'll be after me every night, same as he were 'er, but I intend to get something out of it, don't you worry. I'll have me own little cottage afore I'm done . . .'

Eliza nodded, picked up her cleaning cloths and went upstairs. She was not sure what Mags was planning, because the master would flay her alive if she took his money, especially after what his son had done. His temper would be more vicious than ever when he woke up – and they had both best keep out of his way.

When the master woke his temper was no better, though he did not seem to recall the part Eliza had played in what had happened. However, once he discovered that his son had fled, taking the money from the till as well as other valuable items from the house, he raged like a frustrated bull, knocking Mags aside when she spoke to him and overturning a kitchen stool.

Eliza was coming from the pantry with a dish of brawn for their supper when he barged into her and sent the pork jelly flying so that it landed on the floor and was ruined.

'You careless little bitch!' he raged at her and struck her on the side of the head, sending her to the kitchen floor on her knees and while she knelt there trying to recover her senses, he kicked her side and made her cry out in pain.

Eliza got to her feet, eyeing the butcher in fear as he glared at her and she thought he would strike her again, but then the yardman called to him that a pig had arrived and he swore, spat at Eliza and told her to clear up the mess she'd made.

Eliza stood staring after him as he went out and

101

slammed the door. Tears were burning behind her eyes, but she refused to cry. Her fingers curled into the palms of her hands and she felt a surge of rebellion. The ruin of the pork brawn was not her fault; it was his and he was a bully and a brute. She wasn't going to stay here and let him treat her like this! The thought was there in her mind, but the next thought came swiftly. Where could she go? If she returned to the workhouse Mistress Simpkins would only send her back to this man who treated her like a slave.

'Get on with yer work, girl,' Mags said. 'If he comes back and it's not done he'll half kill yer – and me too.'

Eliza looked at her rebelliously. Mags had given her food and seen her clothed but there was no love in her. The only person who had ever loved Eliza was Ruth – and perhaps Joe – and she wanted them. She wanted them so badly but there was no one to help her.

Dropping to her knees, she began to clean up the mess the master had made, resentment burning inside her.

Eliza did not know what woke her that night, but then she sensed someone near her bed and she could smell the blood and fat on him and knew it was the butcher, because the stink never left him even if he washed; it was ingrained into his skin. Shrinking back against the pillows, Eliza hardly dared to breathe as she sensed him coming nearer. Then he was close to the bed and she felt his hands tugging at the blankets. She held them close up to her neck, shaking with fear, but he pulled them from her with one wrench and she could see his bulky shape bending over her.

'Good Eliza, pretty girl,' he said in a foolish voice that made her think he was drunk. 'Pretty little Eliza for me to stroke . . .'

Eliza screamed as she felt his hands on her shift, tearing at it in his eagerness. She wriggled away from his searching hands and jumped out of bed, running on bare feet through the open door towards the narrow stairs that led to the landing below, her frantic screams bringing Mags to the door of her bedchamber as he came after her.

'Yer dirty old bugger!' Mags yelled. 'Get orf her, Fred Roberts, or I swear I'll bloody kill yer. Sweet talkin' me into takin' the mistress's place and now yer want ter throw me over fer that brat. I'll castrate yer, yer filthy swine!'

Mags threw herself at Fred as he hurtled down the narrow attic stairs towards her. She was a big woman and strong, well able to fight and wrestle him, and Fred Roberts had been drunk ever since his wife died and his son ran off.

'Get out of me way, yer old hag,' he muttered and tried to wrestle her away from him, but Mags had him in a bear hug and was determined not to let go of him. Eliza stood sheltered in the doorway of the late mistress's bedroom while the two fought, bit, scratched and punched each other. There they stood at the top of the stairs, seemingly locked in an eternal struggle, grunting and swearing at each other, and then, suddenly, Mags gave one almighty push and thrust him backwards; he teetered at the edge of the stair for a moment and then fell, tumbling down and down to the hall below.

Fred groaned once, as he hit the bottom stair with his head and his neck cracked. The force took him forward so that he rolled over in the narrow hallway, his legs twitching for a moment before he lay still. Mags stood staring at him for several minutes and then threw a scared look at Eliza.

'Gawd blimey, I reckon 'e's dead,' she said and went down the stairs gingerly, clearly frightened. She bent down next to him and put a finger to his throat. She sighed with relief as she felt his pulse, and then he snored loudly and Eliza gave a little giggle of relief. For a moment she'd thought the master dead.

'It's a mercy for you he isn't killed,' she said. 'I bet he'll have a nasty bruise on his neck in the morning.'

'Well, you won't be here to see it,' Mags retorted. 'Put yer dress on over yer night-chemise, for 'tis cold on the streets and it's out there yer must go – and afore he wakes.'

'You're sending me away?' Eliza looked at her uncertainly. 'Why – what have I done?'

'I've put up with that bugger fer years and now the mistress has gone I intend gettin' what I deserve,' Mags told her. 'I'm not havin' yer 'ere to cause me more trouble, so off yer go. Dress and put yer boots on and I'll give yer a shawl to keep yerself warm, Eliza. I'll pack some food and there'll be two shillin' from the housekeeping pot, 'cos yer've earned it – but 'tis all I can give yer.'

Eliza stared at her, stunned into immobility. 'Where should I go?'

'Back to the workhouse yer came from if they'll 'ave yer – or look fer work on the market stalls at the corner of Bull Lane. What should I care?' Mags glared at her and Eliza felt as if she'd slapped her. The woman had not been unkind but now she looked at her as if she hated her.

Returning to her room, Eliza pulled on her one dress over the nightshift Mags had given her when she first came then slid on her boots and put her own ragged shawl round her shoulders. Mags was waiting downstairs in the kitchen. She thrust a bundle made out of another old shawl at Eliza.

'Be careful where you eat that food, girl, for there's some as would kill for a piece of bread,' she said gruffly. 'I'm sorry you've got ter go, but if yer stay he'll likely beat the hell out of yer. God knows what he'll do to me in the morning if he remembers what happened this night.'

Eliza nodded. She'd been kicked, beaten and made to work all hours since she came here. Even the workhouse would be better than staying here to be mauled and used by her master.

Eliza brushed the tears from her cheeks. Mags had the door opened and almost thrust her through it. It was only as she was speeding through the yard that Eliza realised she had no idea where to go. The master had brought her here in his cart and she had not seen which way they turned. She did not know where the workhouse was, or the market Mags had spoken of, and even though she could recall the name Mags had given her, she did not know where to find the lane. Glancing back, she saw that the door had been shut and bolted against the night and knew it was no use returning to ask.

Once out of the yard, she looked up and then down

the lane. It was early, still not truly light, and despite it being nearly summer she felt chilled – or perhaps that was just fear. Eliza had longed to be free when she was kept in the workhouse and thought it would be a great adventure to run away, but that had been with Joe. If Joe was with her she would not be anxious or afraid. It would be fun to travel with him – but alone in a huge city she knew only from her journey from the workhouse to here, Eliza was suddenly very alone. She shivered, for a moment so frightened that she could hardly put one foot before the other.

She had no idea which way to go, but hearing footsteps coming from the left, she turned right and began to run this way and that, down one lane, up another, across to yet another, her scurrying feet carrying her in panic and in the opposite direction to the market Mags had told her of and the workhouse where she believed her friends to be.

CHAPTER 9

'How do you progress with your investigation into the running of the Spitalfields workhouse?' Toby asked when they met for luncheon that day at their club. 'I spoke to my father about your conviction that all was not well, and he happens to agree with you. He is all for reform but thinks it will be difficult to bring about. However, he is very willing to lend his support to you – and will engage to speak before the Board if you should need his help. He is acquainted with Bishop Hendricks, who I believe is a member?'

Arthur inclined his head. 'Yes, but in name only. I've never known the Bishop to attend a meeting – indeed, of the ten members only three or four regularly attend and another three come once a year for the budget.'

'That makes it difficult for you if the three are set against you – you should insist on a full board meeting, my friend.'

'I intend to once I have the information I need.' Arthur smiled grimly and glanced at his gold pocket watch. 'I have a mind to visit a certain Mr Fred Roberts this afternoon. He is a butcher and one of the women at the spike claimed that Eliza had been sold to him. Mistress Simpkins gave me a false location, but her brother supplied the true direction. I intend to investigate just what kind of a man he is.'

'A butcher?' Toby raised his brows. 'At least she may eat well there – do you require any assistance?'

'Not yet, though if I'm not seen again you may come looking for me,' Arthur said wryly and Toby laughed.

'I think you well capable of dealing with this butcher,' he said, 'but now there's something important I wanted to tell you concerning the lady I spoke of.'

Arthur wrinkled his brow. 'I'm not sure I recall . . .'

'No, I daresay you have too much on your mind, but the lady has expressed a desire to meet you – and I've told her you will attend my father's evening affair. Now you can't refuse me, Arthur. I believe you will find Miss Katharine Ross a lady after your own heart.'

Eliza's first night on the streets was spent wandering from one lane to another, looking for somewhere to rest. It was not until the sun had been up some hours that she found herself in a busy street where the pavements were wide and thronged with people shopping and going about their business. Carriages rattled over the cobbles and horses jostled each other in the press of traffic; some well-dressed children were rolling a wooden hoop down the road, followed by their nursemaid, and two dogs quarrelled in the gutters. As she wandered further, Eliza saw a small park next to a church and went to sit on a wooden bench, pulling out a piece of bread from the bundle inside her shawl and eating it. She removed the cork from the small glass bottle that Mags had given her, sipping water as she looked about her with interest.

In the sunshine, things no longer looked so frightening, and, as she'd walked, she'd watched laden carts being drawn by heavy horses up the wide street – wider than any she'd ever seen – and wondered where she was. There were shops everywhere and they seemed to sell all kinds of things; some had pots and pans hanging outside while others were dark and dingy places that had wire mesh at their windows. Books, second-hand goods, with everything from a penknife to a pair of boots jumbled up together in the window; a silk merchant's window overflowed with bales of jewel-like materials, and a shop selling hot bread, fresh-baked pies and cakes that smelled delicious and made Eliza's tummy rumble. Everyone seemed to be in a hurry and Eliza was too nervous to ask anyone for help. When she saw someone she knew by his dress to be a vicar leave the church and walk towards her, she almost fled but then decided he did not look unfriendly and stayed where she was.

'Are you lost, child?' he asked.

Eliza considered her words. 'I was sent on an errand by my mistress,' she said. 'I took the wrong turning and do not know where I am. Can you tell me the name of this place, sir?'

'You are sitting in Nelson's Gardens, child – and my church is the church of Saint Peter. If you are alone and hungry at any time, you may visit the church and I will tell you where to find shelter and food.'

'Thank you,' Eliza said and rose with dignity. 'I be looking for the market at the corner of Bull Lane.'

'I do not think I know that one,' the kindly priest said. 'There are many markets and stallholders use odd corners at the end of lanes to sell their wares – the market you speak of is not in Bethnal Green as far as I know.'

'Am I in Bethnal Green?' Eliza frowned, for the workhouse was in Whitechapel and she believed that the market Mags had spoken of was halfway between that and the workhouse. 'Which way is Whitechapel, please, sir?'

He frowned as he thought about her question. 'You have wandered a long way, my child.' He took a watch from inside his gown and looked at it. 'I do not have time to take you home now, but if you will go to the vicarage and wait until I have done my business I will guide you there myself.'

'You are kind, sir,' Eliza said and hesitated, because she was not yet sure what she meant to do. If she returned to the workhouse Miss Simpkins could give her back to Fred Roberts and she would be thrashed for running away – but more than that, he might come to her bed and perhaps next time she would not escape him 'I have remembered where I want to go now.' She jumped to her feet and started to run away, ignoring his call to her to come back and he would help her.

Eliza passed a school as she ran and heard the sound of children's voices raised in song. For a moment, as she paused to catch her breath, she wondered what sort of children went to a school like that. She glanced back at it as she walked on, deciding that she would ask the way to the market as soon as she saw someone who looked approachable.

'What do you mean she isn't here?' Arthur asked of the man. He had taken an immediate and instinctive dislike to the butcher who had a great bruise on his cheek and stank of goodness knows what and looked as if he had not washed his bloodstained clothes in an age. 'Miss Simpkins says you hired Eliza from her.'

'The ungrateful little bitch ran off in the night,' the butcher declared furiously. 'Stole food, she did, and went off while we was asleep. I'll flay the skin from her backside when I get her back.'

Arthur's brows furrowed. 'The terms of hire mean that you have the use of the girl's service for a certain amount of years but you do not own her – and if you beat her too hard you could be punished for it, particularly if she dies – it would be a hanging matter.'

'What's it to you?' the butcher said belligerently. 'What I paid fer her, I bloody mean to get me money's worth out of the brat and you can't stop me!'

'No, she is bound to work for you,' Arthur agreed. 'But I shall be calling again, and if I discover she's been badly treated I promise you, you will regret it.'

The butcher glared at him and then spat on the ground near Arthur's long riding boots but didn't speak again. Arthur tipped his beaver hat to him and walked away, seething inside. He would have liked to thrash the insolent brute but for the moment the law was in the butcher's favour and he could only make threats that he hoped would prevent him punishing the girl if she was caught and returned to him, as she most likely would be, for the streets were not a safe place for a young girl like that and she would probably be taken up as a vagrant by the watch for loitering.

'What are yer after?' the man behind the baker's stall demanded as Eliza picked up a bread roll and sniffed

111

it. 'You'd better 'ave the money to pay fer that or I'll see yer behind bars.'

Eliza ran still clutching the bread, though she wasn't aware it was in her hand. She wasn't sure why she'd touched the roll except that it smelled lovely and was still warm. She'd eaten most of what Mags had given her and there was just a piece of stale cheese and a crust of bread left, and she had wondered how much the fresh bread cost, but she hadn't intended to steal it.

'Come back yer little bitch!' the irate stallholder yelled, but Eliza ran on until she bumped into a man who grabbed her shoulder and turned her round, leering at her.

'Been thievin' 'ave yer?' he muttered and she smelled his foul breath. ''Ungry I'll bet. Come along wiv me, girl and I'll give yer somethin' ter eat when I've done wiv yer.'

Eliza was in no doubt that he wanted the same from her as Fred Roberts had wanted that night. She kicked him in the shin and wrenched free of his dirty hands, running as fast as she could. Once again, Eliza was driven by fear and she ran on for as long as she could, brushing past people who turned and stared at her and avoiding more than one pair of hands that tried to catch her.

She was numbed with misery as she wandered down alleys and through wider streets, looking at buildings and streets in despair because she was thoroughly lost. Eliza couldn't even find her way back to the butcher's yard now, even if she'd wanted to. The afternoon was nearly done; it would soon be dark and she was afraid of sleeping rough on the streets, because wherever she went people stared at her and she didn't know where to go or what to do.

If only she'd been able to read the street names, Eliza thought as she began to realise that each street or lane had a name. She stood looking at one sign so long that a youth came up to her.

''Ere, you lost?' he asked and lifted his greasy cap to scratch his head. 'Yer in Kite Place – where do yer want ter go?'

'I'm looking for the market at the corner of Bull Lane,' Eliza said hopefully. 'I was goin' ter ask for work.'

'Never 'eard of 'it,' the youth said. 'Is it a special place – or are yer just lookin' fer work?'

'I want work and somewhere to sleep. My master turned me off . . .'

'Yeah, I fought yer looked lost,' he said and grinned at her. 'I'm Tucker. Me and a few mates work the markets, see, and we know lots of places to sleep – if yer want ter come along o' me, I'll show yer what we do. It ain't 'ard.'

'All right,' Eliza said. 'I'm called Eliza – and I've been scrubbin' and cleaning in a butcher's house. It smelled so bad there it made me sick and he beat me.'

'Still, I bet he fed yer – yer can't work if yer starved,' Tucker said and grinned. 'We don't eat every day, 'cos we don't always get lucky but we ain't starved yet.'

'Are you hungry?' Eliza asked. 'I've got some bread I'll share.' She thrust the stolen roll at him.

'Would yer?' He looked at her with eager anticipation as she took out her bundle and gave him most of the cheese Mags had wrapped for her. She ate the last scrap of stale bread herself. 'Thanks, Eliza. Yer all right. I'll give yer some of my food when I earn it.'

'Thanks.' She looked at him shyly and then passed the water bottle, which he drained and then tossed into the gutter. 'We don't need that – we'll get tea and beer when we've done our work. Need to be light on our feet, see, and no baggage. We're nippers, see; we have ter be able to run fast when the time comes.'

Eliza went along with him, feeling happier than she had since leaving the workhouse and her friends. She was trying to memorise things, like the church, the park, the school and the shops so that she could find her way back.

'That over there is the seaman's mission,' Tucker told her and pointed to a large grey building. 'Sometimes they give us food if we go early in the mornin' – but yer want ter watch out fer the sailors when they're drunk. They'll give yer a beatin' soon as look at yer – and more than that if they're feelin' randy.'

Eliza nodded. She understood what Tucker meant now. More than once men had leered at her as she wandered the streets and she'd felt afraid of what they might do to her. In the workhouse she'd remained innocent of the brutality of that side of life, because Ruth had protected her, but Mags had left her in no doubt of what the butcher meant to do to her and she knew that he wasn't the only man who would take advantage of her if given the chance. It was lucky that Tucker had noticed her; she could learn her way about the streets and how to take care of herself from him.

Eliza wondered how she could contact Joe in the workhouse without falling foul of its mistress. If she could just get a message to Ruth she would tell Joe – and perhaps he knew how to escape by now. The thought crossed her mind that Joe could have got away long ago and that made her sad because she might not see him again, but for the moment she had a new companion and she was going to learn all she could from him because she did not want to be sent back to her master, the butcher.

'If you've got 'er 'ere I'll take her wiv me,' Fred said and glared at Joan Simpkins as if he thought she'd spirited the wretched girl way. 'Ran off with bread and the boots I give 'er, she did – a little thief she is.'

'Did you throw away her old boots?' Joan demanded and saw the answer in his eyes. 'You've worked her for weeks on end and I know you didn't pay her – so the boots were her pay. Clothes and food and a bed they are the terms on which we give you our workers.'

'Well, now she's run orf and I want 'er back. I paid fer 'er and I want 'er or the money.'

'You can't have either,' Joan said secretly relishing his discomfort. She had no doubt in her mind as to why the girl had run off. It didn't bother her that he'd abused the girl, but if he couldn't keep hold of his servants it was not Joan's fault and she had no intention of returning his money. 'The girl isn't here and I never refund the money. You took her in good faith and it was up to you to subdue her. I told you not to feed her on meat. Bread and gruel and she would've been no trouble.'

Fred glared and spat on the ground. 'She belongs to me and I want 'er back. Yer haven't seen the last of me, so don't forget, if she turns up remember she's my property.'

Joan looked down her long nose at him. 'You have the use of her services but no more. After three years she will be free to leave your service if she wishes.'

'That ain't true,' Fred muttered. 'I bought 'er.'

'You paid me a pittance for her services, but she is not your property and that was the agreement you signed,' Joan said, knowing that he'd scribbled his mark without reading the few lines above it. Most likely he could reckon numbers better than he could read and had not even bothered to look. 'If she returns I shall of course let you know – unless you would like to purchase the services of another of our inmates?'

'Ah, I daresay you'd like that,' he said and spat again. 'I'll swear the wench is hid somewhere here and you'll sell 'er to someone else – but you can't cheat me. You've not heard the last of this.'

Joan watched as he stormed out of her office and walked across the courtyard without looking back. A little smile touched her mouth, because he was quite right. If Eliza returned to the workhouse she would find another master or mistress for her. Why should she give the girl back to the butcher when there was further profit to be made?

Joan was about to open the locked drawer where she kept her money when the door opened and her brother walked in. She could instantly see that he was angry with her.

'What's wrong?'

'Why did you lie to Mr Stoneham? He asked you where the girl Eliza had gone and you gave him a false address. I informed him of Roberts' whereabouts myself – but I know he was annoyed. I've told you to be careful,

Joan. Arthur Stoneham is an influential man and rich. He can do things for us, but he can also break us. I'm not ready to retire. I haven't got enough savings – so just be careful, Joan. I hope nothing bad has happened to that girl.'

'I'm sure I have no idea,' Joan said. 'I was paid a paltry amount for her clothing, as is my due, and Mr Roberts claimed to be a respectable tradesman.'

'Well, perhaps he is,' her brother said and sighed. 'You've been warned, Joan. I only need a few years more before I can retire with my own pub and that will do me nicely for my last years, but you're younger. You could be the mistress here for years to come.'

Joan didn't answer and he went away with a shake of his head, but his words had made her think. She did not want to spend the rest of her life as mistress of the workhouse and it was obvious there would be no place for her with her brother when he left here. If she was going to retire with a nice pension for herself she must make sure she got decent money for those she passed on – both for legitimate work and other things. With any luck all the fuss over young girls being used in houses of ill-repute would be finished by the autumn and there were several girls that Joan had been saving for that purpose. When the time came, she would sell them to the highest bidder and if there was any trouble, leave quickly before she was exposed. She had in mind a nice little seaside boarding house where she could take in paying guests, choosing those she preferred and employing maids to do all the work, or a cottage in the country where she could grow fruit and vegetables and sell her produce in the market. It would be a quiet,

117

pleasant life and there was always the chance that she might meet a wealthy widower who needed a wife to care for him.

CHAPTER 10

Arthur glanced around the large and very elegant drawing room. He'd gone straight from his meeting with the master of the workhouse earlier that day and confronted the butcher. Fred Roberts had blustered and raged, protesting that he'd done nothing to make Eliza run off, but Arthur's instincts told him that she'd been abused in some way, that she'd run because she was afraid of her brutal master.

It was a pleasant society gathering that evening. He'd met his host, Toby's father, and chatted to several ladies and gentlemen and was wondering how much longer he need stay before he could escape. The talk of Queen Victoria's speech to the Houses of Parliament, spoken by the Lord Chancellor on her behalf, was on everyone's lips, as well as the more scandalous activities of her eldest son, Bertie, and his current mistress. After the tragic death of Prince Albert on 14 December 1861, the Queen had plunged herself, her family, and the nation into deepest mourning – a period of mourning that went on far too long for the safety of the monarchy and caused unrest. It was only the severe illness of the Prince of Wales in 1871 and the urging of Disraeli that had induced Her Majesty to attend a thanksgiving service and appear in public again. An abortive attempt on her life a few days later had brought her the overwhelming support and sympathy of her people.

The Queen had by then begun to recover slowly from the loss of the man she had loved and mourned so sincerely, and with the return of Mr Disraeli as her Prime Minister, she became more visible to her people, and she'd been upset when he'd recently been voted out and Mr Gladstone returned to power. She wore the deepest black still, but she was now accepted as a respected and much-loved figure; renowned for her dignity as a matriarchal widow, proclaimed Empress of India at the Delhi Durbar on 1 January 1877, and the model by which English men and women took their stand. Her life now centred on her children and grand-children, in whom she took a great deal of interest, delighting in drawing their pictures for her albums and having their photographs taken; anyone fortunate to catch sight of Her Majesty driving in her carriage in the park with one of her brood thought they were fortunate to be able to call themselves Victorians.

'Arthur, I wanted to introduce you to Miss Katharine Ross.' Toby's voice cut across Arthur's thoughts and he focused on the woman his friend was presenting to him. At first glance she looked no more than twenty but when she extended her hand and smiled, the corners of her eyes crinkled and he was aware of tiny lines and of an air of hidden sorrow. Her hair was a pale honey, coiled like a skein of heavy silk in the nape of her neck and held by a circlet of fresh roses that were slightly perfumed, their scent wafting towards him with every slight movement of her head. She had a beautiful neck and her skin was pale, her eyes large and dark blue; she was beautiful, but not in the conventional way for she had a quiet, almost private air about her.

'Charmed to meet you, Miss Ross,' Arthur said and gallantly took the hand she offered to air kiss it. She smiled, and her face lit up for an instant, flooding with light that seemed to dazzle like the sun. 'I was growing a little tired of the same old faces this evening and needed some diversion.'

'I too am charmed to meet you, sir,' she said in a voice that was light and musical. 'I asked Toby if he could arrange an introduction for he told me about the house you are contemplating setting up for women in difficulty and I have an interest in those who have met with misfortune and share their sorrows in the harshness of a cruel world.'

'Surely you are too young for such things to have touched you?' Arthur asked, his look a caress that praised her beauty. She laughed softly and arched one mobile eyebrow mockingly. Her laughter sent little thrills of pleasure through him.

'I am nine and twenty years, sir, past the age where I think of little but dresses and dancing; it was someone dear to me who suffered, and I have never ceased to mourn her. I am on the verge of purchasing a property for the purpose of supporting young women in trouble.'

'Indeed, are you very rich, Miss Ross?' Arthur arched his left eyebrow, quizzing her mischievously.

'I fear my fortune is not large. I had hoped that perhaps you might help me – indeed, I wondered if we might not pool our efforts or at the very least you would contribute to mine.'

'Now that is an interesting proposition.' Arthur smiled at her warmly. 'I imagine you have other ways of raising funds?

'My father was a country parson,' she replied, and he saw shadows pass across her face. 'I was his helper and because his health deteriorated after my sister . . . in later life I organised everything in the parish for him until his death last year. I am but recently out of mourning. Our local squire was very good in holding garden parties for church funds, but of course I organised them each year.'

'And what is it that I may do for you?' Arthur asked.

'I have thoughts of a charity ball, sir,' Katharine suggested but Arthur shook his head. 'You could not see your way clear to host such an event?'

'I am not a man for such affairs,' he said and shook his head. 'However, I do not think it beyond you to think of another affair that I might lend my name to – and I am willing to consider we join forces to buy and endow this establishment of yours.'

'What if I asked for a garden party? I could arrange it all – in your large gardens. Toby told me that you had beautiful gardens.' She gave him a smile that took his breath and he felt himself melting in its warmth.

'Indeed?' Arthur smiled oddly. 'As it happens, I have been known to open my gardens for a worthy cause, and if I could leave it all in your beautiful hands . . .' Arthur knew he was flirting with her but could not help himself. One of the reasons he did not often socialise at events such as this was that his hosts invariably tried to match him with a woman they thought suitable – but this one was so delightful that he did not mind even if that had been Toby's aim.

'Of course,' she said and moved closer to him so that he smelled the perfume of her roses once more. 'I shall call on you one day to discuss these matters and take a tour of your gardens, with my aunt – if you will permit me?'

'As far as I am concerned, you may do anything you wish in my garden, Miss Ross,' Arthur said and saw the delicate flush in her cheeks. She lowered her gaze and then their host came up to them and all chance of private conversation was gone as Katharine Ross was led away to meet someone else.

Arthur watched her go and knew that he had not felt so interested in a woman for years, and yet even as he felt the quickening of his loins, he remembered. Katharine Ross was a young woman of beauty, intelligence and charm – she would not give herself to a rogue such as Arthur Stoneham. If she ever knew what he'd done, she would turn her face from him in disgust. Feeling the pain of loss strike, because he knew himself unworthy, he turned and left the elegant room without looking for her again and did not see her watching him nor the disappointment in her face as he left.

'What's goin' on in there?' Eliza asked as they stood outside a large inn. Lanterns hung over the door and there was a queue of people waiting to enter. 'Why do they all want to get in there?'

'That's a hall of music,' Tucker said and grinned at her. 'They 'ave singin' and music and stuff in there –

and booze too. I like the blokes wot stand up and tell jokes best . . .'

'You mean like hymns?' Eliza asked, because that was the only music she'd ever heard, and she had no idea what a joke was – unless it was when someone mocked you.

'Didn't they teach yer nothin' where yer were?' Tucker asked, looking at her strangely.

'All we did was work,' Eliza said. She looked about her at the activity in the market place. In the few days since she'd joined Tucker and his gang she had become used to the various markets; there were some selling old clothes, spread out on the ground if they weren't much better than rags, and hung up on stalls if they were better; markets that sold fruit and vegetables, the bird market where wild birds in cages were sold some days and then the general market stalls that sold everything from earthenware dishes to leather bags and shoes to knives and forks and silk roses for fine ladies to sew on their dresses or wear in their hair. Petticoat Lane was very busy, especially at the weekends; there were shops on either side of the road, pawnbrokers and jewellers, butchers and Jewish shops selling special food, also one displaying colourful saris, and a myriad of different stalls lined the road itself. Here the sellers would call out in loud voices, sometimes auctioning their wares off, getting lower and lower until the last one was sold.

There were so many different peoples mingling in Petticoat Lane: men with dusky skins and turbans, women in long saris with their heads covered by filmy veils. Eliza had never seen a person with brown skin before and she stared until Tucker told her they came from India and owned a shop nearby. There were also Chinamen, who wore a single plait hanging down their backs and long robes that looked like dresses to Eliza's eyes; Jews with pale skins, long black coats and felt hats, ringlets of hair on each side of their faces, and men with skin nearly as dark as coal. They spoke in different languages, which amazed Eliza and made her wonder at how big the world must be.

Tucker told her all she needed to know. He was giving her an education in life on the streets. It was he that showed her where they could safely sleep in derelict buildings and a maze of little alleys to dodge down when the watch was after them. The work he and his friends did was a mixture of thieving and running errands for men of dubious reputation; Tucker had a good relationship with a man who took bets on horses and he ran between the bookmaker and punters, placing money on various horses. But there were other forms of gambling too on the streets. Cards played on upturned orange boxes in old warehouses, dog fighting in out-of-the-way corners which led to lots of gambling and cursing, because the men drank as they watched the poor creatures tear themselves to pieces. There were bare knuckle fights, rat baiting, and all manner of dice and other games on which men gambled their wages.

Once, they saw a man being taken away by the constables; his hands were chained and several men in uniform were brandishing their truncheons as they escort him to a horse-drawn van.

'I shouldn't want ter be 'im,' one of the gang said. 'I reckon they'll toss 'im in prison and throw away the key.'

Eliza asked why and was told the man had been caught stealing from one of the shops and he'd hurt a constable badly when trying to escape. A shiver ran down her spine, because she realised that if she or any of the gang was caught stealing, they too could go to prison – and Tucker told her it was like the workhouse, only worse.

'They beat yer ter teach yer a lesson,' he said, and his eyes looked scared. 'I got beat when I was in the spike too – but one of me mates died in prison after they beat 'im and then worked him till he dropped . . .'

Life on the streets was precarious, because they had to be quick and clever to keep from being taken up by the watch, and it was often cold and dirty, but prison sounded even worse than the workhouse. Eliza thought she would rather starve than go to that awful place.

Eliza was learning to find her way about by memorising various landmarks, and Tucker told her the names of streets and gradually she learned to recognise them. It wasn't that she could read, but she was quick to learn and soon knew shapes and letters. She was learning about the world, things she'd been ignorant of in the workhouse. Sometimes she felt angry because no one had told her all these things. Ruth had told her of her life and so had Cook and some other inmates, but she hadn't known what it was like to live in the real world and, despite the hardships of sleeping rough, Eliza was enjoying herself. She'd tasted different food and drunk beer and tea and a fizzy ginger beer that sent bubbles up her nose; she'd also ridden on a horse-drawn bus and stared in wonder at a weird contraption that banged and popped as it bounced along on high, thin wheels. Tucker said it was a horseless carriage and it ran on steam, but smelled worse than the horse excrement that the sweepers were forever clearing away from the busy streets.

Men selling newssheets stood at the edge of the market and called out for people to buy a sheet. They lured folk with talk of a grisly murder and the latest horse-racing results. To a girl who had not known a world outside the workhouse, it was vivid and alive and made her feel glad to be free and young. She wished that Joe might have been with her to experience it all and thought often of the apple pie she'd shared with him in the cellar. They'd sworn to be true and Joe had told her that one day they would be together, but she did not know how that could be. Fate had parted them and Eliza's world was centred here, in the mean streets of the city, often sleeping under railway arches or in disused warehouses. Tucker's gang wandered all over the East End of London, sometimes working for a few pennies, sometimes forced to steal their bread.

Some days she was cold and hungry and her stomach ached, but she'd known hunger in the workhouse and she endured it, never thinking of returning to that place of misery, though Tucker would have shown her the way had she asked. Instead, she let herself be as dirty as her companions were, scratching at the lice that infested her hair and wiping her dripping nose on her hand, but happy despite all. She was free and there was no one trying to abuse or beat her. Tucker and his friends looked after one another and he'd taken her under his wing, so none of them would have thought of hurting her; she was one of them and they all shared what they had.

In some ways it was an idyllic life and yet it was bound to end. It happened one hot summer day when Tucker told her she had to steal a gentleman's kerchief or something from a market stall.

'You've bin wiv us fer a while,' he told her, 'and it's time yer did yer share – some of the others don't like it 'cos yer just watch. We're goin' ter raid a stall and yer must do yer bit, Eliza.'

Eliza nodded, because she'd known it was coming. 'I'd rather be part of the raid than take a gent's kerchief,' she whispered.

'Yeah, I fought so,' he agreed, 'but yer will 'ave ter do more one of these days. It's the way we live, Eliza. Look at that gent over there, his kerchief 'anging out his back pocket. Watch what I do . . .'

Eliza watched as Tucker sauntered over the road, making out he was looking at something in the window of a shop, then just sidled up to the man, drew the kerchief gently free and hid it inside his jacket. The gentleman never even turned around and Tucker walked back to her jauntily.

'There you are,' he said. 'It's easy, but be careful 'ow you choose yer mark.'

Eliza nodded, but her stomach felt hollow, because one thing Ruth had told her was that pinchin' stuff never did anyone any good.

Ruth smelled the stew and nodded, because even though it was mostly vegetables it was good and Cook had made lovely fresh bread that morning.

'They say Joe has run off,' Ruth said as she helped Cook to move the heavy pan from the heat. 'Some of the women think he's dead and that *she* done it – but one of the men told me he'd run.'

'I hope he did – he was a good lad,' Cook said and gasped because the mistress had just entered the kitchen and a lady walked behind them – a very elegant lady. Cook stood staring as Mr Stoneham followed them in. Ruth dropped a hasty curtsey to the lady and gentleman but the lady smiled and shook her head.

'Good morning,' she said in a pleasant voice. 'I am Katharine Ross. Mr Stoneham tells me that you may be available to work in a house that he and I are setting up for unfortunate women?'

'Yes, ma'am,' Ruth said and saw the look of fury in Miss Simpkins' eyes. 'I'm ready to join you whenever you say . . .'

'Then I shall ask you to come with me tomorrow morning,' Miss Ross said, taking Ruth's breath. 'We have this day purchased a house and I would like your advice on various matters. I shall call at ten in the morning – if that is convenient? You will have your own room immediately and I need you to help me prepare for the first inmates . . .'

'Yes, ma'am,' Ruth said, but glanced at the mistress of the workhouse and saw her mouth tighten. 'But I need to pay what's owed to Mistress . . .'

'I have arranged that,' Mr Stoneham said easily. 'Cook, if you would be willing I shall arrange for your release in two weeks – Mistress Simpkins has asked for that much time to replace you. I trust that is convenient?'

'Aye, sir, and you'll pay nothing for me,' Cook said.

'I work fer me wages and I owe nothin' to mistress.' She looked hard at the mistress as if daring her to say different.

Ruth drew her breath as she saw the spite in Miss Simpkins' eyes but averted her gaze as the mistress glared at her.

'I shall be in my office,' Mistress Simpkins said. 'You will come and sign before you leave in the morning, Ruth.'

Ruth inclined her head, watching as she left before turning to Mr Stoneham. 'Have you heard anything of Eliza, sir?'

'Have you heard that she ran away from her master?'

Ruth looked at Cook and then nodded. 'We heard a rumour, sir – but we wasn't sure it was the truth.'

'I visited her place of employment but was informed both by Mr Roberts and his maidservant that she had run off. I shall continue to make inquiries – and if anything is discovered I shall let you know.'

'I be grateful, sir,' Ruth said. 'Both for Miss Ross comin' 'ere today and your kindness.'

'I believe you to be a hard worker,' Arthur replied. 'I shall do my best to find your friend.'

Ruth nodded and thanked him. Miss Ross had been discussing the meals served here with Cook and looked perturbed.

'If what you say is true, the rules are not always adhered to,' she said and frowned. 'I shall see that you have sufficient funds to feed our people properly – and I intend to have a word with some friends of mine concerning the menu here.'

'I shall enjoy working for you, ma'am – some days

it be just gruel here without even a bit of bread and that ain't enough to feed any man or woman.'

Miss Ross inclined her head, looking as if she agreed and she and Mr Stoneham took their leave.

'Mistress will not like this,' Ruth said after they'd gone. 'She can't do much to me afore the mornin' but watch yer step, Cook – she won't want ter lose you.'

'I'm a match fer her,' Cook said stoutly. 'I might 'ave left afore had I wished it – but I stopped 'cos of our friendship, Ruth, and I'll be glad to shake the dust of this place from me shoes . . .'

Ruth nodded. 'I'm glad to be leavin' but I wish I knew where my Eliza was.'

Tucker signalled to Eliza to watch as they diverted the stallholder. This particular coster was a mean old devil and yelled at them to go away if they even asked the price of food from his stall, so it was his own fault that they'd planned a raid that morning. Most of the market people were friendly and often gave the street kids food: cakes and bread that were two days old, fruit a little on the turn but still eatable, and they gave them half-pennies and farthings if they did errands, and in return the kids left them alone to carry on their business, but this man wouldn't give them the time of day.

Eliza watched as a small boy suddenly ran forward and threw a rotten tomato at the bulky stallholder, who gave a cry of rage and came out from behind his stall to catch the culprit. He ran, and the stallholder followed for a short distance, realising too late that it had been a diversion. As soon as his back was turned, all Tucker's gang rushed forward and grabbed pies, bread and cakes from the stall, filled their jackets and pockets and then scarpered in different directions. Instead of watching as she often had in the past, Eliza joined the grab and fled with her shawl stuffed with food just as the stallholder returned and made a grab for her. Evading his grasp by the skin of her teeth, she made off down one of the alleys that she knew so well.

A woman dressed in sober grey was standing watching them, her eyes on Eliza. For a moment Eliza feared she might try to stop her, but she moved aside to let the children run past her.

Eliza ran as fast as she could to the rendezvous, a deserted warehouse they had been living in for some days. A large corrugated iron fence had been erected all around the compound, which was soon to be pulled down, but the kids had found a way to pull a section aside and they scrambled through it one by one until the whole gang had arrived. They looked at each other in elation as they emptied pockets, jackets and Eliza's shawl and spread out their haul on a waterproof sheet. There was enough to feed them all for a week, more than they'd ever snatched before. Tucker had planned it and it had turned out perfectly.

'It must be worth a lot of money,' Eliza said in awe because the big pork pies were two shillings each and even the large cottage loaf was one shilling and sixpence. She counted on her fingers, which Tucker had taught her to do, and thought there must be more than four pounds' worth of stolen food. 'He will be so angry.'

'Serves him right,' Tucker said. 'If the ole misery guts'd ever give us a bun, or spoke as much as a kind word we'd never 'ave done it.'

Eliza nodded and accepted her share of the day's food. The rest of it would be well wrapped up against the inroads of rats or flies and stored in their special place, to be shared equally amongst them all. She felt a little guilty when she thought of all the hard work the stallholder had put into making his bread and pies. Yet she shared in the food earned by Tucker and his friends and could never have refused to take part in the raid, but it was a lot of money to steal and she hoped it would not make too much trouble.

'We'll go somewhere else fer a few days,' Tucker said. 'We don't need to steal while we've got food – and maybe we can find work somewhere, perhaps on the docks.'

Eliza nodded, refusing to let her conscience distress her. It was a harsh world and they did what they had to in order to survive.

CHAPTER 11

'I like Ruth very much,' Katharine told Arthur when she had installed their new housekeeper in her rooms. 'We shall get on – and since Cook is her friend I believe they will run the house well between them.'

'Yes, I am certain they will – and we may leave it to them,' he said and took her hand, which was covered in a pretty lace glove, to kiss it. 'You are an angel, Miss Ross – just as Ruth said.'

'And I think you are flirting with me,' Katharine countered and laughed up at him, her eyes dancing. 'I do not dislike it, though I am reliably informed that you are a wicked rogue.'

'How could you say it?' he questioned, the light of devilment in his eyes, for she had that effect upon him, and despite his resolve never to marry a young and lovely woman, she made his body tingle with need and longing. 'I assure you that you have nothing to fear from me, Miss Ross.'

'I know it,' she said, and her smile was warm. 'I but tease you a little for you have looked so serious of late that I wondered if I might have offended until you told me that you had found a house for our unfortu-nates.'

'I am concerned for a child,' Arthur said and sighed. 'She is one of many – but somehow her fate pricks at me. She ran away from a cruel master to whom she had been sold – at least that was his claim. Miss Simpkins says she was hired to him, which is her legal right – but the man strikes me as one who knows what was truly intended. So he treated her ill and she ran and now she may be in terrible danger.'

'You are worried, my dear friend,' Katharine said and laid her hand on his. 'Have you considered hiring an agent to look for this child? I know that sometimes it is impossible to find a missing person . . .' A little sob escaped her. 'But you will not rest until you have done all you can to find her.'

'You are perfectly right,' Arthur said. 'I have one agent looking for her already, but I shall hire more – as you say, I must do all I can to find her before it is too late.'

Why the need to find one particular child was so urgent Arthur could not say, but it nagged at him, refusing to let go day or night, and he knew that he would not forgive himself if she came to harm through his neglect.

It was the morning after their daring raid, before they had woken up properly, that it happened. Tucker suddenly came rushing in and started yelling at them to run.

'They've found us!' he said. 'It's that bugger from the market got a constable after us.'

The gang split in different ways, because there was

135

always more than one way out of the compound. Tucker had taught them never to use a hideout that had only one way of escape. Eliza ran around the side of the warehouse and away across a pile of rubble. Part of the building had already been pulled down and left ready for the wreckers to come in and clear it. She could hear screams and yells as many of the children were caught, but she got clear and was out into a lane further down before she realised that she had cut her leg in the scramble to escape. These industrial wastelands were always dangerous, with broken glass and old metal hidden amongst the rubbish and Eliza's leg stung, the blood trickling down her flesh and into her boots.

She was hobbling by the time she stopped to rest in Nelson Gardens. The blood had stopped dripping but her leg was sore and she felt scared and very alone. A lot of her friends had been caught and she did not know if Tucker was amongst them. Bending her head, she covered her face with her hands and felt the tears falling. Living on the streets had been exciting with Tucker's gang, but she did not know if she dared to go back. The raid had been planned to catch them unawares and Eliza knew that those of her friends who had been caught would be sent to prison. Tucker had warned her that it could happen, but boasted that they were too quick and too sharp for the plodders who tried half-heartedly to catch them. It was because of the raid on the baker's stall that the constables had come after them. They had stolen too much and the coster had demanded that it be stopped.

Eliza knew she dare not return to the old haunts in the hope of finding some of her friends. She must move on and try to find work – but who would employ her looking as filthy as she did now?

Eliza raised her head, ready to move on, just as a hand descended on her shoulder. She looked up and saw that it was the vicar who had spoken to her weeks before.

'Well, my poor child, by the look of you, it is time you came to us and let us help you,' he said and smiled kindly. 'My housekeeper will bathe your leg, wash you and clothe you in something better than these rags – and of course we shall feed you.'

'Thank you, sir.' Eliza did not have the energy to resist this time. She felt the pressure of his hand on her shoulder as he guided her across the road to the church and a house next to it, which he told her was his home.

His housekeeper was in the kitchen and looked at Eliza in dismay. 'Whatever, will you bring home next?' she clucked and shook her head at the vicar. 'Gawd have mercy! What have you done to your leg, child?' She was very plump and her three chins wobbled as she fussed about Eliza and marched her up the stairs to a room such as Eliza had never seen before.

Accustomed to the bathhouse at the workhouse, which was a line of tin baths that had to be filled and emptied by hand and had only a thin sheet hung between them for modesty, she was at first amazed by the shining white tub. The butcher's wife had bathed in a tin tub that Eliza had carried upstairs to her room, filled and then emptied after it had been used. This tub still had to be filled by jugs, some of which Eliza had carried up herself, but there was a plug in the bottom at one end and it was easy to let the used water run away through hidden pipe beneath it.

'Have you never seen a bath before?' the housekeeper scolded as she hesitated. 'Well, by the look of you it is a long time since you've washed yourself.'

'I washed before I was on the streets,' Eliza said, stung by the scorn in her eyes. 'I was clean until I had no home.'

'The Reverend is a good man but it's me that has to cope with his misfits,' the woman scolded. 'Well, in with you then and wash yourself, girl – don't expect me to do it for you. And make sure you clean the cut on your leg well or it could turn nasty.'

'Yes, ma'am,' Eliza said and accepted the bar of soap she was given. She held it to her nose and was surprised that it smelled of something sweet. 'Oh, that's lovely!'

'Yes, it's scented with rose essence – and wasted on the likes of you. Well, get on with it – whatever your name is. I haven't got all day.'

'My name is Eliza, ma'am, and thank you.'

'I'll fetch you a clean dress and shawl – these others are rags, fit only for the fire, crawling with lice and fleas, I daresay.'

'Yes, ma'am, they haven't been washed for weeks – ever since I lost my place.' She made a grab for her shawl. 'Don't take this – my mother gave it me when I was a babe.'

'Keep it if you wish, though it's no more than a rag.'

'Thank you, ma'am...'

'Well, Eliza, your manners are better than a good many. Make sure to scrub your hair and wash all over. I'll bring you some clothes and I want to see the colour of your skin under all that dirt!'

Eliza thanked her and ducked under the water. It felt

138

so lovely and she'd never had such a luxurious bath in her life. The soap lathered beautifully and smelled wonderful and she rubbed it well into her body and her hair, rinsing it out and then soaping it again. The cut on her leg stung so much that it brought tears to her eyes, but she took notice of the housekeeper and washed it well. Soon, standing up, she looked for something to dry herself on. All she could find was a piece of soft white material that she knew was a towel, but so much softer and thicker than anything she'd ever seen or touched before, other than in Mistress Robert's house, and even her late mistress's linen had not been so fine. Was it really for her to use?

'What are you standing there shivering for?' the housekeeper said bringing in a cotton shift and a gown of dark blue wool with a white collar. 'Dry yourself and put these on. We've no boots to fit you, but I've cleaned yours, though the soles are all but worn through.'

'I put paper in to stop the water comin' in,' Eliza told her and the woman clucked her tongue.

'Well, I daresay my master will see to it,' she said. 'Come back to the kitchen when you're dressed and you can have some apple pie and bread and cheese.'

'Thank you, you're very kind,' Eliza said, and the woman sniffed.

'It's nothing to do with me. Reverend told me to wash, feed and clothe you – and I am carrying out his orders.'

Eliza nodded. She realised that this woman must have looked after many others before her. The owner of this house was rich and he was also kind, taking folk in from the street. She wondered if he would set her to work in his kitchens and was feeling happy when she went down to the kitchen. The apple pie was delicious and she had just eaten the last scrap of her portion when the kitchen door opened and the vicar walked in. Eliza jumped up and was about to thank him for his kindness when she saw the woman entering behind him and her heart sank.

He'd fetched Mistress Simpkins from the workhouse! Eliza had thought him kind and a good friend to her, but he'd betrayed her.

'Well, that is an improvement,' he said and smiled benevolently. 'She looks decent now – is this the young girl you mentioned, Mistress Simpkins.'

'Yes, this is our Eliza,' Mistress Simpkins said with a false smile. 'The naughty girl ran away from her master – but thanks to you, sir, we have her back, safe and sound.' She approached Eliza, the friendly smile dying from her eyes as she held out her hand. 'Come along, young lady. No need to be frightened. You will not be punished. Your friends have been anxious for you and would give me no peace.' Eliza hung back and Miss Simpkins took her arm firmly, her fingers gripping tight. 'Say thank you to this kind vicar for rescuing you, Eliza.'

Eliza sent him a look filled with reproach. 'Thank you for the food and the bath,' she said but did not smile.

'You will be safe with Mistress Simpkins,' he said in a kindly manner. Clearly, he had no idea what it was like in the workhouse and imagined that she was going to her home where she would be cared for, fed adequately, and given work suitable for a girl of her age. Eliza wanted to resist, to scream and tell him that this woman's smiles were false and that as soon as they were out of sight, she would be beaten. However, she knew it was useless to protest because these good people would not believe her. They, like so many others, believed that the workhouse was there to protect the poor, whereas in so many cases it was used to abuse them and take advantage of their plight.

Eliza was no longer the innocent girl who had been sent to the butcher's house as a skivvy. She knew the perils of the streets and, despite her reluctance to go with Miss Simpkins, accepted that it was slightly better than prison. She would be patient and wait, and perhaps her chance to escape would come – and she did want to see Ruth and Joe. Eliza had missed her friends and had thought of them often when she was in the butcher's house and running wild on the streets with Tucker and his gang.

Now that she had some experience of how to live on the streets of London, Eliza thought that she and Joe could find a way to escape together. They would hide out and beg or earn their food until Joe's father was freed from prison, as he must be once his innocence was proven, and then they could go travelling in the caravan Joe had told her about, pulled by a strong black horse.

Nursing her hopes for the future, Eliza made no attempt to pull away from Mistress Simpkins as they left the Vicar's house and crossed the street. Once out of sight, Mistress Simpkins produced a thin rope from inside her coat, which she tied around Eliza's waist and then attached to her own belt.

'I'll have no more of this running off, my girl!'

'I wasn't goin' ter run orf,' Eliza muttered resentfully. 'I ain't a criminal.'

'No? You were bound to your master for three years, girl. I've had him making a nuisance of himself for weeks – three times he's come demanding you be returned to him, Eliza.'

'I won't go back to him,' Eliza said stubbornly. 'If you send me there I'll run away again. He's a dirty, horrid man.'

'Well, behave yourself and perhaps I'll protect you from him,' Miss Simpkins said sternly. 'Cause me no trouble and I'll find you another place – with a mistress this time, maybe.'

'I ain't goin' back to Roberts,' Eliza said stubbornly. 'I shan't be no trouble – but if he comes fer me I'll kick him where it hurts and I'll make *you* sorry.'

'You've learned a few things since you left us,' Miss Simpkins said and smiled sourly. 'Well, behave yourself and I shall see what turns up.'

Eliza nodded and hung her head. She looked about her as she followed meekly behind the workhouse mistress, taking note of which way they turned and how far they walked, noting landmarks and the signs that proclaimed street names. They passed Bull Lane, which was marked with the painted sign of a bull just as Tucker had told her it was, and she saw a few market stalls, although nothing like the big markets she'd been haunting with Tucker's gang. Had she come here, her master would have found her easily. The busy lanes and streets of Bethnal Green and the markets had been a good hiding place for her and she believed she could find her way back there if she chose.

Eliza had a good memory and she had learned so much during the weeks she'd spent on the streets. The summer had almost fled now, her thirteenth birthday having passed with no one to remark it, but now the nights were colder and she could feel a bite in the air despite the sunshine. It was the end of summer and it would soon be autumn and then winter. Eliza thought that life on the streets would be worse in winter, even bitterer and harder than in the workhouse itself.

Still, a chill went down her spine as the gates of the workhouse clanged behind her and she was once again locked in. She wondered about Tucker and whether he was now languishing in a police cell, but accepted that she might never know. Eliza was learning that life changed and she must learn to move on.

Eliza was given an old dress and the lovely wool gown she'd been given by the vicar's housekeeper was taken away, though the mistress didn't bother over her shawl for it was worthless to her. She knew that Miss Simpkins would probably sell it and she would never see it again, but since it had never truly been hers she did not mind.

'You can work in the laundry for now,' Miss Simpkins told her. 'I shall find outside work for you soon. Until then behave and we'll say no more of this nonsense.'

Eliza just looked at her and did not answer. She went straight to the laundry and one of the women gave her an apron to put on and then set her to rinsing the clothes after they'd been washed, which was less unpleasant than stirring the hot tub.

'So yer back then,' Sadie said sourly, coming up to

Eliza as she pounded her stick on the clothes to make the soap scum rise to the top. 'A high fuss there's been over yer an' all.'

'Why?'

'That butcher's been 'ere creatin' – and one of them toffee-nosed guv'ners has been kickin' up 'ell over yer.'

'I know Mr Roberts wants me back, but I don't know about the governor.' Eliza was puzzled. 'Why is *he* angry with me?'

''E's the one wot took Ruth and Cook orf somewhere,' Sadie said gleefully. 'Yeah, Ruth's gorn an' left yer. Yer'll get no more favours 'ere, girl, no more titbits from the cook – bloody food's worse than ever now. The muck they serve us these days ain't worth eatin'.'

'Ruth has gone?' Eliza's heart sank. 'Where? Do you know where she went, Sadie?'

'Nah; didn't tell me – no one tells me nuthin'.' Sadie gave a cackle of malicious laughter. 'Yer on yer own now, girl. That bloody gypsy lad is gorn too – dead, he is, I reckon, and buried in the cellar from what the men 'eard.'

Eliza swallowed hard, blinking back the rush of tears. The one thing that had kept her spirits up was that she would see her friends soon. She'd believed that she and Joe could run off together but now Sadie was saying that Joe was dead – and buried in the cellar. Why buried in the cellar?

'What makes you say he's buried in the cellar?' she asked Sadie.

'The men heard digging there for several nights and then it was quiet and no one has seen the boy since just after yer left.'

Joe dead and buried in the cellar. For a few moments Eliza was numbed with grief and then she remembered giving Joe the key to the cellar. He'd told her the rats were clever and that he'd found a way out of the workhouse – of course, that had to be it! The rats were free to come and go as they pleased; they came there to find shelter and somewhere out of the weather to breed, but they came and went as they pleased – and Joe, clever Joe, who could see in the dark, had watched them and discovered their secret.

Joe wasn't dead and buried in the cellar. Joe had found a way to dig himself out and he was free. He must have found some kind of tunnel that he'd made big enough to scramble through and escape.

Joe, her Joe, was alive and outside the workhouse somewhere! He might even be looking for her. Eliza wondered if he had found the butchers where she'd been taken and whether he'd gone there to look for her. Had he continued to search for her – or had he gone to find his father and his family?

Joe had told her that his mother and younger brother and his aunt were in Ireland. They had some land there where they kept horses. Joe had explained that they travelled during the spring and summer but in the autumn and winter they lived on their land and broke young horses to sell at the horse fairs in the spring and summer. It had been due to a fight at one of the horse fairs that Joe's father had been arrested and imprisoned on a false charge.

Eliza thought that if his father had been given his freedom, he might have taken Joe to Ireland. Would he stay there and forget her – or would he come back one day to look for her again? Remembering his promise, she smiled and nursed the thought inside. Joe was special to her and she was special to him. One day, perhaps when they were older, they would be together.

'Stop dreaming and get them clothes out fer the mangle,' a woman's voice cut through Eliza's thoughts. 'Yer back in the workhouse now so start workin' or yer'll feel me 'and about yer ear.'

Jerked back to reality, Eliza used the tongs to lift the heavy wet clothes into a large zinc bath. From there she had to lift them to the mangle and hold them while her fellow worker turned the big handle that made the rollers grab the material and squeeze the water back into the tin bath beneath. It was hard, back-breaking work and Eliza soon forgot everything except how tired she was. The mind-numbing hopelessness of life here stole over her once more, making her regret the loss of her friends, and she wondered if she would ever be free again.

Joe watched the butcher's yard for several days, judging that he would be wise to keep clear of the butcher and the surly yard man. It had taken him weeks of searching to find it and when he had, he had hoped to see Eliza and attract her attention, but not once had he seen her at the window or in the yard. Then, one late summer afternoon, he saw the plump woman come into the yard to peg out her clothes on a bit of rope strung between two posts. She jumped as he crept up on her but did not cry out.

'What be you 'ere for, lad?' she asked. 'If it's work, run away now, for the master is a cruel devil.'

'I'm looking for Eliza. She's here, ain't she?'

'Nay, lad, she did run off weeks ago. Be you 'er friend?'

'Yes.' Joe glared at her from disappointment. 'Do yer know where she went?'

'Nah, I can't 'elp yer.' Mags hesitated, then, 'Clear orf afore the master comes and beats us both!'

Joe hesitated but had no reason to think she was lying about Eliza running off. He'd managed to find work at a stable yard but was determined to find his friend if he could.

'If you see her, tell her I was asking,' he said, and ran off as he saw the butcher approaching

Eliza wasn't here; he was satisfied that the woman had told the truth, but Joe was determined to continue his search. Had she still been here, he could have found a way of rescuing her, but now he had to start again, yet he knew she must be somewhere hiding on the streets with the other kids he'd seen lurking in the shadows. They often hung around the markets, taking the opportunity to steal an apple or a piece of bread.

CHAPTER 12

'Tell me, Molly,' Robbie Simpkins said that night as he carelessly caressed her ample rump with his hand. 'The child you gave away this time – was it mine?'

'You asked me before,' Molly said and looked at him oddly as she flicked her full skirt away and reached for the jug of ale, refilling both their pewter mugs. 'Besides, I never give none of my babies away – yer sister sells them. She says I'm privileged to come and go as I please and I put up wiv it 'cos I don't 'ave no choice.'

Robbie frowned. 'What do you mean? I wouldn't let her sell yer babe if I'd known it wasn't what you wanted.' He saw the look of accusation in her eyes. 'You thought I knew?'

'She said you knew! She told me you didn't care.' Molly's eyes flashed with anger. 'The first time it *was* your child, Robbie. Yer knew I was virgin when yer 'ad me first, just afore yer wife died. Yer forced me then and yer sister told me I was a dirty slut and claimed I'd broken yer wife's heart – and she said it was my punishment fer leadin' yer astray.'

Robbie's expression darkened to one of anger. 'It was

148

never your fault, Molly. I may have forced yer the first time – though you were ripe for it . . .'

'I'm not complainin',' Molly said and smiled, though inside the resentment burned. He and his sister had made her what she was and one day she would make them both pay for it, but for the moment she intended to use him for her own advantage. 'Yer all right as men go; it was yer sister that gave me the choice – an asylum or a brothel. I chose the whorehouse for it was where I was bound to end and better than a house of correction.'

Robbie looked at her hard. 'I thought your first child died – Joan swore that it was so.'

'She told me the same but I discovered later that she sells the children of any women who give birth in the workhouse, whether they be honest or whores like me. She tells them the child has died, like she did me until I threatened I'd kill 'er – and then she agreed to give me what I wanted if she got to sell the babies to good homes.'

'Why didn't you come to me?'

'I thought you wasn't bothered.' Molly looked him in the eyes. 'I'm a whore, Robbie. Men like me because I make them laugh and I like them; I give them what they want – but they don't want tears and complaints.'

He nodded. 'One day, in another year or two, I'm goin' to retire from this wretched place and buy a pub. I'd like you to be my barmaid – and my bedmate, Molly.'

Molly raised her eyebrows. 'You want me to work fer yer?'

'It's why I asked if the babe was mine,' Robbie said and looked at her intently. 'I'd like a son, Molly – and if I was sure I had one I would look after yer both.'

Molly regarded him in silence for a moment. She despised him for his weakness and knew that he was less to blame for her predicament than his sister but she intended that they should both pay. Robbie thought he'd had his way with her and got away without penalty, but she was learning his secrets and those of his sister and when she knew something truly important she would go to the one person she was certain would punish them both.

'I'd like that fine, Robbie,' Molly said and laughed. 'Yes, I'd like that fine.'

Outside, unknown to them both, Joan listened and scowled. It had suited her to keep her brother in ignorance of what she did. Now that Molly had told him, he would either demand that she share some of what she made with him – or he would stop her, and she had no intention of giving up any of the little schemes that brought her extra money. Her brother was busy planning the future for Molly and himself, but he had never given a thought to her.

It was Joan who had to deal with the wretched families when they came in. Her brother merely signed them in and left it to her to sort the groups out. Joan had to put up with the screaming as children were wrenched from their mothers and the mothers weeping and begging not to be separated. The men usually seemed beaten by poverty and accepted their fate, and the old were too ill and too devoid of hope to argue, but mothers argued, wept and clung to their children and it was Joan who had to threaten and bully to sort them out. It was she who got fetched out in the middle of the night when one of the elderly vagrants died, and she who had to make sure they were all fed, clean and healthy. Her brother just amused himself with his whores and left the bulk of the work to her.

Walking the darkened corridors, peering through her spyholes and watching the private lives of the wretches she held so much power over usually gave Joan a great deal of pleasure, but that night she was angry. If her brother had so much money put away he had no right to grudge her the little she made from her side of the workhouse. She needed to make more and quickly, because time was running out . . .

It was so hot and damp in the laundry and Eliza's eyelids drooped as she moved her dolly stick up and down to loosen the clothes in the hot water. She could hardly wait until it was time to stop for their break and the cup of strong tea they were allowed at mid-morning.

'Stop dreamin', girl!' Mistress Simpkins boomed at her, making Eliza start. She'd been taking a little rest, because her back ached so much, but she stirred the hot water with renewed vigour, knowing that if mistress thought she was lazy she would get no supper and her stomach felt empty after the thin soup, which was all she'd been given that morning. 'You can stop that now, Jones. You're wanted in the warden's office. Follow me.'

Eliza's heart raced, because whenever she was summoned these days it was for punishment and the beatings could be severe, depending on what sort of mood Mistress was in. She walked behind the warden's sister, feeling breathless and afraid, because mistress had looked very oddly at her, as if she were pleased about something.

As they neared the warden's office, Mistress Simpkins stopped and turned to look at Eliza. 'You be careful now; speak only if Miss Richards asks you a question. Do you hear me? If you speak out of turn I'll flay the skin from your hide, girl. Remember, I can do as I like with you – and I could send you back to the butcher if I chose.'

Eliza swallowed hard. She guessed that someone was willing to pay the mistress good money for her and the woman was eager to take it. If Eliza let her down, she would be beaten. Her mouth felt dry as she entered the warden's room and saw a tall thin woman dressed in a long black coat standing near the window looking out into the yard where they were allowed to exercise and take the air for short periods. For a moment no one spoke and Eliza was on thorns. Had the lady decided she no longer wanted a girl?

'Here is the girl you picked out earlier, Miss Richards. I do not know why you want her in particular for she's a lazy slut, but she's young and strong and if you beat her regularly she will work hard for you.'

The woman turned sharply at her words, her face harsh with what looked like anger to Eliza. 'Thank you, Miss Simpkins, you may leave us.'

'Leave? But the girl is my responsibility. She might do something foolish if I ain't here—'

'Wait outside the door if you must,' Miss Richards interrupted with a note of command in her voice. 'I wish to speak to the girl alone.'

'Yes, ma'am.' The mistress turned and went out, though her cheeks looked puce and she was clearly furious. Eliza thought that the least she could look

152

forward to that night was being banished to her room with no supper.

'Come here, child, and do not look so nervous.' Miss Richards spoke gently, easing some of Eliza's fears. 'I am not angry with you. I saw you this morning in the assembly hall, though you did not see me for I was behind a screen and I have a question for you – would you prefer to live in my house as my ward or remain here?' Eliza's tongue stuck to the roof of her mouth and she could not find the breath to answer. 'Surely that is not too difficult a question? You may be asked to help me in my work sometimes – and you will be expected to learn to read and write so that you are useful, but—'

'Yes please!' Eliza gasped the words out as she realised her hesitation was causing the lady some annoyance. Whoever she was, she did not have much patience. 'So shocked be I, milady, that I knew not what you said.'

'I am not a lady, child. You may call me Miss Richards for the moment and we'll see how we go on.'

'Thank you, Miss Richards,' Eliza said and dipped an awkward curtsey. Her action brought a laugh to the lady's face and she shook her head.

'No need to curtsey to me, girl. What do they call you here?'

'Eliza; I'm called Eliza, Miss Richards, Eliza Jones. Jones is the name of the woman who cared for me here, for no one knows where I be from.'

'Hmm . . .' She gave her a considering look. 'No, I imagine not,' she said and once again that quick smile made her look younger. 'Well, is there anything you wish to ask me?'

'I don't know, miss . . .' Eliza felt puzzled. 'How long will you keep me – if I'm good and work hard?'

'It is my intention that you shall live with me, Eliza. If we suit I shall certainly keep you as long as you wish – and I promise you shall never return here. You will have a good home and I hope we shall like each other.'

'Why did you choose me, miss?'

'I have seen you before – at the market with some street children – and there was something about you that appealed to me. I would have spoken to you then, but suddenly you all started to steal bread and cakes and then you ran away.'

Eliza hung her head; she was ashamed that this lady should have seen her stealing food. 'I didn't want to steal but we were hungry . . .'

'Yes, I am sure you were, though that does not excuse it,' Miss Richards said sternly. 'I saw your face that morning and you looked so anxious that my heart caught for you – and I was determined that I would save you from yourself. I came here to discover if there was a chance you had been brought here and I was happy to see you.'

'Thank you,' Eliza said, looking at her in awe. The parson had once told her that somewhere there was a God, and a place called Heaven, though she had not believed him then, but now she wondered if she'd wandered there by mistake. 'I shall try to suit you, Miss Richards. When will you take me?'

'Have you anything you wish to take with you?'

'I have only this dress and my shawl . . .' Eliza clutched her ragged shawl to her shoulders.

'How foolish of me to ask such a question! Of course you have nothing of value, my dear. Then we shall go now for all the forms are signed. I have only to pay Mistress Simpkins and we shall be on our way home.'

'I'll have my money if you please, ma'am!' Mistress Simpkins entered the office, showing that she'd been listening outside. She held out her hand in an aggressive manner.

Miss Richards gave her a hard look and counted several coins into her hand, making Eliza gasp, for she had never seen so much money and could not believe anyone would pay that for her. 'That concludes our business,' Miss Richards said. 'Come along, Eliza; the sooner we are out of this foul place the better.'

With that she swept Eliza out of the office, down the hall and into the exercise area. As they approached the tall iron gates, which were always locked, the elderly keeper looked at Eliza and winked.

'You'll be glad to see the back of this place, girl,' he said and opened the gates to allow them to pass through.

Outside a small black carriage awaited. It looked like the kind of gig that the doctor drove when he visited the inmates. A lad of perhaps twelve was at the head of the bay horse; he'd been leading it up and down and relinquished it into Miss Richard's hands, touching his disreputable cap eagerly.

'Looked after your 'orse, miss,' he said. 'Ain't let nobody near 'im.'

'Thank you, young man,' she said and smiled slightly as she pressed a shiny florin into his grubby palm. 'If you would care for some more work you may come to me at Silk House at the corner of Halfpenny Street – do you know the area?'

'Yes, miss – it's them posh places what used ter belong to the rich merchants, I reckon?'

'Well, compared to these streets I daresay it may be posh,' Miss Richards said with a nod as she motioned to Eliza to climb in and took the reins herself. 'I am called Miss Richards, boy – come to me if you wish to earn an honest coin and I might find permanent business for you.'

The lad grinned, touched his forelock and moved back as she took her place in the driving seat. Her manner was assured and confident and she was clearly accustomed to driving herself.

Eliza caught her breath as the gig moved forward with a jerking movement. She'd never been in a carriage before, only the pig cart the butcher had thrown her into when he took her.

Eliza glanced back at the forbidding walls of the workhouse. Once the heavy iron gates were closed it was possible to see only the slate roof, a slightly darker grey than the stone walls. She was relieved to be leaving a place that had become bleak and friendless since Ruth and Joe were no longer there, and prayed to the God Ruth said really existed that she would never have to return to that awful place.

Glancing at Miss Richard's profile, Eliza wondered about her new mistress. She'd been terrified when the butcher dragged her off to his house, bewildered and apprehensive of what life held for her, but Miss Richards was different. She seemed stern and yet Eliza thought she would be a good mistress. Her spirits lifted as the workhouse was left far behind. She did not know what awaited her at her new home, but nothing could be worse than what she had left behind.

CHAPTER 13

'Eliza seems to have disappeared,' Arthur said to Ruth when he came back from his latest visit to the workhouse. 'No one has heard of her since she ran away from that disgusting fellow.'

''E must 'ave done somethin to 'er, sir,' Ruth said and looked anxious. 'Are yer sure Mistress Simpkins doesn't know more than she lets on? She'd lie while she looked yer straight in the eyes.'

'Yes, I imagine she might. However, I asked Master Simpkins if he'd heard anything of the child and he claimed not to – and I do not see why he should lie to me.'

'No, but he might not 'ave known if mistress kept it from him.'

'Well, I think we must look further afield,' Arthur went on thoughtfully. I visited the magistrates' court yesterday and saw some street children who had been rounded up for thieving from a baker's market stall. Apparently, they made a concerted raid some weeks ago and stole more than five pounds' worth of food, which is a serious crime. In the last century, a person might have been hung for stealing more than forty shillings, though we are more lenient now.'

'Eliza wasn't with them?'

'No, if she had been I would have paid her fine and brought her to you. The magistrate was unusually lenient with them. Often these thieving children can be sent to prison but there have been voices raised in parliament recently against the harsh treatment of children and so they were either fined or sent to a workhouse.'

'How many paid their fine?'

'One boy's was paid for him. I heard the name the lad gave – something like Tucker. He was paid for by a man named Reece and I believe that gentleman runs some gambling houses in the East End so I daresay the boy works for him. A lot of boys run errands for such folk and earn themselves the name of nippers, because they are fleet of foot.'

'I am sure he does work for a master, for the fine would not otherwise have been paid. Were they all boys?'

'Yes.' Arthur was still thoughtful. 'I asked the constable who had caught them if there were any girls amongst them. He said that there had been a girl for a few weeks prior to the arrest but that she had escaped along with several of the others.'

'Oh, sir, do you think it might be Eliza?' Ruth asked, looking at him hopefully. 'I think of her often, sir, and worry for her – alone on the streets at night, and the winter coming on us . . .'

'Yes, I am sure you must,' Arthur agreed. 'I am anxious for her myself. If she has been running with this gang, she will have learned much from them. The boy Tucker was very sure of himself, very streetwise. I think Eliza would've been safe enough with him – but he was in prison for two or three weeks before his trial so there is no way of knowing where she is now.'

'No . . .' Ruth wiped her eyes with her apron. 'She was like my own daughter, sir. Ever since her mother brought her in . . .'

Arthur nodded sympathetically. 'I shall not give up my search for her, Ruth. And now – tell me of our guests. Are they all well and content?'

'Yes, sir, they are. Miss Esther 'as been a little poorly. She suffers with her chest as soon as it gets chilly in the evenings, but I 'ad the doctor to 'er as you asked, sir, and she seems better this mornin'.'

'I think she would not have survived another winter on her own,' Arthur said and smiled. 'I made a wise choice when I chose you to look after my guests, Ruth. Miss Esther will be comfortable and happy here in her last days.'

'Yes, sir. You and Miss Ross have done a good thing in opening this house, sir.'

Arthur smiled and took his leave of her. Miss Ross was often in his thoughts these days, more than he'd intended when he'd agreed that they should take on this project together. She was a lovely young woman and he knew that she meant more to him than he ought to have allowed, for he could not ask her to wed him. He did not deserve that kind of happiness because he had caused the ruin of a young woman once and could never forgive himself for what had happened to her.

Miss Richards had driven her gig into the mews behind a row of buildings. She gave the reins into the hands of a young boy, who ran forward to take the horse away, and led Eliza through a narrow passage to a wider street. This consisted of shops and business premises, but the buildings were old and still had an air of faded grandeur that impressed Eliza.

'This is my shop, and I live in the back and above,' she said, indicating one of the shops.

Above the window was a sign with gold lettering on a black background, which moved and creaked a little in the breeze. The window itself was dark, with black curtains shutting off the inner sanctum, and there were only two large bell-shaped jars standing on the shelf inside the faintly grey glass. A bell jangled as Miss Richards opened the door and, once inside, Eliza was mesmerised.

Eliza stared in wonder as she followed Miss Richards into the dark interior of the shop, for she had never seen anything like it, the shelves lined with blue glass bottles in all shapes and sizes; there were gold letters on them, a few of which she recognised, but could not put together to read. Set at each end of the shelves were two long wooden cabinets with lots of tiny drawers and on each drawer a brass surround held white cards with more letters neatly written on them. The smell was spicy and yet sharp and the young man who stood behind the counter was wearing a white apron over dark trousers, his shirt sleeves rolled up to the elbows and held with wide black bands. Miss Richards introduced him as her cousin Malcolm. He stared at Eliza but did not smile in welcome and his eyes were not in the least friendly.

Eliza turned in a full circle, taking in all the wonders

of large brass scales and tiny ones. She'd seen the coke merchant use a crude form of scales when he delivered to the workhouse, for Miss Simpkins demanded full measure before she paid the tradesmen, but his were of wood and rusted metal, crude besides these beautiful things.

'What do you think of my little apothecary shop?' Miss Richards asked when Eliza remained silent. 'Papa called us apothecaries – though these days most would say we were chemists. A lot of our preparations are made of herbs and natural things, which can be dangerous unless used in the right way. That is why he taught me how to use them. I helped him make up his preparations in the evenings when the shop was closed and during the day I did what Malcolm does now.'

'May I go for my dinner now, Cousin Edith?' the young man behind the counter asked.

Miss Richards looked at the wooden clock on the wall. 'It is but three minutes to one, Malcolm. We never close our doors until one, as you well know – but go along. I shall use the time to show Eliza where things are.' He took off his apron and grabbed a jacket from a hook at the far end of the counter. 'Have you no welcome for Eliza, cousin?'

Malcolm glared at Eliza as if he hated the sight of her, but he mouthed the words, 'Welcome, Eliza . . .' before bolting out of the door.

Miss Richards shook her head resignedly. 'I fear Malcolm will never make an apothecary, but I have higher hopes for you, Eliza.'

'I know nothing of such things, miss.'

'Well, I shall teach you everything, but in return I

162

expect loyalty. No stealing from me,' Miss Richards said sternly. 'This house was once the residence of a wealthy silk merchant, but it has been divided into three separate properties. We are number fifteen, Eliza. The milliner next door is number fourteen and the confectioner's is number twelve; there is no number thirteen, because it is considered unlucky. Three doors down is what was once another silk merchant's house and is now the Fever Hospital. This was a thriving community of Huguenots, who came to England to escape religious persecution, but in time the wealthy merchants moved away and much of the property has become shabby. Just up the road there is a Jewish synagogue and beyond that a workshop where women make garments.'

'I've seen such places in Bethnal Green,' Eliza said. 'Tucker called them sweat shops and said the women were treated like slaves.'

'Yes, I believe that is true,' Miss Richards agreed. 'Now pay attention, Eliza. We keep all our medicines in these jars and drawers.' Edith Richards frowned as her cousin shot off to find his midday meal, setting the bell jangling. 'You will learn where everything is in time, Eliza – but the powders and pills we make ourselves are kept in the drawers, and the jars contain liquids. We have several poisons and great care must be taken with dispensing those – and a note is made in a special book of every half ounce of arsenic we sell. People have been known to use it for wicked purposes rather than to kill rats and pests, which is its proper use. Occasionally, Papa used the tiniest amount in a medicine, but that can be dangerous, for if it is used carelessly and taken too frequently it might induce illness rather than cure it.'

'Can it do good as well as evil?' Eliza asked.

'Assuredly, or Papa would not have used it. Henry Richards was a great and good man, Eliza. One day, when we know each other better, I shall tell you about my dear papa, but not just yet. You have much to learn and it is a vast pity that you were sent to that terrible place. I do not think Papa was aware of it until shortly before his death, but no more of that for now.' A thin smile touched her mouth. 'I daresay you will be hungry, Eliza. It is one o'clock now so we shall put the lock on the door and go through.'

As she moved purposefully towards the door, it opened, setting the bell jangling as an attractive young woman rushed in. Edith frowned and asked what was needed in a severe tone.

'Some of that mixture yer give me afore,' the woman said and made a wry face. 'The stuff what gets rid of unwanted brats.'

'Maggie Jackson, I've told you before, we do not deal in such things here, nor did I give you anything of the sort – you asked for an emetic because you were constipated and that's what I gave you.'

'Well, it worked anyhow,' Maggie said and winked at Eliza. 'I shan't tell anyone you give me it.'

'You must come back this evening at six. I do not have time to make it up for you at the moment.'

'If I must – but give me the same as last time, 'cos I'm up the duff agin – the ole bugger won't leave me alone, Miss Edith.'

'You should leave his employ, Maggie – or tell his wife what he does when she's sleeping.'

'She'd say I was lying and lay the stick about me

shoulders – and I'd find another job if I could, but 'tis like as not 'twould be the same. They either starve you or rape you – and if you complain 'tis thrown out you'll be and only the workhouse left for shelter.'

Edith shook her head as the shop door closed behind Maggie with a little bang. She locked the door and turned to Eliza with a sigh.

'I think the workhouse was the devil's invention. Did you know that before they had such things decent folk made it their business to feed and help the destitute, and there were laws meant to keep them from starving? When folk stayed at home in their parish where they belonged, the system worked well enough, so Papa told me, but when everyone began to move to the towns there were just too many people, causing overcrowding in bad housing, poverty and health problems, and so someone thought of the workhouse.'

'Why do they send people there?' Eliza asked her. 'Mistress said we be there to learn to be disciplined and respect our betters so that if we be fortunate to be taken out we would know our place.'

'The workhouse would be a good thing if people were treated more kindly,' Edith said as she led the way through to what was a large kitchen at the back of the house. It was twice the size of the front shop and the first thing Eliza noticed was that it looked very clean and neat. 'This is our kitchen. The smaller room at the end is where we cook and eat, and this part is where I make up the preparations. It is where you will be working with me.' She gave Eliza a little push towards the domestic end and took off her coat, revealing a serviceable dark grey dress. 'As for folk knowing their

165

place – Papa believed that all men were created equal under God and the place we had in life was the place we had worked for.'

Eliza's nostrils twitched as she caught the most enticing smell. Edith had donned a large white apron and she set two plates on the scrubbed-pine table with forks, knives and spoons, and then bent to take a brown pot from the oven which was heated by a large iron range. She set the pot on the table and took off the cover, allowing the delicious smell to escape and tantalise Eliza even more for she had never smelled its like.

'What is that?' she asked in awe. 'Is it one of your medicines?'

Edith looked at her and smiled. 'That is chicken and vegetables in a rich gravy, child. I cook everything in the same pot because it is easy and allows me to get on with my work without fussing. It simmers in the oven all morning so that I never have to stop and see to it. Sit down and eat now – but wash your hands first in the bowl there. A jug of water is under the stand.'

Eliza followed the direction of her nod and saw the marble-topped washstand in the corner. A pretty blue-and-white china bowl stood on top and underneath was a jug of a similar though not matching pattern. She poured a little water into the bowl, rinsed her hands in the water and wiped her hands on the piece of towel hanging on a rail underneath.

'Show me,' Edith said when she came to the table and inspected her hands. 'They will do for now, but I will train you how to wash your hands properly, and to scrub your nails. When you help me with the herbs

166

you must have clean hands at all times – do you understand me, Eliza?'

'Yes, Miss Richards.'

'Good, now sit and eat.'

While Eliza had been cleansing her hands, Edith had ladled the food into two bowls and beside the now steaming bowls were two small plates made from the same blue-and-white china with chunks of fresh bread. Eliza's stomach rumbled and she blushed for shame, but Edith seemed not to notice. They both sat down and Edith said grace, something Eliza was used to at the workhouse for the master always told them how thankful they must be for their food – even though it was never enough and never tasted half as good as this smelled.

The first mouthful made Eliza's eyes open in wonder. She held the chunk of soft, meltingly-good chicken and gravy in her mouth, reluctant to swallow because the taste was so wonderful.

'You're not eating? Is it not to your liking?' Edith looked at her severely and Eliza chewed and swallowed, before daring to answer.

'It's so lovely – I didn't want to eat it too quick, because I've never tasted food like this before, miss.'

'Well, you may soon tire of it,' Edith said briskly not wasting time on sympathy. 'You will eat the same meal again this evening, and if we don't finish it, I may warm it up again for tomorrow. The day after, it will be rabbit or a piece of braising beef. Only on Sunday do I prepare a different type of meal – my cousin doesn't care for my cooking, which is why he goes out for his dinner.'

'Does your cousin live 'ere with you in your 'ouse, miss?'

'You must begin to speak properly, Eliza. Do not drop your aitches, please. It is house and here, not 'ouse and 'ere – do you understand, Eliza? I want you to speak properly when you serve my customers.'

'Yes, miss. The vicar and the doctor speak posh like you. Ruth says it's so we know our place and we shouldn't try to be better than we be.'

'It's than we are, not than we be – and you most definitely should try to speak properly, Eliza. Listen to the way I speak, and copy it. However, in answer to your question, Malcolm lives with his widowed mother in the house his father left to them. Mrs Richards is a widow and cannot control her son, I fear.'

'So your father and his were brothers, miss?'

'Yes, that is so – and I had hopes of Malcolm taking over from me one day when he first came here, but I fear he does not apply himself. He would rather be off to the tavern with his friends than learn how to grind shells to a powder and blend herbs.'

Edith had finished her meal. She glanced at Eliza's bowl, which was empty. 'Have you eaten enough, child?'

'Yes, thank you, Miss Richards.'

'Very well, you may clear these things into the sink, using the bowl you will find underneath. There is hot water in the kettle and soda crystals in the jar on the drainer. Do you know how to wash dishes?'

'Yes, Miss Richards. I helped Ruth in the kitchen sometimes, when I'd finished in the laundry. I wasn't supposed to, but Cook didn't mind – she sometimes gave me a cup of milk.'

Eliza cleared the dishes to the sink, and then fetched hot water from the kettle, added a few crystals of the precious soda that made the water soapy, and then added a little cold water from the can. She was unaware that Edith was watching her and when she finished drying her hands was surprised to be told there was a cup of tea waiting for her.

'Tea, miss?' she asked and turned to see that a blue-and-white patterned teapot stood on the table; there was also a jug containing milk, a sugar box with a lid and two cups. Eliza knew that Mistress Simpkins had offered tea to the wives of the guardians who had come once a year to inspect the workhouse, but she'd never tasted it. 'Isn't that expensive?'

'Yes, very,' Edith replied with a smile, and took down the small mahogany box which had a paler wood strung through it and an impressive lock. Edith took the key from her apron pocket, unlocked the tea caddy, and then allowed Eliza to look inside. There were two compartments which held different blends of tea and a glass bowl in the middle. Edith took three spoonfuls from each tea and mixed them in the bowl and then transferred two spoonsful to the pot. 'I always warm the pot first, Eliza. The mixture left in the bowl is my allowance for the day. I never use more, because, as you say it is very expensive.'

'I've never tasted tea before.'

'I daresay there are many things you have not done, but you will have your chance in the coming months and years – if you behave and try to please me.' She relocked the caddy and placed it back on the mantel, pocketing the key. 'I am giving you a chance in life, Eliza, but I expect

169

you to show me respect – and not to cheat me. If I find that you deceive me in any way I might not be so happy to have you here – so never lie to me. Do you understand?'

'Yes, Miss Richards. I don't know why you chose me – but I thank you for your goodness.'

'I consider it my Christian duty to help those I can.' Edith shook her head and a glimmer of tears was in her eyes. 'Now, come and taste your tea. I shall serve it as I like it, with a little milk and one spoon of sugar. You must tell me what you think.'

Eliza picked up the cup that her employer pushed towards her. The liquid was a pale golden-brown in colour and the china felt hot in her hands. Holding it with care, she sniffed doubtfully and then smiled, because the aroma was pleasant. Ruth had told her it was nasty stuff – but she'd only tasted the dregs from the warden's pot. She sipped carefully, letting the liquid roll over her tongue – and then swallowed.

'Well, what is your verdict?' Edith asked, a faint smile in her eyes as Eliza drank another mouthful and then another.

'It's good, miss,' Eliza said. 'It's warm as you swallow and it makes you feel nice inside – a lot better than water or the beer they gave us for special days, but I like milk.'

'Then perhaps you would like a little more in your tea,' Edith suggested. 'You may have milk for your supper and your breakfast, but I shall let you join me for a cup of tea sometimes – and perhaps you will learn to appreciate it.'

'It's too good to waste on the likes of me,' Eliza said shyly, but Edith shook her head.

'No, Eliza, I do not consider it a waste to teach you the finer things of life. Perhaps you will not always share my tastes, but my hope is that you will grow to like the things I like so that we may enjoy each other's company. I need a companion, not a servant, my dear child – and it would please me to bring you back to the kind of life that ought to be yours.'

'I don't understand, miss.'

'No, but you will when you learn that there is so much in life to enjoy,' Edith said. 'I know Papa would say I was right to bring you here – and I intend that you shall be happy. And I think you may call me Edith. Miss Richards is so formal and I want us to be friends.'

Eliza's throat tightened. Ruth had been kind to her, but they'd been thrown together by the harshness of their surroundings. This lady came from another world and she was offering to let Eliza share it with her. She could not believe her good fortune. Surely at any moment she would wake up and discover that it was all a dream?

CHAPTER 14

In the days and weeks that followed, Eliza often wondered if she was dreaming. After the years of despair in the workhouse and the horror of what had happened the last time she'd been sold to a master, Eliza could not believe what was happening now. She'd been given a room to herself, a room that was as big as the butcher's wife had slept in; it was furnished with a comfortable bed, a chest of drawers for her clothes and a chair and table where she could sit and practise her letters. Eliza was learning to write and to reckon numbers, because Miss Richards wanted her to, and Eliza studied hard for she would have done anything to please her mistress.

She now had three dresses hanging from hooks on the wall. Two for every day and one for Sunday best. They had been Miss Edith's when she was Eliza's age and were made of lovely material in a pale blue, a navy blue with a white collar and long sleeves with cuffs, and a dark green heavy material for Sunday. Eliza's feet did not fit into any of the shoes Miss Edith had saved, so the very next morning she took Eliza to the market and purchased two pairs of sensible black boots with shiny buttons and a pretty pair of house slippers. She had also given Eliza underwear and some cotton stockings to wear so that the new boots did not rub the skin on her feet.

Every day, Miss Edith worked in her big kitchen, making mixtures and pills to help people with common complaints; there was a green minty liquid for wind and indigestion, pills for bad breath, pills or mixtures for headaches, for hay fever, also stomach upsets and sickness. She made creams and lotions for various skin conditions and lotions to keep the complexion clear of spots as well as many other things that would take stains from a dress without spoiling it or lift a water mark from wood, as well as poisons to kill rats and pests. She also made the potion that Maggie Jackson had asked for when Eliza first came to the shop.

'It helps constipation,' Miss Edith told her. 'I believe if taken in large quantities it might cause a woman to lose a child in the early stages of pregnancy – so be very careful who you sell it to, Eliza. If you are ever left in charge of the shop, you must always take great care what you dispense. This mixture is an emetic and that is it's only use, do you understand? If we sold it for any other purpose we might be in trouble with the law.'

'Yes, Miss Edith.' Eliza nodded, because she remembered that her employer had been very reluctant to sell it to Maggie, and yet she had done so because Eliza had seen her give it to the woman and warn her.

'You must be very careful, Maggie,' she'd told her. 'In small doses this relieves chronic constipation but in large doses it could be dangerous for women who are with child.'

'Yeah, I know,' Maggie said. 'I've got chronic constipation all right.' She'd laughed, paid over her shilling and gone out grinning.

Eliza knew that Miss Edith worried about selling the medicine to Maggie. She'd shaken her head over it, looking at Eliza as if to excuse herself.

'What should I do when she is in trouble? Her employer's wife would turn her out on to the streets if she carried the child to full term. She has nowhere to go and no one to care for her. What else can I do, Eliza?'

'Maggie knows the risks she runs,' Eliza said because she could see it troubled Miss Edith. 'If forced to bear the child, she would only end up selling herself on the streets or perhaps in the workhouse, and she could die in childbed, as so many women do.'

'Yes, that is what I tell myself,' Miss Edith said. 'Now, Eliza, I have done my work for the morning. I want you to read this list for me – and to learn not only the words, but what they mean.'

'What are they?' Eliza asked looking at the long list. She realised that she'd seen some of them on the jars in the shop. 'These are the names of ingredients you use.'

'Can you read them?'

'I can remember shapes and I recognise them,' Eliza said, 'but I want to learn to read and write properly, Miss Edith.'

'Good, that is excellent, Eliza. We will begin with this list and you will copy them out in your own hand. I shall say them, and you may repeat them after me.'

'Feverfew . . . mint . . .' She began to read down the long list. 'Mercury . . . zinc . . . arsenic . . .' She took a pencil and underlined it. 'This one is very important, Eliza, because it is poison. Never forget that. We only sell very small portions of it, never more than an ounce, and the customers have to sign their names in our book. It is used for many things, killing pests is what most people buy it for but we must never sell too much in case it is used for murder.'

Eliza nodded. She wrote the name out six times so that she could recognise it at once and would not mistake it for antinomy or something else beginning with the same letter.

'You learn quickly,' Miss Edith said. 'I can see you will be an excellent pupil, Eliza, and of much help to me in my work. And now, since you've worked so hard, you can help me prepare our meal for the evening – and then we shall have a little music.'

Eliza nodded and smiled. Miss Edith played the pianoforte in the evenings and she was allowed to sit and listen. The music she played had been a revelation to Eliza and Miss Edith had promised that they would go to a concert in the church at Christmas.

'I do not care for the halls of music, which are common, vulgar places,' she'd told Eliza. 'Sometimes the theatres give concerts which we may attend, but that is expensive and a rare treat – the church is free for all, and we may give what we can afford in the collection.'

Eliza nodded. She knew that her employer lived frugally, not out of meanness, but because she did not make a great deal of money from her shop. She did have some money put by for a rainy day, in a secret place in the cupboard in the corner of the kitchen which she didn't think Eliza knew about, but usually she had a few coins in the metal box on the mantel and that was eked out to last her the week.

'Yes, Miss Edith, it will be a treat to hear the carols. Sometimes, I was allowed to go with the others but often the privilege was withdrawn as a punishment.'

'I am sorry you were treated so harshly, Eliza – and before Christmas we shall go shopping together. I shall buy a few treats for us and you shall choose something you like from the market.'

Eliza could not believe what she was hearing. Miss Edith had already given her so much and now she was to receive a gift as well? It was too good to be true and she wondered when she would wake up and find herself back in the hell of the workhouse laundry.

'I want Christmas to be a happy occasion for our guests,' Arthur told Ruth as he gave her twelve gold sovereigns. 'This is to buy special food and small treats for your ladies. I shall provide some small gifts for them so there is no need for you to stretch your budget. Miss Ross is going to help me choose what is most suitable – and she wishes to make some small contributions herself.' He hesitated, then, 'She would like to provide a hamper of food and to join us here on Christmas Eve for a supper – do you think you could provide something, Ruth?'

'Yes, of course, sir. Cook will make some warming soup and we'll have a cold meal of ham, pickles and fresh bread, and perhaps some potatoes cooked in their jackets. We can have some fancy bits and pieces as well; mince pies, chocolate truffles made with almonds, and little sweet comfits, for Cook be happy to make them if she has the ingredients.'

'Yes, that sounds exactly right,' Arthur said. 'It will be an informal meal, one that we can all enjoy – and I know Miss Ross has gifts for everyone.'

'She be a kind lady, sir. A lady after yer own heart.' She smiled knowingly at him, but he shook his head.

'Miss Ross is far above me,' Arthur said and laughed softly. 'I could never aspire to match her goodness – but I do my best to be honest and decent and that must suffice.'

'Well, me and Cook think you'm the best,' she said and folded her arms over her chest.

'I'm only sorry that I have not been able to trace Eliza for you,' he said. 'I had hoped to have news of her before this, but Miss Simpkins is adamant that she knows nothing of her.'

The smile died from Ruth's face. 'I fear for her, sir. If she be on the streets in this bitter weather she could die – and if that woman has sold her again, she could be anywhere. Even in the whorehouse.'

'Surely she would not dare to do such a thing? I know that you suffered at Miss Simpkins hands – and I should like to dismiss her – but some of the Board members believe that she is a good warden and think that I misjudge her. If I had proof of wrong doing – but her brother refuses to condemn her and no one else will speak out against her.'

'Aye, sir, I know,' Ruth said. 'But they are afraid of her – afraid of being starved and beaten.'

'Well, we are having a special meal for the inmates on the day before Christmas Eve. While I am there I shall see if some cider and ale will loosen tongues – and if I find anything, Miss Simpkins shall feel the full force of the law. I promise you.'

'Make her tell you what she's done with Eliza, sir. I don't believe she's just disappeared.'

'Unfortunately, many children do every year,' Arthur said sadly. 'Children run away and are never seen again. Some of them are taken into brothels, some die of starvation and their bodies are buried in a pauper's grave – others just never turn up.'

'Yes, sir, I know – but I keep praying Eliza be not one of them. I love that girl and I'd give my own life for her.'

He shook his head. 'I blame myself, Ruth. I should have done something that day she was in your care. I should have taken you both away then, but such interference is frowned on. The workhouse is an institution that many feel does a wonderful job of keeping vagrants from our streets and preventing more deaths.'

'The workhouse is a sentence of living death,' Ruth said and set her mouth grimly. 'Well-meaning folk send us there, but they have no idea what hell it is for those who are not strong enough to endure it. I've seen the way the old folk just wither away and die – and I'm never goin' back.'

'I did not know when I first met you what I know now,' Arthur said. 'I was one of those who believed we were doing our best for unfortunate people who would otherwise starve. I know better now, because of what you've told me – and I promise I will never give up looking for Eliza.' He smiled at her. 'You taught her to be strong – and I feel that she will survive whatever fate has thrown at her.'

'I've been asked for some special merchandise.' The man looked craftily at Joan Simpkins that night three weeks before Christmas. 'My customer will pay well – and he would willingly take more than one.'

Joan's eyes gleamed with avarice. 'I have three ready at the moment – and there will be another three soon, but I dare not send too many at once lest it is noticed. There is to be a special meal for the inmates this Christmas and the children are to receive a small gift paid for by the governors. I have been asked for a list of names and ages so that suitable gifts may be purchased.'

'Will their interference never cease?' her visitor snarled. 'That wretched man and his friends are ruining my business.'

'And mine – but you shall have three of the girls. Their ages are thirteen, fifteen and sixteen; all are of an age to be sent out to work and their absence will not be noticed.'

'Well, they will suit most of my clients,' Drake said, 'but my special client wants them younger – eleven or twelve at most and he prefers them much younger if he can get them.'

Joan pulled a face of disgust. 'Even I would hesitate to sell a girl under eleven,' she said. 'For such a favour as that I would want as much as fifty guineas. If it were discovered, I would be instantly dismissed – I might be imprisoned.'

'It's risky, especially after the recent campaigns in parliament and the newssheets,' he agreed. 'I've told him we want more money because of the risk and he promised that he would pay a hundred guineas for a young, fresh girl, especially if she was fair and pretty.'

'Very well.' Joan frowned, but she was tingling with excitement at the thought of so much to be earned. 'There are no girls like that here at the moment. The three I will let you take are dark and skinny little things, but they are innocent and should please most of your clients.'

'Keep my special client's request in mind,' he said. 'When can I take the other girls?'

'A week on Tuesday is our best chance. I shall tell them they have been chosen to work in a lady's house and you may collect them at four. My brother will be out that day and it is better if he does not see – but I want payment first.'

'Here . . .' Drake took the money from his pocket and put it down on the table. The gold coins glittered in the light of her lamp. 'It doesn't matter about their clothes, because we shall give them something to wear – but make sure they're clean and healthy.'

'Yes, of course,' Joan said. 'Now you'd best go before someone comes.'

She smiled as she scooped up the money and locked it away in her drawer. Her brother would be out, and he took little notice of the women's side. No one was going to bother about three workhouse orphans, who had neither mother nor father to miss them. Her pile of money was growing. If she could find a pretty child to sell to Drake's special customer, she would be able to leave this place and set herself up for life . . .

Outside in the corridor, Molly turned and fled before the door opened and Joan's visitor left. She did not wish to be caught listening to Mistress Simpkins' conversations, but her eyes gleamed with excitement at the news she'd overheard. That evil woman was up to her tricks again, but this time Molly intended to do something about it – her time in the workhouse had paid off and it was her chance for revenge at last!

CHAPTER 15

'You've been with me nearly two months now, Eliza,' Edith Richards told her when they started work that morning. 'Things have turned out better than I imagined, for I did not expect you to learn your letters so quickly or that you would be clever with figures.'

'Ruth told me I had a good memory,' Eliza said, smiling at the woman she had come to trust almost as much as she'd once trusted Ruth. Every day with Miss Edith had been a pleasure, marred only because she did not know what had happened to her friends. 'She could reckon figures in her head but she could not write much more than her name unless she copied it, though she could read very slowly. The rector taught me my name and Tucker taught me place names. Perhaps that is why I have learned quickly from you.'

'Yes, perhaps,' Miss Edith agreed. 'I wish you had been given a proper education from the start, Eliza. It was very unfair to you, for you are an intelligent girl.'

'I think I am luckier than most, Miss Edith. Most employers would not treat me as kindly as you do.'

Miss Edith merely shook her head and told her to

fetch the pestle and mortar. She began to grind herbs and berries together, explaining each step as she did so and naming the healing herbs as rosemary, juniper and mint amongst many others. Each time a preparation was strained and decanted into a small bottle, a label was stuck on and the cure for which it was intended written in capital letters.

Mint was one of the main ingredients in a cure for a burning in the chest, caused, Miss Edith said, by eating too much fat. It was a failing rich people indulged in too often and it made their digestions uneasy, especially at night when they were prone to consuming several courses of rich food.

'In ancient times women sometimes used incantations when preparing cures; certain herbs and berries had to be gathered at a particular time of the night or morning, some with the dew on them. It was rituals like these that led to many women being named as witches, though of course that was all nonsense,' she told Eliza.

'Some of the women in the workhouse spoke of witches and black magic that ill-wished folk,' Eliza said. 'Ruth said 'twas nonsense and spite.'

'Yes, and so it was,' Edith agreed. '*It was* nonsense, Eliza, not 'twas, my dear. Your speech is improving but you lapse when you think of the workhouse. I've told you, you shall never return there. Now, fetch me the tincture of belladonna, for I need one drop of it in my preparation. Too much could kill – it is one of the poisons of which I told you – but it can also help when someone is suffering from terrible toothache and cannot sleep for it induces slumber, but it must never be given in larger doses.'

'How do you remember all these things?' Eliza asked. 'You're so clever, Miss Edith, and I want to be just like you.'

'For that you may have to go to a special school when you are older. I suppose that you ought to go to school now, but I prefer to teach you myself. At school they do not allow you to open your mind – and I was educated by my own father. He was a clever man, as I have told you. Papa studied as a chemist and passed many exams, but he always believed in the power of herbs and natural things.' She looked up as Eliza passed her a large stone jar of honey. 'Yes, I need honey to sweeten the bitterness of the herbs – how did you know that, Eliza?'

'Because you told me so yesterday and the day before.' Eliza grinned at her. 'It is easy to learn from you, Miss Edith. If I went to school I should not learn half so much for I should be there but a few hours – and I am here all day with you.'

'When I brought you here I thought to rescue you from the harshness of your surroundings, but now I wonder if I have been fair to you, keeping you here as my companion, making you work with me . . .'

'Please do not send me away,' Eliza begged. 'I love being with you, Miss Edith. I want to learn everything so that one day I can do all the things you do.'

A thin smile touched Edith's lips. 'Well, I doubt I shall have anyone harassing me, demanding that you attend school, Eliza. When you are older you will know as much as I can teach you, and perhaps it is enough. I have made a good life for myself and there is no reason why you should not do the same.'

'It is all I want,' Eliza declared fervently. 'I'd die if you sent me back there.'

'No, no,' Edith said and laughed. 'I was just wondering if I ought to send you to school for a few hours – but perhaps we shall go on as we are. Now fetch me the basil and the feverfew.'

Eliza scurried away to obey. For a moment she'd feared Miss Edith was displeased with her, but she had only been thinking of her good.

'This is the last of the feverfew, Miss Edith,' Eliza said, showing her how little remained of the dried plant in its jar. 'And I noticed that your stock of lavender is low, as is the agrimony, and the blackberry root is all gone.'

Edith made a ticking noise with her tongue. 'It is time Bathsheba, the Romany woman visited me again,' she said. 'Some of the herbs and roots she brings me are rare. I can buy the common herbs fresh from the markets, but only from the travelling woman can I purchase more important plants and herbs. Always remember that dried herbs lose much of their healing power; they need to be fresh if you can find them – fresh-picked if possible to reach their full potential.'

'How often does she call on you?' Eliza asked.

'Perhaps once or twice a year,' Edith said and shook her head over it. 'Well, I must use what I have . . .' She glanced up at the clock. 'The morning has almost flown. I do not have time to visit the market this morning. Well, you must go for me, Eliza.'

'Go to the market alone?'

Eliza stared at her apprehensively. She'd visited this particular market with her employer on several occasions,

185

but it was a long way to walk there and back alone, and a big responsibility to choose and buy the shopping. Eliza had loved the markets when she was with Tucker; they were filled with strange and exotic smells and there were so many things to see. Always, when she visited the shops with Miss Edith, she longed to linger by some of the stalls selling pretty things, but was hurried along by her impatient companion who never had time to stand and stare.

'I need a loaf of bread, butter, carrots – and you may buy me some fresh herbs if you can find any – also a rabbit, but only from the stall we always buy our meat from, Eliza. Now, write a list and I will give you the money.' Edith took up her purse and counted four half-crowns into her hand. 'That should be enough.'

'It is so much money,' Eliza said nervously. 'I am feared I might lose it, Miss Edith.'

'Tie it into a corner of your handkerchief,' Edith said, 'and tuck that inside your bodice. Be careful to ask the price of everything and make sure the trader does not cheat you of your change.'

'Yes, Miss Edith,' Eliza said, but she was nervous as she fetched her shawl and the rush basket they used for the market. It was easy enough to reckon the prices of things in Miss Edith's kitchen, but would the traders cheat her because she was not quick enough to notice how much change they gave her? 'I will do the best I can.'

'I trust you, Eliza,' Edith said. 'I must finish this mixture for Mrs Trent, as she is calling for it this afternoon. Since I cannot visit the market, you must. Go now, and do not waste time for we have much to do today.'

Eliza nodded and went out without another word. She felt proud to be allowed to shop for Miss Edith, though a little daunted. As she entered the shop, Malcolm was putting something into his pocket and glared at her. She thought she caught sight of silver coins but wasn't sure. Used to his dark looks, she took little notice normally but this time he seemed angry.

'Where are you goin', workhouse girl?'

'I've been sent on an errand,' she replied warily. 'And my name is Eliza.'

'Brat from the workhouse – that's what you are,' he said. 'A filthy little child of a whore from the workhouse, and one of these days I'll make you sorry you came here.'

Eliza refused to let him scare or intimidate her; she'd faced bullies in the workhouse and was used to standing up to them. 'And you're a sneaking little coward,' she hissed. 'You wouldn't dare say a word if your cousin was here. Now get out of my way and let me pass or I'll go back and tell her what you called me.'

'Tell-tale bitch,' he muttered and pinched her arm as she pushed past him. 'Just you wait – one of these days I'll make sure she sends you back where you came from.'

Eliza lifted her head and ignored him. She was too nervous and too excited at the prospect of her adventure to bother about such empty threats. Malcolm worked for his cousin but had little influence with her. Only if Eliza seriously displeased Miss Edith would she be sent back in disgrace, and that she would never willingly do.

There were less than three weeks to Christmas and the scents of holly and fir trees were the first to reach Eliza's nostrils as she entered the market that frosty morning. A thin grey smoke issued from a fire in some kind of brazier on which chestnuts were being roasted, adding to the scents of spices and hot drinks being sold to the people shopping.

Eliza's apprehension faded as she wandered about the stalls, looking at candies being sold for use on the Christmas tree, and small wooden dolls, trains, bricks and lead soldiers which made a splendid array on a stall selling toys for the festive season. Eliza lingered, looking at some of the dolls, especially one with a beautiful wax face and hair that looked real. She'd never seen anything like it or realised that some children were given things like these to play with.

'Get your ma to buy you her for Christmas?' the stallholder said, noticing the looks she gave the doll.

Eliza shook her head and tore herself away. She must get on with her shopping, for if she was too long Miss Edith might be cross. The stall her employer always bought her meat from was just across the street. Its owner recognised her and found her the best rabbit he had. She took her money out and paid him the one shilling he asked and kept the change from her first half-crown in her hand as she went on to the stalls selling carrots, bread and butter. She managed to buy all she needed and there were still two half-crowns in her handkerchief. The only other thing Miss Edith had asked for was some fresh herbs, but Eliza walked all over the market before she found a stall selling dried flowers and herbs. She hesitated whether or not to purchase anything, because Miss Edith had told her that fresh herbs were far more effective, though she knew that some of the herbs were always dried – indeed, it would be impossible to buy fresh at this time of year.

Approaching the woman standing by the baskets of dried lavender and various herbs, Eliza hesitated, and then asked the price. The woman's skin was swarthy, as though she had either come from a land where the sun was harsh or spent much of her time outdoors. She had bright eyes rather like those of a bird, but dark and fierce, her black hair hanging from beneath a red scarf that she wrapped around her head, and there were gold loops in her ears.

'How much are they?' Eliza asked, pointing at the bunches of lavender in her basket.

'Sixpence each or three for a shilling,' the woman said in a voice that had a lilting sound and reminded her of Joe. 'All the herbs be the same price.' The woman's eyes narrowed, seeming to bore into Eliza. 'And what be you wanting with herbs, little mistress?'

'I've been asked to buy them for my mistress, Miss Edith. She is an apothecary and she is teaching me all she knows.'

'And what have you learned?' There was laughter in the strange woman's eyes and Eliza's skin flushed.

'I know that you have lavender, agrimony and dried rosemary but I am not sure of some of the others.' Eliza lifted her head proudly.

'Ah, so she tells the truth,' the woman said and suddenly reached out and caught Eliza's hand. 'Open your palm and I shall tell you what the future holds for you, little mistress.'

Eliza wanted to withdraw her hand and run away, but the woman's brown fingers held her fast and her eyes locked with hers. Against her will, Eliza was mesmerised. She did not resist as the woman traced her palm with a long fingernail.

'You'm a long road to travel,' she said in that strange tone which was a little like Joe's. 'Yours will never be an easy life, for pain and sorrow stalks you like a shadow. Yet you be strong enough to endure whatever comes – and your mother loves you . . .'

'I have no mother,' Eliza said. 'I was taken to the workhouse as a babe and I've never known my mother.'

'Yet she loves you,' the woman said, and the glitter in her eyes made Eliza shiver. 'There are others who care for you as well as those that hate you – and one day you will find peace with the one you will love for all your life . . .' She let go of Eliza's hand and bent to select three bunches of lavender and one each of the other herbs. 'Give me a half-crown and these are yours.'

Eliza made no move to pay her, though the offer was generous. 'Please,' she begged. 'Tell me more of my mother. You say she loves me, so she must be alive – but how do you know her or me?'

'I do not,' the woman said. 'I have the sight and I can tell only what is revealed to me. Give me the half-crown or be on your way; I have no more for you.'

Reluctantly, Eliza took the money and paid her. She put the herbs on top of her other shopping and walked away quickly, feeling a little afraid of the woman who had looked at her so oddly. It was as if she could see into her heart and knew the secret longing that Eliza had kept hidden for so long.

Tears pricked her eyes for it was cruel of the woman

to say such things to her. She did not know her, or her mother, so why did she claim that Eliza's mother loved her?

Because she was crying, Eliza did not notice the man standing in her path until she almost bumped into him. He reached out and grabbed her arm, glaring at her in a way that made her heart race.

'Mind where yer goin',' he muttered, and she caught the smell of strong drink on his breath. 'Little whore. I know yer sort. Yer lookin' ter steal me purse!'

'No, sir. Forgive me I did not see you,' Eliza said as his hand curled around her wrist and he started to drag her towards a narrow alley that ran between rows of shops and houses. It was a rundown area and dark, the road pitted with holes and filled with icy puddles. 'Let me go!' Eliza aimed a kick at his shin. He gave a cry of pain and let go and she ran further down the alley, looking for a way of escape. The man was coming after her and despite his size and his inebriation he was gaining on her.

She turned the corner into a broader street and gave a cry of alarm as she saw that it was a dead end. The brick wall of a warehouse closed off the street and her only way out was he way she'd come. She saw her pursuer coming purposefully towards her, and knew that he would beat her and perhaps do vile things to her if she could not escape him. Screaming, she ran at him and tried to get past, but he caught her about the waist and knocked her back against a wall. Eliza screamed again and dropped her basket as she fought him, but he was pressing his foul beery mouth against hers and he felt him pulling at her dress, lifting it and

191

scrabbling underneath it. Then, quite suddenly, he was dragged off her and sent flying.

Eliza hardly saw the face of the man who had rescued her, though she knew him to be a gentleman by his smart frock coat and his long shiny boots worn over pale breeches. She called a warning as the brute who had attacked her produced some kind of truncheon and came at him from behind. Unable to move for fear, Eliza watched as the two struggled, and then her rescuer had the other man on his knees. Her saviour now had the heavy stick, which he threatened her attacker with, making him cower and blubber.

'I didn't know she were yours,' he muttered. 'She's just a little whore.'

'Get out of here before I beat your head in,' the gentleman said sternly. 'You know of me – believe me when I say that if I hear you've touched her again I'll make sure you pay for it. You'll die before you see the light of another day.'

Her attacker lurched to his feet and set off down the lane in a hurry. Eliza was too shocked to move until the man who had saved her returned and picked up her shopping, restoring it to her with a little smile.

'Are you all right? He didn't harm you?'

'No, sir, you were in time,' Eliza said and smiled nervously at him. 'I did nothing to entice him, sir. I was lost in thought and almost bumped into him but he called me a whore and t-tried . . .'

'I know well what that brute intended,' her rescuer said. 'Do you live far from here? Would you like me to see you safely home – though I do not think that scum will touch you again today.'

'No, sir, you thrashed him, thank you,' Eliza said. 'I must go home for my mistress will think me lost and be angry.'

Her rescuer was looking at her intently. A little tingle of apprehension went down her spine. Why did he look at her so oddly? And could she trust him even though he had helped her?

'May I know your name?' he asked, his eyes seeming to take note of everything about her.

'My name is . . . Edith,' Eliza said, not sure why she lied. 'I live not far from here. Please let me go now, sir.'

'Of course you may go,' he said and stood back. 'I would not harm you, child. Not all men are brutes – though you are wise to be wary for we can all fall from grace given drink and uncertain fate.'

Eliza gave him an uneasy look and began to run. All she wanted was to get home with her shopping and be safe in Miss Edith's house. At the end of the lane she looked back and saw that he had not moved. He was just standing there, watching her. She lifted her hand and then turned the corner and retraced her steps so that she knew where to go to find her way home.

Arthur Stoneham stood staring after the girl until she was out of sight. He'd thought for a moment that he'd found the girl he was looking for, the girl Ruth was still fretting over. What a lovely surprise that would have been to take home for her, but the child had said her name was Edith. Something in her manner at that moment had made him think she might be lying, but why would she lie to him? He had just rescued her from that brute – surely she would have trusted him enough to tell him her name?

Yet he'd sensed her fear – fear that had come from past experience and too much knowledge of a cruel world – and so he had not pressed her. There was something about her, something that had touched a chord in his memory and his heart and he'd felt as if he'd known her all his life. Even if she was the girl from the workhouse, he'd only seen her that once before and she'd looked very different this time – her freshly-washed hair, wound into tight plaits about her head, shone like spun silk.

Why did something about her ring a bell in his memory? Arthur was not certain. Did she look a little like someone he knew, or someone he had once known? The thought took hold in his mind and a little groan passed his lips because it could not be possible – and yet, impossible or not, she did remind him of Sarah, the lovely and innocent woman he had betrayed as a callow youth.

CHAPTER 16

'Ruth, I want to talk to you,' Arthur said later that day. 'You know that I only saw Eliza briefly, and she was in a terrible state and filthy from the cellar – can you tell me what colour her hair would be when it was clean?'

'I always thought it was the colour of moonlight,' Ruth said and moved towards him, an eager look in her eyes. 'Have you seen her?'

'I think perhaps I may have – but, if it was her, she lied to me, told me her name was Edith. I imagine she did not think she could trust me even though I had helped her.' He explained his thoughts to Ruth and she nodded.

'She might lie if she was uncertain whether to trust you,' Ruth said and sighed. 'To think you were so close, sir! Do you believe it was her?'

'I don't know, but there was something about her. Something that rang a bell but I can't be certain . . . However, she told me that she did not live far away from the market and I think it should not be difficult to find her. She told me that she had been shopping for

195

her mistress and I noticed that she had several bunches of lavender and also some herbs in her basket. Who do you think would want so much lavender?'

Ruth shook her head. Most housewives bought lavender to make into little bags to keep their drawers fresh and sweet, but not several bunches at a time.

'I am not sure, sir.'

'I have it!' he exclaimed. 'An apothecary would need many herbs, and lavender is used in cures for headaches as well as other remedies.'

'An apothecary?' Ruth stared at him in surprise. 'You mean someone who uses natural things to make cures for folk?'

'Yes, Ruth. I have been turning it over in my mind and I've an idea that I've seen such a shop in Spitalfields, not too far from the market. I do not recall exactly where but it is not too far from where I saw her.'

Ruth looked at him in sudden excitement. 'We might find her at last, sir!'

'Yes, we might. Of course I do not know for certain if it is the same girl – I could be quite wrong. She did look very different to the poor child I saw at the work-house.' He frowned. 'I have cursed myself a thousand times that I did nothing, Ruth. I should have taken her with me that day – found a good home for her, but I was not then so certain that Mistress Simpkins was, and is not, a fit person to have charge of that place.'

'I should've told you then,' Ruth said and looked sad. 'It might have saved my dearest Eliza much suffering. But I feared retribution and I did not know then what a good man you are sir.'

Arthur shook his head and turned away from her

admiring glance. Little did she know that he had once done a terrible thing – a crime so heinous that he had never forgiven himself nor could he ever. It was the reason that he did not deserve happiness, the reason that he could not follow his heart and court Miss Katharine Ross as he wished. The warmth he'd seen in her eyes would turn to disgust and then hatred if she knew what he'd done – the more so since he'd learned from Toby that her dear sister had disappeared after being attacked in the woods near their home.

Katharine had never given up searching for Marianne, though it was more than twelve years since she was lost, and he knew it was a sorrow she would keep in her heart until her death and that the secret that shamed him would make her turn from him if she ever learned it – and he could not wed her with such a secret between them. She was his friend now, and she shared his passion for helping unfortunate women, but he kept her at a distance, never letting her see what was in his heart. It would wound her if he had to tell her that he had been the cause of a gentle girl's untimely death. No matter how many young women and children he helped, it would never wipe away the stain of what he'd done to an innocent girl by seducing her, robbing her of her virtue with sweet words, and then deserting her. Although, she had not conceived a child, she had felt used and shamed, and she had become an invalid, refusing to eat until she wasted away to a shadow of herself and died one winter of pneumonia.

How could he have used a beautiful innocent girl so falsely? Youth, pride and the selfish desires of a wild young man were no excuse for what he'd done. What

197

had he been thinking when he rode away and left her weeping for love of him? She was the daughter of a school teacher while his uncle was a rich landowner, Arthur his sole heir, and a match between them would never have been approved. He'd known that when he'd wooed her with sweet kisses and so carelessly stolen her innocence. What had possessed him to treat such a gentle girl so cruelly? No fortune was worth such regret as he felt now.

Wracked with remorse after her death, he had embarked on an orgy of drinking, gambling and whoring. Yes, to his infinite shame he had once used those unfortunate women he now protected so fiercely, and it was one of them who had nursed him back to health. He had stood on the edge of a black hole, his sanity almost gone, his health ruined. Arthur thought that he had subconsciously been determined to kill himself the way Sarah had, save that Hetty, a whore but a loving woman, had brought him back from death's door, nursing him and holding him as he wept out his bitter hatred of himself in her arms.

As he grew stronger, his health gradually restored, she'd told him her own story, a story that might have belonged to so many unfortunate girls. Betrayed by a man she trusted, Hetty had fallen for a child. The man wanted nothing to do with her and told her to find someone to get rid of it for her, but Hetty refused. She'd borne her child despite all the hardships and she'd placed her daughter with a decent family in the country, far from the life she was forced to live to support the child.

'I must make certain she is well and happy, it no longer matters about me,' Hetty had told him and smiled.

'Sometimes, I'm lucky enough to find a man like you, Arthur Stoneham, and that makes up for all the rest.'

'Don't you hate me for using you – for using your body like all the men who so mistreat you?'

'I don't feel used by you,' she told him and smiled. 'You made me feel love for the first time in years, Arthur. The men you speak of are beasts and do not deserve to be spoken of in the same breath as you. I care for you and I thank you for making me realise that I am worth more than this.'

In saving Arthur's life, Hetty had also saved her own, for she was determined to begin again, to lead another life and be the woman she had been meant to be until a rogue destroyed her.

Arthur had given her money to start over somewhere new and she was now teaching needlework to girls at an exclusive school. He had not seen her some years, but he knew where she lived and worked and would never forget that it was her love and kindness that had made him realise that he too could begin again. He could never forgive himself for killing Sarah with his careless cruelty, but he could make amends – he could help other women who had been ill-treated, and perhaps one day he might be able to redeem himself in his own eyes.

'Where are you going, workhouse brat?'

Eliza stared at Miss Edith's cousin but did not answer him. She had known he disliked her from the moment she came to his cousin's house, but he lost no opportunity to call her names and to pinch her. Whenever she fetched something from one of the jars or passed by him behind the counter, Malcolm took the opportunity to pinch her or tug at her hair if it was not wound tightly into a plait about her head.

'I'm speaking to you, slut,' Malcolm snarled and pinched her arm as she took down a glass jar from behind the counter. The shock of the sharp pain almost made her drop the jar but she clutched it to her chest, staring at him defiantly. Tears of anger and pain were building inside her but she would not let him see.

From experience in the workhouse, Eliza knew that once a bully sensed he or she was getting to you they never ceased to torment you. To let Malcolm reduce her to tears would mean that she was at his mercy.

'Please let me pass. Miss Edith needs this jar.'

'Please let me pass,' he jeered, making faces at her. 'Miss Prissy. Anyone would think you born to decent folks but you're a workhouse bastard, that's what you are – and if you think you're going to worm your way in here and take what's mine, you'll be sorry.'

'Please, let me do my job,' Eliza said refusing to be drawn.

'Eliza, surely it doesn't take all day to find the rose-water?' Miss Edith was looking in at them from the kitchen door and her eyes narrowed as she took in the situation. 'Malcolm, let her pass. I hope you haven't been teasing her again. Don't think I haven't noticed. Please behave decently or I may have to let you go.'

Malcolm's eyes narrowed with malicious hatred. He moved aside in obedience to his cousin's instructions, but Eliza knew that she would pay next time she was alone with him.

'Does Malcolm often annoy you?' Miss Edith asked

when they were alone in the kitchen. She measured three drops of rosewater into the mixture she was preparing, and then added some scented oil. The cream she was dispensing into small glass pots was used for both the hands and face, to keep them soft and smooth and she'd given Eliza a pot for herself when she first came to live with her. It smelled and felt wonderful on the skin and smoothed the roughness of hands that were red and sore from having them in hot water too often in the workhouse laundry.

'He does not like me,' Eliza said at last since her employer was waiting for an answer. 'I do not know why.'

'I daresay Malcolm is jealous,' Miss Edith said looking thoughtful.' She shook her head and indicated that Eliza could now place the lids on the pots. 'You must tell me if he goes too far. I believe he keeps bad company. His mother cannot control him since his father's death – and I think at night he goes drinking with rough creatures. I do not approve but I should be loath to send him away for his mother needs him to work.'

'Oh, you must not do that for my sake,' Eliza said. 'I do not let him upset me. There were many unkind people in the workhouse.'

'Yes, I daresay.' Miss Edith looked at her sadly. 'Come and sit down, Eliza. I want to speak to you – to tell you why I came to the workhouse that day and asked for you.'

Eliza went to sit in one of the chairs next to the kitchen range. Miss Edith stood looking into the fire for a few moments, and then she sat down opposite Eliza.

'My father was a kind and generous man. I remember when I was small he would sit me on his lap and tell me that my mother was a sweet angel and that his heart had broken the day she died . . .' Miss Edith took out her handkerchief and blew her nose daintily. 'I believed that he spoke of his wife and grew up believing that I was his flesh and blood – but it was not so, Eliza, though I was named for her. Edith's baby daughter died soon after she entered this world and it broke her heart because the doctor said that she was too delicate to carry another. Indeed, she made herself so ill that my father thought she would die – and so he went to the workhouse and he bought a girl child, a baby of a few weeks, and brought that child back to his wife. She loved me from the moment he placed me in her arms and I was brought up as her own until she died of a fever when I was just five years old.'

'Miss Edith . . .' Eliza looked at her in concern, for the story brought a lump to her throat. 'When did you discover this?'

'Not until my father was close to death. He gave me a letter from my mother and told me to read it. She told me that the happiest day of her life was when I was put into her arms.'

'Did you cry? I think I should've cried . . .' Eliza brushed a tear from her cheek.

Miss Edith smiled and inclined her head. 'Yes, I cried, and I mourned her all over again, and I mourned my father who had never been able to tell me the truth for fear of hurting me. He loved me, you see.' She wiped away a tear from the corner of her eye. 'My father left everything to me. The house, and the business, and as I have told you, he gave me all the schooling I needed to carry on his work – which is what I have done.'

'Is that why you chose a girl from the workhouse, because *you* came from a workhouse?'

'Yes. It was not the one that I found you in, for my father found me somewhere in the country. I never knew where. I think Father was afraid that I might try to find my family, but I thought that foolish. My parents were the people who had raised me and given me love; I needed no other.' Miss Edith smiled at her. 'I asked Miss Simpkins about you – because of all the girls there I thought you special. There was something fine about you, about the way you held your head so proudly. Miss Simpkins told me your mother was gentle born but said she did not know her name or where she came from – only that she said she would return for you but had never done so.'

Eliza blinked hard. 'Ruth told me my mother was a lady, because my shawl was so fine – but I thought she just said it to please me.'

'I cannot tell you the truth of it, Eliza. I think if your mother could have returned for you she would have done so long ago – but if you wished to look for her when you're older, I should never try to stop you.'

'When I was cold and hungry and hurt from a beating I longed for my mother to come for me,' Eliza said truthfully, 'but she never came. And I do not think it would be possible to find her unless she came looking for me.'

'You are a sensible girl,' Miss Edith said. 'I did not

try to look for the woman who left me in the workhouse and I have been happy enough – especially since you came to join me.'

'Thank you for telling me,' Eliza said but frowned. 'Your father left everything to you – but did his family mind that? Did they know that you were adopted and resent it?'

'How did you become so wise?' Miss Edith said and smiled oddly. 'My uncle told me that he had never resented me because I gave his brother peace of mind – but I think when he died and left his widow the house but very little money, she *did* resent me. She asked me to give Malcolm a job and I agreed – but I fear he does not enjoy his work here.'

Eliza nodded, but said nothing. It was not her place to say that she thought Malcolm considered that all this ought to be his and was concerned that it should be one day. Miss Edith's story explained why Malcolm resented Eliza so deeply. Her father had adopted a child from the workhouse and left all his possessions to that child – and Malcolm was afraid that she might do the same.

'Well, I wanted you to know the truth,' Miss Edith said and stood up. She took her little cash box from the mantelshelf and unlocked it with the key she wore on a little chain about her neck. 'Here are four half-crowns. I have written a shopping list and I want you to go to the market for me, Eliza. I have several prescriptions to make up today, and I have no time to shop but we must eat, so you must go.'

'Yes, Miss Edith.' Eliza looked down the list. It was easy for her to read simple words now and she nodded.

'I will hurry back because I know how busy you are – and we must not keep our clients waiting.'

Her employer nodded her approval. 'Off you go then, Eliza. Mind you buy only fresh meat and fish and be careful with the change.'

CHAPTER 17

Molly stood outside the house in Coke Street and hesitated. She'd been told she would find Mr Stoneham here, because it was his refuge for fallen women and his housekeeper had said that's where he'd gone that morning. Taking a deep breath, she stepped forward and rang the bell twice. A few moments passed before the door opened and Molly sighed with relief when she saw a woman she knew well.

'Ruth,' she said. 'May I come in please? I have a message for Mr Arthur Stoneham.'

'Molly!' Ruth looked astonished. 'Are you in trouble, lass? We're full to bursting but I can let you sleep on the couch if yer've nowhere to go.'

'It's not me,' Molly said in a rush. 'I've come because of some young girls. That bitch is goin' ter sell them to a bloke this afternoon and he'll take them straight to the whorehouse – and you know what will 'appen then.'

'You'd best come in,' Ruth said and led the way through to a small parlour where Arthur and another woman were speaking. The woman looked surprised, but Arthur was instantly alert. 'Begging your pardon, sir, but may I speak with you? I be sorry to intrude but Molly wants to speak with you urgently, sir,' Ruth said.

'I've seen you before this, haven't I – at the workhouse?' Arthur said to Molly and frowned. 'Have you come asking for a place here?'

'No, sir,' Molly said. 'I've heard you're a good man, sir – and I know you were interested in the child Eliza, but Mistress Simpkins sold her to the apothecary and she's all right there – it's three others I'm worried for.'

'You know where Eliza is?' Ruth asked, catching hold of her arm urgently.

'Yes, she be not far from here – with Miss Edith Richards, the apothecary. She's all right – it's the girls that witch Joan Simpkins means to sell to the whorehouse this afternoon that need help.'

'Quiet, Ruth,' Arthur warned as Ruth would have asked for more details of Eliza. 'This is important. You know for certain that the girls are to be sold this afternoon – how?'

'I heard them talking the other night,' Molly confessed. 'I wasn't sure what to do. Robbie might have stopped her if I'd told him, but then she would've done it another day. She needs to be stopped for good – so I remembered that you were concerned for Eliza and thought if I told you, you might do something. If she is allowed to get away wiv it, she'll keep on doin' it – and there's lots more I can tell you, sir. I know all their secrets, enough to bring them down and they surely deserve it, the both of them.'

'Yes, I agree with you. Now, Molly, please tell me exactly what you heard. I need the names and ages of the girls and what is meant to happen.'

'Master Simpkins will be away at four this afternoon,' Molly said. 'That's when she plans to send them off with Drake – and once he's got them they'll be sold to one man after another and used for their pleasure. The youngest be thirteen and the eldest sixteen and they were talkin' about finding some younger ones.'

Arthur swore and looked angry. He took a turn about the room and then came back to her. 'We must prevent the girls being handed over. Molly, give me their names and Ruth, can you find room for them here until I can make other arrangements?'

'I can find them beds for a while.' Katharine Ross spoke before Ruth had time to answer. 'My aunt will allow it. I might be able to place one of the girls in our kitchens if she is willing to do such work – and I am certain I can help you find places for the others.'

'Thank you, Miss Ross, that is generous of you,' Arthur said. 'I must act at once. I need another of the governors with me – and Toby – in case they try to stop us taking the girls.'

Molly looked at him. 'You won't let them know who told you, sir? If either Robbie or Mistress Joan knew that I'd betrayed them, I'd be in trouble, but I didn't want her to do to them what she did to me.'

'You can trust me – and you must tell me what she did to you another day, Molly, and everything you know,' Arthur said and looked at Miss Ross. 'I must leave at once if this crime is to be prevented. You will excuse me . . .' He inclined his head and left at once.

'Well, you did those girls a bit of good,' Ruth said and clutched Molly's arm urgently. 'You said Eliza was

208

with Miss Richards, an apothecary – can you tell me where she be livin'? I've worrit meself to death over her.'

'There be a house in Halfpenny Street in Spitalfields. 'Twas one of a row of grand houses that belonged to the silk merchants, long ago.' Ruth nodded impatiently. 'Well, one of them grand houses 'as been divided into three shops and the apothecary has one of them.'

'You're certain Eliza is there?'

'Aye, for I saw a friend of mine who visited the shop to buy medicine on the day Eliza was took and her description intrigued me – so I went and asked for some medicine for my chest. I do get a bad cough sometimes in this bitter weather and I see Eliza for myself. She didn't see me for she was upstairs at the window but she was smiling and I thought she looked happier than I'd seen her of late.'

'You did not speak to her?'

'No, but you could go to see her for yourself.'

It was what Ruth wanted more than anything, but she hesitated; if Eliza was happy she might not wish to be reminded of her time in the workhouse.

'If you should visit to buy medicine again, you might tell her I would be happy to see her.'

'You should seek her out,' Molly said. 'She asked after you when that witch fetched her back to the workhouse.'

'Eliza was brought back to the workhouse?'

'Aye, she was, and put to work in the laundry, but then she was sold again. I reckon mistress didn't want the butcher to 'ave 'er 'cos he wouldn't pay no more.'

Ruth was angry. 'Mistress told Mr Stoneham that she had not seen Eliza since she sent her to work for the butcher.'

'That was a lie, and you must know she would never confess to her wickedness. She claims that she asks only for the cost of the clothing the inmate is wearing when she leaves.'

Ruth made a scornful noise. 'She sends them out in the rags they brought in if she can. You know that she cheats those in her care, Molly. She is evil and so I've told my master, but he needs proof.'

'Well, I have brought him proof this day,' Molly said. 'He knows that three girls are being sold to a man who will force them into a life of prostitution – what more proof does he need?'

'I pray that it is enough to send her packing,' Ruth said and nodded. 'Will you take a drop of tea with me, Molly – or something stronger?'

'I'll have a drop of gin if yer 'ave any,' Molly said. 'You've found yerself a good place 'ere, Ruth.'

'Well, I must be going,' Miss Ross said. She had been listening to them intently, but now prepared to leave. 'I shall call again next week, Ruth. Goodbye, Molly. It was nice to meet you – please let us know if there is anything we can do to help you.'

Molly looked at Ruth as she went out. 'Sweet on Mr Stoneham, is she?'

'I don't know, and I wouldn't discuss it if I did,' Ruth told her. 'She's a lovely lady and she helps us with the poor souls that come here to rest.'

'God bless her for that,' Molly said and drank her gin straight down. 'Tell Mr Stoneham I'll be back, and next time I'll give him all the information he needs to bring that witch down – and her brother with her.'

'What do you intend to do?' Toby asked when they met at Arthur's club early that afternoon. 'Demand that the girls are given to you – or let the handover take place and catch them in the act later and have the brothel closed down?'

'I am not intending to close the brothel,' Arthur said. 'It would cause an outcry and the owners will have powerful friends who would find some way out of it. No, I shall go into the workhouse and ask to see the girls and then tell Mistress Simpkins that work has been found for them. It is her response to my request that will show me whether this story is true, for so far we only have Molly's word.'

'The word of a whore and few would believe her,' Toby said and nodded grimly. 'I would have liked to catch them in the act of subduing the girls, but I daresay you are right. These places have their supporters and we should likely be told the girls were willing participants.'

'Exactly! It has happened before when some such attempt at rescue has been made. Only in a few cases has the prosecution been successful – and that is the lower end of the scale, where no one of influence is concerned. Some of these houses have rich men as their backers – men of our own class, Toby.'

'It is the suppliers that are the worst,' Toby said, frowning. 'Women like this Joan Simpkins who sell innocent girls for profit for themselves for I believe women who choose to enter such a house of their own volition may do so if they wish.'

'Yes, I agree. I have asked Major Cartwright to accompany us. He is one of the doubters and supports Master Simpkins. I have tried to convince him that everything is not right in that place, but he refuses to believe me. It is his opinion that unless the poor are kept in their place we shall have anarchy.'

'God save us from the Major Cartwrights of this world,' Toby said and rolled his eyes. 'So what do you hope to prove?'

'I am hoping that, robbed of the chance of profit, our Miss Simpkins will show her true colours.'

Toby nodded and looked thoughtful. 'Your plan may well save the girls, but I am not sure we shall pry our quarry from her nest. I believe that we should follow them to the whorehouse and then pounce.'

'And all that would prove is that the man who bought them runs a brothel but not that Joan Simpkins knew of it,' Arthur said. 'I've enough evidence to convict her six times over in my own mind, but the Board must be convinced, worthy men that they are, and a court of law must convict.'

'I had difficulty in convincing my father that there was a white slave trade in England. He is a true gentleman and would not believe it possible that young children were being abducted, sometimes from the streets where they live. I argued with him for three hours before he would accept that there might be something in it. For months he would not speak in the House, but then at last I persuaded him and you know there has been much publicity because of it.' Toby smiled oddly. 'My father is honest, as straight and clean-living as any man, and yet he was so horrified when I told him that children the age of my brother's son and daughter were being used so despicably that his mind refused to admit it for months.'

'Your father is one of the few men I would completely trust,' Arthur said. 'He has done what he can to help us since you convinced him.'

'I had to take him to the infirmary and show him what can happen to these wretched children and then a nun told him the unvarnished truth. I can tell you, Arthur, he broke down and wept. I had never seen my father weep before – even when my mother died he bore it with dignity, but when he heard of how the child had been abused and saw her filthy, diseased and deranged, despite all the good nuns had done to help her, he was broken. I was almost sorry I had shown him the child – but now he is as determined to see this foul practice stamped out as we are.'

'Yes, I know. He told me when he gave me money for a refuge. He wants a house for children similar to the one I have for my ladies – so the next house will be for mothers and children.'

'Yes, I think—' Toby was about to continue when he saw the man standing outside the workhouse gates. 'I believe that must be Major Cartwright – my God, Arthur. No wonder you said that these worthy men drive you mad. I believe you shall have your work cut out this afternoon.'

'Yes, so no more such remarks, Toby. We want the good major on our side if we are to stamp this filthy trade into the ground.'

Joan looked at the three men confronting her and clenched her hands at her sides. Fury was building inside

213

her as she realised that she had no alternative but to release the three girls to Mr Stoneham. His paperwork was in order and signed by a prospective employer and by two members of the Board.

'I can assure you that the girls in question have already been found proper employment,' she said through gritted teeth. Reason told her she must give in with a good grace, but her rage was at boiling point and she could hardly contain it. If Drake did not get the girls he'd paid for, he would demand the return of his money – and he might not trust her in future.

'Can you give me the names of their prospective employers?' Arthur asked and she squirmed beneath that stern yet mocking gaze. Joan did not know how such a man could be so damned interfering and high-minded. He looked as if he were a red-blooded male, one who ought to enjoy the services of a whore as much as the next man, but he was so damned righteous! What harm did it do to earn a little from the sale of a few workhouse brats? They would only end up in the whorehouse once they left here anyway, because for girls such as these there was only a life of servitude or a brothel, and most of them preferred life on their backs to their knees.

'I really must protest,' she said drawing herself up, a picture of outrage. 'Major Cartwright, I appeal to you. Do I have the authority to release female inmates to suitable employers or not?'

'Naturally, you have the right, and you may charge the cost of whatever clothing you have provided whilst they were in your care – but no more. I've been informed that you sold these girls to a person not fit to have charge of them and that he will be here at four – which is in just ten minutes. I think we do not have long to wait for the proof either way, gentlemen.'

'You can't question him!' Joan blurted out hastily and realised immediately that she'd made a mistake. 'I mean, what does it look like? How does it make me appear? As if I am not to be trusted.'

'And are you to be trusted, madam?' Mr Stoneham asked, looking at her in such a way that she wished the ground might open and let her through. 'I believe we shall know in just a few minutes.'

Joan stared at him, her mind seeking desperately for a way of escape. If they insisted on waiting and confronting Drake it would be the end of a lucrative deal for her. He would deny all knowledge and was unlikely to trust her enough to buy from her again.

She could hear the black marble clock on her mantelshelf ticking as the minutes passed. And then the solution occurred to her. She looked at the faces of the three men, reading her fate in their stony glances. Drake would either bluster or lie about his business or cut and run – either would seal her fate. She heard his footsteps outside the door and then the door opened and Drake entered; he was five minutes early and eager to see the girls she'd promised.

'Where are they?' The question died on his lips as Joan gave a little sigh and fainted, crumpling dramatically into a heap. Drake's eyes travelled to the expectant faces of the men and knew that he was trapped. He turned and ran, down the long passage way and into the courtyard. Halfway to the gate he felt a heavy force hit him in the back and then next second he was brought down in a rugby tackle that had him winded.

Hauled to his feet he looked into the angry face of a man he knew as Arthur Stoneham. There was no point in lying, because this man had confronted him before this and was well aware of the business he'd grown rich from.

'I've no need to ask what you expected to find here this afternoon,' Arthur said. 'Don't trouble to deny it, Drake Arnham. I know that you intended to take three young girls from this place this afternoon and imprison them in a house of prostitution where they would be used and abused until you threw them out.'

'Prove it!' Drake raised his head defiantly and laughed as he saw the answer in the other man's eyes. 'I came here to buy some old clothes and that's all.'

'You run a brothel and the world knows it,' Arthur Stoneham snarled. 'If there were real justice in this country you would have been thrown in prison long ago and the key to your cell would be at the bottom of the river.'

'I own a house that may be used by whores,' Drake leered at him mockingly, 'who live there and carry on their trade. But all I receive is rent each month – and you can prove no more than that. I may suspect what they do, but I am not their keeper and I do not interfere with the lives of others.'

'Yes, I am aware of all the excuses that your fancy lawyers come up with for you,' Arthur said. 'I also know that you have influential clients who would help you avoid punishment.'

'You may as well let me go then.' Drake grinned in

triumph. 'All the women that live in my house are over eighteen and able to choose for themselves whether they live there or leave – just ask them.'

As Arthur hesitated, Toby joined him. 'He knows we can't prove anything much against him, Arthur. The girls are safe; let it go at that.'

'So that he can come back another day and take three others in their places?' Arthur said but stood back, jerking his head. 'Go on then, before I give you the thrashing you deserve.'

'Self-righteous prig,' Drake Arnham said and spat on the ground. 'Watch yer back or one of these dark nights yer might find a knife in it.'

Arthur made a lunge at him, but Toby held him back and Arnham walked off, laughing. 'Take no notice of idle threats, Arthur. He'll think twice about coming here again. Either he won't trust her or he won't dare to risk it.'

Arthur looked at his friend. 'I wish we could be sure of that, Toby. Has she recovered from her supposed faint?'

'You think she feigned it?' Arthur nodded, and Toby scowled. 'Cartwright was fussing over her and calling her his dear lady and she was weeping into his shoulder. I don't think you've finished her yet, my friend.'

'We'll see about that.' Arthur turned and walked purposefully towards the warden's office. When he entered, Miss Simpkins was sitting on a chair sipping a glass of water and Major Cartwright was indeed fussing over her. 'That man is a known brothel-keeper, madam – what have you to say to me now?'

'I have told Major Cartwright that I had no idea of

his terrible intentions. He said he needed three girls to work in the kitchens of a nobleman's house. It seemed a wonderful opportunity for them.'

'Madam, you lie,' Arthur said, his anger at being unable to stamp out a vile trade making him careless.

'Mr Stoneham!' the major said sharply. 'You are distressing this lady. I do not think your case proven. Even if that villain is who you say he is – this poor lady can have had no knowledge of it. You saw how overcome she was by the horror of being accused of such vileness.'

'Indeed, I was, sir,' Joan simpered at him. 'I promise you that I shall make certain to obtain sufficient references before I hand over any of my girls again.'

'If I had my way you would have no further say in the lives of these poor unfortunate women,' Arthur said. 'Had I the final say, you would be packing your bags this instant.'

'No, no, sir, I think you wrong Miss Simpkins,' Major Cartwright said pompously. 'These people have to be dealt with firmly – firmly but within the law. It is not Miss Simpkins' fault if she was deceived by that rogue.' He smiled at her and she held his hand-kerchief to her lips and smothered a sob. 'You will learn from this, dear lady. In future you must consult with others and make sure that you hand your girls over to respectable citizens – now, will you promise me to do that?'

'Oh yes, sir, I promise faithfully. I will leave nothing to chance – and consult with my brother and with you, sir, if it would not trouble you too much.'

'I should be only too delighted to advise you,' he

said and looked very pleased with his solution. He turned to Arthur, who was fit to burst but managed to hold his tongue. 'I am sure you must agree that this has all been unfortunate – and since no harm has been done and the girls are safe, we should give Mistress Simpkins a chance to prove herself worthy of our trust.'

'I think we'd better take the children with us now,' Toby said before Arthur could trust himself to speak. 'Miss Ross is expecting them, and we do not want to take up too much of your time, Major.'

'No, no, quite, quite,' the major said, smiling at Miss Simpkins.

Arthur bit back the angry words he could have let fly, knowing that for the moment he was beaten. He had saved three young girls from an unhappy fate, but it was a drop in the ocean. Yet for the moment there was no more he could do.

'Perhaps you will send for them?' he said looking coldly at her.

She inclined her head, picked up a bell and rang it and the door opened. Three girls were shepherded in by an old woman who looked sourly at them.

'You three – you have been found positions with a Miss Ross. These gentlemen have come to take you to her.'

The anger in Joan Simpkins' face was unmistakable. She'd been thwarted and she did not like it, but she also knew that she'd been lucky to keep her place here. Had she not conveniently fainted at the right moment, thereby warning Drake to say nothing more, he might have blurted out the damning truth, which would have condemned them both. She'd got away with it this time, thanks to Major Cartwright, but she knew that she was being closely watched and it would be dangerous to try anything else again for a while.

CHAPTER 18

Eliza entered the kitchen to see Miss Richards standing before the mantelshelf with her cash box in her hand. It was open, and she was staring at it in dismay. She turned to Eliza as she heard her pick up some dishes to start setting the table and the doubts were in her face.

'Eliza, have you taken anything from this box?'

Eliza felt a chill at her nape. 'No, Miss Edith. I-I've never opened it. I only take what money you give me for the shopping.'

'I was sure I had three pounds in change and there is only one shilling and two florins.' Miss Edith shook her head. 'Yet how could you have had the key? No, no, forgive me, Eliza. I must have taken the money myself but I cannot think when . . .'

She sighed and went to a cupboard on the wall. Eliza turned away, because she knew there was another secret place where her employer kept money hidden, though she'd never seen it and did not know exactly how it was secreted.

'No! It cannot be – all my savings have gone!' Eliza

whirled round as she heard the cry of distress. Miss Edith had taken down some jars of bottled fruit in the corner cupboard and behind them was a wooden panel which she'd lifted out, revealing a small secret shelf. In her hand she had a velvet purse with draw-strings and Eliza could see that it was flat and empty. Miss Edith shook it in a vain attempt to find the lost money. 'I had twenty gold sovereigns and two five-pound pieces,' she gasped, her face as white as a new-washed sheet. 'My life savings gone . . . all of it!' She raised her eyes to look at Eliza accusingly. 'I knew you stole from that market stall but I did not think you would steal from me. How could you – how could you take so much? Have I not given you all you could need?'

'I did not know it was there,' Eliza said the words seeming to stick in her throat and choke her so that they came out as a whisper. 'I would never take your money. You have been so kind to me . . .'

Tears stung behind her eyes because the accusation cut her to the quick. How could Miss Edith think that she would betray her trust like this? Eliza would be frightened of having one gold sovereign, let alone a fortune such as Miss Edith was describing. She would never dare or wish to touch her employer's money.

'You cannot have spent it. Please tell me you have it hidden in your room,' Miss Edith's voice rose hyster-ically. The loss of her savings had distressed her so much that she was incapable of coherent thought and she looked at Eliza accusingly. 'Without this money we shall not manage the winter for I cannot buy what I need to carry on and there are expenses to pay of which you can know nothing. I gave you all I could afford, Eliza – how could you steal from me?'

'No, no, I did not!' Eliza said and she felt sick as Miss Edith moved towards her with the speed of lightning. She raised her hand and struck Eliza once across the cheek, her own face pale with distress. Eliza jerked back but made no attempt to save herself from her employer's anger, though the tears dripped silently down her cheeks. 'I'm so sorry . . .' She was offering sympathy not regret for she had done nothing, but her words seemed to make Miss Edith even angrier.

'Go to your room and stay there until I allow you to come down,' Miss Edith said. 'You are a wicked, ungrateful girl and if I lose my home it will be your fault.' She took hold of Eliza's arm and half dragged, half propelled her up the stairs to her room, pushing her inside.

'Where have you hidden it?' she demanded bitterly. 'Show me instantly or I shall thrash you.'

Eliza raised her head, looking her in the eyes. 'I would never steal from you. You are unjust,' she said but Edith ignored her protest and began to pull the covers from the bed. She threw the pillow down and searched beneath the mattress and brought out a silk kerchief tied in a knot. Her eyes were accusing as she looked at Eliza. Opening the kerchief she revealed several half crowns and a florin. 'How could you? After all I have done for you? And what have you done with the rest?'

'I've never seen that money or the kerchief before!' Eliza said, her eyes stinging with unshed tears. 'I swear that I did not take it – someone else must have put it there.'

'I should have known you were set in your ways,' Edith said sadly. 'I was there that day in the market when your friends raided the baker's stall and I was told you were a wicked girl – and yet I believed there was good in you.' She looked at Eliza coldly. 'You cannot have spent so much money; it must be hidden somewhere. I shall give you a little time to come to your senses and return the money to me.' She turned and left the room, leaving Eliza alone.

Eliza sat on the edge of the bed and bowed her head, letting the tears flow. She felt as if her heart was broken, the pain so sharp that she did not know how to bear it. Miss Edith had treated her as if she were her family and Eliza had known happiness for the first time in her life, but now it was all destroyed. Miss Edith thought she was a thief. She believed Eliza would take all her money and then lie to her so how could she have ever truly liked or trusted her? It was unfair and it hurt so much to know that she was not truly trusted or loved.

Eliza was sitting with her head bowed when the door of her room was thrust open and, as she looked up, she saw Malcolm's gloating face.

'I told you I'd get you sent back to the workhouse where you belong,' he crowed. 'She won't keep you now you little slut. You're in for it good and proper, work-house brat!'

Eliza stared at him but would not give him the answer he craved. She brushed her hand across her wet cheeks, refusing to let him see how broken she was. He was laughing as he shut the door and ran back down the stairs.

Eliza looked about her at the room she'd come to think of as home. It smelled of the lavender bags she'd made and placed in her drawers. She loved it and the little things that Miss Edith had given her – a journal to write her letters in and simple books to learn from, as well as the hand cream, soaps and her clothes.

She could take nothing with her. Nothing in this room was truly hers. Eliza felt so alone and this time the hurt of rejection was strong and painful, because she had loved Miss Edith. She was torn between staying here and standing her corner. She had not touched a penny of Miss Edith's money, had always given her every farthing of her change when she returned from shopping and never looked for payment, thinking herself fortunate to be given a comfortable home, clothes to wear and good food to eat – and she had loved the work she'd done. Now she was to be sent back to the workhouse in disgrace, accused of theft. If she was not sent for trial, she would be condemned to a life of drudgery at the workhouse, for who would ever want to employ her now?

Eliza's heart ached, and her pride was hurt. She had stolen food when she ran wild with Tucker, but only when she was told it was necessary and forced to take her part. Eliza had her own sense of justice and the last thing she would ever do was hurt someone she cared for.

Yet she could not let Miss Edith send her back to the workhouse as a thief. She would rather starve on the streets. It would be better to die of hunger than live in the workhouse after she'd known what life could be like in a real home. Eliza wondered if she could find Tucker or any of his friends in their old haunts. Time had passed and she'd become used to good living, but she would prefer to take her chance in the back alleys she'd known so well to a life of misery in the workhouse.

Miss Edith had burned her old things, save her shawl, which had been washed and mended, so Eliza had no choice but to take the clothes she was wearing. As her determination not to return to the workhouse hardened, Eliza made up her mind. She would write a note to Miss Edith and tell her that one day she would send back the things she'd run away in.

I swear I would never steal from you. I loved you as my friend, but I can never return to the workhouse, she wrote and signed her name.

Folding the paper from the journal, Eliza left it on her bed. She looked through the back window and saw that Miss Edith was out in the back yard. Now was her moment. She must leave now before Miss Edith had the gig ready to take her back to the workhouse.

Running down the stairs, Eliza took a deep breath before opening the door that led through the shop. No one was there and Eliza realised that it was time for Malcolm's dinner hour. She breathed a sigh of relief and slipped out of the side door into the passage that led into Halfpenny Street. Once out in the streets, she headed towards the market, following the small winding lanes and alleys with the sureness of familiarity. She had no money to buy food, but she had learned to read and write and reckon numbers during her time with Miss Edith. If she asked politely, surely someone would give her work. She did not mind what she did, but she would start by asking the stallholders if they had work for her.

'Eliza, where are you?' Edith opened the bedroom door and looked in. She had been thinking since her outburst

226

earlier and realised that she'd been unfair. In her sudden fear and distress she had attacked the nearest person, but she ought to have thought things through more carefully. Eliza had worked honestly and diligently all these weeks, so why would she suddenly steal from her? And surely if she had she would have run away before the theft was discovered? Besides, Edith wasn't sure that the girl knew she had money hidden in the corner cupboard.

She should have taken her savings to a bank or bought a heavy strong box and hidden it under her bed, but she'd never trusted banks and thought they would despise her small savings. Besides, no one had ever stolen from her before. Although the takings in the shop till had seemed to be rather less than usual of late, she had not thought to question it, blaming herself for inattention. But was it possible that someone had been stealing from her? And if not Eliza, it could only be Malcolm. But why would her cousin suddenly take from her – unless it was because he feared that Edith intended to leave her property away from him? Because he resented Eliza being taught all things he ought to have learned . . .

Remembering the look of resentment in his eyes when she'd brought Eliza to her home, Edith realised that he'd been surly over it from the start and that anger had built. If Eliza had not taken her money it could only have been her cousin.

'Eliza . . .' Edith glanced around the room. The girl was not here. Why had she disobeyed her? Seeing the piece of paper torn from Eliza's journal lying on the bed, she quickly moved to pick it up and read the few words in Eliza's careful hand. 'Oh, Eliza, you foolish girl. I would never have sent you back to that place. Surely you could not think it?'

Tears stung her eyes as she went along the hall to the parlour where they had spent so many happy evenings by the fire, checking all the rooms one by one. Of course Eliza was not there. She must have run away when Edith was out in the yard.

Hearing the shop door bang, Edith went downstairs and saw Malcolm enter. He had his arms filled with parcels and was about to stow them under the counter. When she spoke to him, he jumped and looked at her, guilt all over his face, and in that instant she knew what she had begun to suspect earlier was true. Of course it wasn't Eliza that had stolen from her. The girl had no reason to steal; her cousin, on the other hand, had expensive tastes.

'What have you been buying?' she asked as he tried to hide his packages. 'And where did you get the money for so much?'

'I've been savin' for Ma's birthday,' Malcolm said but she could see that he was lying by the way his eyes avoided hers and the red flush in his neck. He was lying, and he'd been caught in the act.

'Show me what you've bought – and any money you have in your pockets.' Malcolm shook his head and tried to dodge past her, but Edith caught his arm and grabbed hold of his jacket, turning both pockets out. The gold coins came tumbling forth, three sovereigns and one five-pound piece. 'Is this all you have left of my money? What did you spend it on?'

She let go of him and scooped up the money, thrusting it into her apron pocket, and then she began to open the parcels: whisky, brandy, expensive cigars and a box of chocolate truffles.

'I suppose these were for your mother,' Edith said and thrust the chocolates at him. 'You can take them, because it is all you will ever get from me. Get out and don't return. I do not employ thieves!'

'You brought that workhouse brat here and were planning to leave it all to her,' Malcolm shouted furiously. 'This belongs to me and my mother – it should have been left to us when Uncle Tom died – not you, a bloody workhouse brat.'

Edith opened the door, her face white with temper. 'Give me the keys. You may leave now, Malcolm. If I ever see you near this shop again I shall tell your mother what you have done – and I shall report it to the constable.'

'Workhouse slut!' he yelled as he threw down the keys and ran past her, thrusting her out of the way. 'I never wanted your rotten job and I hope you both rot in hell.'

Edith stared after him for a moment, closing her eyes in distress. She pocketed the keys he had discarded and looked at the parcels he'd abandoned on the counter. She could use the brandy for medicine and cooking, but the cigars were of no use to her. It had taken her so many months to save a little nest egg and Malcolm had spent most of it in a single day – and worse than that, Edith had blamed Eliza and now the child had run away. Where would she go – not back to the workhouse, that much was certain. She'd lived on the streets for weeks once before and perhaps she was capable of doing it again, but it was winter now and the weather was bitter. If all she'd taken was her dress and that old shawl she'd kept despite the newer one Edith had given her, she could freeze to death in this weather.

Edith's cheeks were wet with tears as she realised how much she had come to love the child she'd taken in. Eliza was like the daughter she would never have and she was going to miss her. She would miss her every day . . .

CHAPTER 19

'I have found the youngest of those girls work in my house. She wishes to work in a kitchen and our cook is willing to teach her. Mary is a gentle girl and my aunt approves of her. The middle girl is called Bella and she has become apprenticed to a milliner, because she is good with a needle – and Rosa, the eldest, has found work as a scullery maid with my aunt's friend.' Katharine Ross paused and sipped the tea Ruth had made for her. 'I came to tell Mr Stoneham for I thought he would wish to know.'

'My master will be sorry to have missed you,' Ruth said, understanding that her mistress was disappointed that he was not there. 'I shall give him the good news.'

'I shall bring the Christmas gifts for our ladies later this week,' Katharine went on. 'There are gifts for Cook and you too, Ruth. You do such good work here and we are both happy to leave things in your care. I am sure you know that as well as his work trying to reform the workhouse, Mr Stoneham is busy negotiating the purchase of a new property, which will be a home for women and children.'

'Yes, ma'am. Mr Stoneham and his friends are always helping others. It is kind of you to think of us, ma'am. Cook and me be lucky to have found such a place – and we think the world of Mr Stoneham and his friends.'

'Yes, I imagine so.' Katharine sighed. 'My aunt and I have tried to tempt Mr Stoneham to various evenings of pleasure over Christmas, but he seldom bothers with such affairs.'

Ruth inclined her head but made no comment. She continued to look after Miss Katharine until she took her leave, and then went into the kitchen to speak with Cook.

'Did Miss Katharine like those almond comfits I made special for her?' Cook asked looking at the plate, which was empty.

Miss Katharine had eaten three but Ruth had taken the rest and wrapped them in a bit of muslin. She had made up her mind to visit Eliza and thought she would give her the rest of the sweet biscuits as a little gift. Ruth had another special gift for Eliza in her coat pocket, but she was in two minds whether she should give it to the girl. If Eliza was content where she was, such a trinket might stir up restless feelings and a longing for something she could never have.

'I'm taking what Miss Katharine left for Eliza,' Ruth told Cook now. 'Molly said she was living at the apothecary shop in Halfpenny Street. I spoke to Mr Stoneham about it but he was busy and said it might be better if he talked to Miss Richards first, but 'tis almost Christmas and I want to be certain she is safe and happy.'

'Do you doubt what Molly told you?'

'No, but she only glimpsed her smiling at the window.

232

I want to be sure she is all right – and I'd like to see her.'

Ruth said nothing of the trinket in her pocket. She knew it was valuable for the mount was gold and set with what she thought were diamonds, even though it only held a halfpenny that had been minted in 1867. The copper had gone dull now, but the gold and the diamonds were still bright, and the halfpenny could be cleaned and made to shine. It belonged to Eliza, for it had been attached to the inside of her shawl the day she was brought into the workhouse and Ruth had always meant to give it to her. She'd kept it hidden from Mistress Simpkins because, had she seen it, the warden would have taken it and sold it for herself. Ruth would give it to its rightful owner gladly, if she was sure that Eliza would not have it taken from her – and that it would not make her long for a mother she had lost long ago.

Half an hour later, Ruth stood outside the apothecary's shop and looked up at the landing window. No one was there and when she entered the shop, she saw a woman of perhaps thirty-something behind the counter. She was serving a customer and giving her strict instructions on how to use the medicine. Ruth waited her turn, thinking that the apothecary looked pale and tired, her eyes a little red as if she'd recently been crying.

'Yes?' she asked as Ruth hesitated. 'How may I help you?'

'I wondered if I might speak to Eliza Jones. I'm her friend, Ruth.'

The woman looked as if she'd been slapped and her face went even paler. She hesitated a moment, then, 'I'm afraid Eliza isn't here any longer. She ran away two days ago.'

'Eliza ran away?' Ruth felt coldness at the nape of her neck. 'What did you do to her? I was told that she was happy here – what made her run off?'

The woman blinked hard, perhaps because Ruth's voice was harsh with disappointment and worry. 'I fear it was my fault,' she said at last. 'You said your name was Ruth? And you are Eliza's friend from the work-house?'

'I nursed her from a babe,' Ruth said, 'and loved her as if she were me own. I give her me own name of Jones for she was my child in all but blood. I be worried for her for months after Mistress Simpkins sold her to that man – and then I be given a good job and I had to leave, but I still think of my Eliza and hoped to find her here today.'

Miss Edith came round from behind the counter and locked the shop door. 'Please, will you come into the kitchen, Ruth? I should like to explain to you what happened. It is my true desire to find Eliza and I wondered if you knew where I might begin my search?'

Ruth trudged back to the refuge with a heavy heart. She made herself a pot of tea and took it into the parlour she called her own and sat down to think. Miss Edith had seemed genuinely upset because of the misunder-standing and regretted what she'd said in her first distress at losing her savings.

She had explained, with tears in her eyes, 'My first thought was that it must be Eliza because she had access to the kitchen at all times, but I should have known that she would never do such a thing. My cousin must have sneaked in when we were both out and taken the money. He counted on me blaming Eliza and sending her back to the workhouse – he always resented her, because he thought he was entitled to all that my father left me.'

Seeing Miss Edith's remorse for her unkindness in accusing an innocent girl, Ruth felt able to forgive her and told her all she knew about Eliza's background.

'I saw her mother bring the babe to the workhouse that day. She was a person of gentle birth and modest dress – she must have been a girl betrayed, for she was no whore. She wept to give her child to Mistress Simpkins and I'd swear she paid for her to be well cared for – not that Eliza saw a penny of the money.'

'I know she was ill-treated in that place and I wanted to help her but now . . .' Edith dabbed at her cheeks. 'I do not know where she could have gone.'

'Nor I, but there is little we can do but pray and hope my master can find her.'

Miss Edith looked thoughtful. 'Why do you think her mother took her to the workhouse? Surely a convent or a church might have been better?'

'What would they have done but hand her on to a workhouse?' Ruth said. 'Nuns seldom care for the children unwed mothers take to them, unless they run a school, and then they do not want babes. Sometimes they find good homes for them, but often they simply give them to the officials to deal with and the result is the same.'

'Yes, I daresay you are right,' Miss Edith agreed. 'I believe my own story was much the same, but I was luckier. My father's child died and so he took a babe from the workhouse and brought her up as his own – and I meant to do the same.'

'Was Eliza happy here until this happened?'

'I believed so,' Miss Edith sighed and held back a sob. 'If I could only take back those cruel, cruel words.'

'Perhaps she will return to you,' Ruth suggested. 'She must know you were upset.'

'I suspect she thinks I meant to take her back to the workhouse, but I would never have been so cruel.'

Ruth had found herself comforting the other woman, but there was no hope she could offer. Eliza had no friends that Ruth knew of or anywhere she could take refuge. It meant that she was on the streets in the bitter weather and would have to beg for her food, unless she was able to find work. If she stole to feed herself she could fall foul of the watch and end up being sent to prison – and the alternative was to die of starvation or the cold.

Now, sitting in her parlour, Ruth realised she was crying. She fumbled for her handkerchief and took out the one in which she had wrapped the trinket that belonged to Eliza. Its sale would keep the child alive for weeks – long enough to find a home perhaps, but Ruth had kept it safe and now she felt guilty. It ought to have been Eliza's long ago.

'What is wrong, Ruth? Has something upset you?'

Hearing Mr Stoneham's voice, Ruth looked up. She dabbed her eyes with the handkerchief and the trinket dropped to the floor and rolled to his feet. He bent to pick it up and then stood staring at it for a moment, the oddest look in his eyes.

'What is this?' he asked at last.

'It belongs to Eliza, sir,' Ruth said and blew her nose. 'I went to visit her at the apothecary's shop today, for I believe it valuable and intended to give it to her if she was settled and happy – but she'd gone.'

'Gone?' Arthur drew out a chair and sat so that he could look at her face. 'What do you mean?'

Ruth explained all that she'd been told and he nodded. He was turning the halfpenny over and over in his fingers, seeming a little distracted.

'That was unfortunate. We must see what can be done to find her, Ruth,' he said, and then, leaning towards her, an intent look in his eyes, asked, 'Why do you say this trinket belongs to Eliza?'

'Because it was tucked inside her shawl when she was brought to the workhouse. I did see her mother, sir – a young and gentle woman – and the shawl was of the finest spun wool. Mistress Simpkins gave the babe, who was wrapped in a blanket so mistress never saw the shawl, to me to care for because her cloths were wet and she was screaming. Later, she took away the fine clothes Eliza was wearing, but I found the trinket in her shawl and I kept it – and the shawl – hidden, for it is Eliza's from her mother and she must have it.'

'Yes . . .' Mr Stoneham frowned and placed the trinket on the table. 'It looks quite valuable. I wonder why her mother placed it in her shawl.'

'She must have had her reasons, sir. It be valuable I know that. I reckon it be gold that holds the halfpenny and diamonds on the clip.'

'Yes, I am sure it is – a watch fob, I daresay.' Ruth wondered at the look in his eyes.

'Yes, sir. A trinket a gentleman might wear. Do you think it belonged to Eliza's father?'

'No! It could not,' Mr Stoneham said and then put a hand to his forehead. 'God forgive me, it could not!'

'Is something wrong, sir?'

He looked at her for a moment and she thought he meant to tell her something important, but then he shook his head. 'No, Ruth. It just reminded me of something that happened long ago . . . but as to your question, I think it unlikely. If the young lady had been deserted she would not wish to give her child something that had been her father's, would she? Perhaps she found it, or someone else found it and gave it to her.'

Ruth was puzzled, because it was obvious that the trinket disturbed him. 'I be right to think it belongs to Eliza, be that not so, sir?'

'Yes, Ruth, this trinket belongs to Eliza no matter whose it once was,' he said and reached across to place it in her hand. 'Take care of it for her and I promise you that I shall find her – somehow I will discover what has happened to her and I shall bring her home to you.'

Arthur walked home through Regent's Park later. Icicles hung from the trees and ice frosted the grass, his breath making white clouds on the air, so bitter was it. To one side of the main path stood an old man roasting chestnuts and the scent of burning assailing his nostrils as he passed the stall by, only half aware of the children clustering for the festive treat, chaperoned by their nannies. He could hear carols being sung as he emerged into the street and crossed the road towards the house his uncle had left him all those years ago; the uncle who had made it clear that if he married beneath him he would lose the fortune that would otherwise be bequeathed to him. A headline on a newsstand casting doubts on Queen Victoria's health caught his eye but at this moment he had no interest in such news.

His thoughts were churning, breaking into patterns like a kaleidoscope. He had never thought to see that trinket again. Seeing it fall from Ruth's hand had been a shock. His lucky halfpenny that he'd had set in gold and diamonds because he believed it brought him luck – but then his luck had run out after he'd heard of Sarah's death and he'd cast it aside in the woods near her home.

Arthur recalled the day that he'd met Sarah's brother, Henry York. He'd been staying with friends near the Yorks' home and was taking a shortcut through the woods, determined to put things right with Sarah, when he became aware that he was being followed. When Henry suddenly threw himself on him and started yelling, accusing him of causing Sarah's death, they had fought until Arthur found himself lying on the ground, his face battered and bruised. He'd got much the worst of it, because he'd refused to fight back from the moment Henry had said that he, Arthur, had caused Sarah's death, reeling from the shock and guilt at the terrible news of Sarah's fate. He'd had no wish to hurt her brother, for he had done the family enough harm. Because of what he'd done, a beautiful, gentle girl had broken her heart and died of her unhappiness.

Lying beaten and sunk in misery as Henry York had poured scorn on him, telling him what a knave he'd been to seduce and then desert the sweetest, gentlest girl that had ever lived, Arthur had wished that he too might die and join her in the cold ground. He'd never believed that Sarah giving herself to him so freely, so joyfully, could end this way – Sarah dead of grief and he knowing that he would carry the burden of it all his life.

After Henry York had walked away, leaving Arthur lying in the woods he'd cast away the halfpenny that he'd considered lucky. A wretch such as he did not deserve to be lucky. Throwing it on the ground he'd walked away and not looked back. Now, all these years later, it was in Ruth's possession and she believed it belonged to Eliza's mother or father.

How could that be? Sarah had surely not given birth to a child? Her brother had said nothing of it that day and Arthur had heard no rumours of her being with child before or after her death. He'd believed she died of a broken heart, nothing more.

Besides, he had not thrown away the coin until after her death. It was mere coincidence. Eliza – that lovely child who reminded him a little of Sarah – could not be his. It was not possible. Yet the thought haunted him. If he believed that his daughter – Sarah's daughter! – had been brought up in a workhouse and mistreated so terribly, it would drive him mad.

No, no, Eliza could not be his and yet . . . how had the trinket been in her shawl and why? Why had Eliza's mother chosen to put it inside her daughter's shawl? Had Henry found it? Would he have known it was Arthur's? Had someone else found it and given it to the child's mother? Another woman who had needed to abandon her child? None of that made sense.

Sarah would have definitely known the coin was Arthur's had she seen it lying in the woods. She might have picked it up and kept it, even put it in her babe's shawl if she was forced to give the child away – but she was dead before he discarded the coin, wasn't she?

Oh God, if she had still lived when her brother had attacked him – if John had lied! But that would be like a blessing, forgiveness of his sin. He could not believe that anyone would lie about the death of his sister, and others had spoken of her death later. Arthur had never visited her grave, because he felt himself unworthy, but he'd never had cause to doubt she was dead until now.

The mystery was tearing at his heart, destroying his peace of mind, and he knew it would not let him rest. He must find Eliza, whether she was Sarah's daughter or not, and make certain she was safe – and then he must discover the secret of her birth. Only that way could he make amends for what he had done to Sarah.

CHAPTER 20

It was so cold that her toes had gone numb and her shoulders and fingers ached with it. Eliza hugged her ragged shawl about her as she crouched in the corner of the deserted workshops where waxed rope had once been made. She'd found this place the first night she was back on the streets, remembering it from her time with Tucker and the others. There had been talk of it being pulled down then, but it was still here and it was a little better than being on the streets, because there were still coils of rope to sit on and make some kind of shelter to keep out the icy cold.

Eliza had tried to find work that first day, but the stalls had begun to sell their wares off cheaply and told her to come back another day. One of the costers had given her a small loaf of bread, which was already a little stale, but it had kept her from going hungry for two days. She'd begged a cup of milk from a girl selling it round the doors, and the girl had given her enough to soak her stale bread and make it soft enough to swallow. Her water came from the tap that filled one of the horse troughs situated everywhere for the many

242

workhorses which served the huge city of London: bakers' vans, brewery carts, coal merchants, hansom cabs – they all needed big strong horses and so there were water troughs everywhere to refresh them.

Eliza did her best to keep herself looking clean, using water from the troughs to wash herself early in the mornings. Sometimes, she had to break the ice and it made her shiver to splash her face in the cold water, but she knew that unless she looked respectable no one would give her work. She'd been lucky on several mornings, given work cutting outside leaves from cabbages to make them look fresher, clearing the debris from round the stalls, and once a kindly man had let her wash the front of his shop down after passing traffic had splashed it with the filth of the gutters, giving her a cup of tea and a bacon sandwich when she'd finished – but no one had offered her proper work.

She was too young to work behind the counter in a shop or one of the many pubs that she'd tried. The owners simply sent her away, and one of them had aimed a blow at her head for bothering him; another had leered at her and told her to come into his back room, but the expression on his face and the smell of him had alerted her and she'd run away before he could grab her. He'd smelled of strong drink and she guessed what kind of work he would offer her – and Eliza would never agree to prostitute herself. She would rather go hungry.

It had rained in the night, which meant it was not quite as cold as the previous days. Eliza knew that it was getting close to Christmas, for the carol singers were everywhere; in the evening the light from their lanterns was to be seen on street corners and the sound of their voices was sweet and comforting. The markets smelled of exotic spices, cinnamon and fir trees, and she thought with regret of her warm home with Miss Edith and the little treats she'd been promised. Wiping the tears from her cheeks, she thrust the disappointment and hurt from her mind. She knew she was not guilty of theft and she was sure she knew who had taken Miss Edith's money. Malcolm had resented Eliza from the moment he saw her and it was a certain way of getting rid of her, because Miss Edith would never suspect her own cousin.

Sometimes at night, when the rats rustled around her feet and she shivered with cold, Eliza had considered returning to the shop and asking Miss Edith to listen to her story, but she knew it was useless. Why would Miss Edith believe her? She was convinced it was Eliza that had stolen from her.

Brushing the tears from her cheeks fiercely that morning, Eliza walked towards the market. At least during the day she could hang around in the hope that someone would need an errand or perhaps give her a stale bun or a piece of fruit that was on the turn. Many of the stalls were groaning with food baked ready for Christmas; rich fruit cakes waiting for someone to carry them home and ice them, jars of mincemeat, big pork pies with bright red cranberries on the top, and almond comfits wrapped in thin tissue, chocolates and mint creams sitting in dishes alongside silver-covered almonds, waiting to be weighed and packed in little boxes tied with ribbons. On other stalls there were chickens hanging upside down, a larger bird that Eliza hadn't ever seen cooked but thought someone had called a turkey, geese and big joints of beef and pork.

She watched as ladies wearing dresses with full skirts that trailed behind them, fur tippets and lined bonnets, expensive rings on their fingers, bought these things, some taking them with them in their baskets, others giving an order for the provisions to be delivered. Just thinking about the kitchens where all this food would be cooked made Eliza's stomach rumble.

She considered asking if one of the ladies needed a kitchen girl, but once or twice when she tried to speak the rich ladies pulled their skirts aside and looked down their noses at her. Her throat tight with tears, Eliza wandered from stall to stall, looking for someone with a kind face – someone who would give her work or food.

She was standing looking at a stall selling freshly-baked bread, cakes and pies when someone grabbed her by the arm. Thinking she'd been caught by the constable for loitering, Eliza tried to pull away.

'Eliza, it's me – Joe,' a voice said and her heart stood still. She turned to look at him, eyes brimming as she saw the gypsy lad she'd known so briefly in the work-house, but would never forget. 'I've been watchin' yer. I wasn't sure it was you, Eliza.'

'Oh, Joe!' Eliza cried, her joy at seeing him again making her cry at the same time as she hugged him. 'They told me you were dead, but I knew you'd run away.'

Joe grinned and nodded. 'I hid in the cellar and only came out at night to steal food from the kitchen. There was a way under the wall at the back of the cellar. I think it was a kind of chute that had been used to pour coal or wood down when they stored fuel there years before; the rats had been using it for ages, making their tunnels in and out, and I found it. It had become silted up with dust and debris so I dug my way through and then I scrambled out and I was at the other side of the workhouse – at the back where all the deliveries used to be made when it was a grand house centuries ago.'

'Oh, Joe, I'm so glad,' Eliza said and brushed the tears from her face. Her hands left dirty marks on her cheeks and Joe laughed. He took out a red kerchief, spat on it and then rubbed at her cheek. 'No wonder you can't find work. They won't take yer on if they think yer a vagrant or a thief. Come on, I've got work fer today. Yer can help me and I'll give yer something to eat and yer can sleep where I do. It's above a stable and it's warm in the hay.'

'Do you work in a stable?'

'Aye, for 'tis honest work,' Joe said and took hold of her arm, pulling her with him as he headed down one of the lanes adjacent to the market. ''Tis no use tryin' for work on the market, for they think you mean to steal from them. I found work with a decent bloke who runs the ostler's on the corner of Friar's Court. They're always busy and people leave their 'orses to be cared for when they have business in town. I sweep the stables out in the mornin' and then I spread clean straw, groom the 'orses, feed 'em and water 'em.'

'I never thought to try the stables,' Eliza said trotting happily by his side. 'I tried the inns and the shops and the pie stall but they all said I was too young.'

'I'm a lad and bigger than you,' Joe told her with a

246

grin, 'and I'm used to 'orses. At first I was turned down and told to clear orf, but I've a way with wild 'uns and they had trouble with one what was left there one mornin'. I was the only one that could calm it and so they give me a job.'

'You're so clever,' Eliza said looking at him admiringly. 'I wish I'd found work like you.'

'Well, you can help me sweep the stable and carry water,' he said. 'I'll share my bed with you, though 'tis only the straw and a blanket in the hayloft, and we'll share the food. I can buy food for us when I'm paid.'

'I should earn my keep.' Eliza looked at him thoughtfully. 'You spoke of travellin' and workin' in the fields, digging potatoes and binding the hay – I could help with that . . .'

'Aye, you could when we leave town,' Joe said and looked sad. 'My pa is serving a year in prison for a fight he never started – but that's 'cos there ain't no justice fer us. Folks don't like the travellin' people; they say we're dirty thieves and we steal children – but that's all lies. I'm waitin' fer me pa to be freed and then we're off to the country.'

'How much longer must you wait?'

'It will be next spring afore he's free. I managed to see him once. I lied and told 'em I was sixteen and they let me in, but I'm only allowed to visit once in two months. Still, me pa knows I be here waitin fer 'im and told me we shan't come back to Lun'un no more.'

'Oh, Joe, I'll be sorry when you go,' Eliza said, trying not to cry.

'Don't yer fret, my Eliza. I told yer we was meant and so it is – you'm ter come with us when we go.'

'Will your father let me come with you – won't I be in the way?'

''Course not,' Joe said and grinned. 'He knows I've got the sight, and when I tell him we be meant, he will agree. You'll like the way we live, Eliza. Out in the fields and riding the 'orses bare-backed. We don't need no saddles, me and pa. We've both got the way with 'em yer see. Pa breaks 'em from the wild and sells 'em but we keep some fer ourselves. In Ireland we have a place where we leave the young 'uns when we travel – and we breed from the best mares.' His eyes lit up. ''Tis a fine life, Eliza. Better than any you've known.'

Eliza nodded but did not answer. In the workhouse Joe's stories had sounded wonderful, because they offered freedom from a life of hardship and cruelty, but she could never forget Miss Edith and how happy she'd been working in her kitchen. It was a fine thing to make cures for people when they came to her for help, and Eliza thought she would like to have spent her life helping Miss Edith. Yet she'd experienced a strong bond with Joe, so she put her memories of Miss Edith to one side, feeling happy that she was with Joe again and that she could eat without begging or running the risk of being caught as a vagrant. If the constable took her, Eliza knew they would send her to prison or back to the workhouse and she doubted that she would ever escape it again.

Arthur was tormented by what he'd seen in Ruth's parlour that day. It might be a coincidence, for anyone could have found that fob lying in the wood – but surely no one but Sarah would know it had been his and only she would have given it to her child.

Was Eliza his daughter? If he was honest, Arthur had sensed something the first time he saw her. He could never have guessed that she was his, for he had not even known then that Sarah had borne his child – and even now, when he suspected that her brother Henry had lied to him, Arthur found it difficult to accept.

Why had no one ever told him the truth?

A man's pride, perhaps, or a vindictive intention to prevent him from knowing that his child had been born. There was so much that was still hidden and all that he suspected was still conjecture, but he knew now that he could never rest until he was sure.

Toby wondered at his leaving town so close to Christmas. 'Where are you going?' he asked when Arthur told him he intended to visit the country. 'It seems a strange time to be leaving on business.'

'It is something I must settle – should have done so long ago,' Arthur told him and smiled. 'Do not be concerned, my friend. I shall be gone only a few days.'

He chose to ride rather than drive and took with him only a change of linen in his saddlebags. It would be easier on horseback, and he needed neither his manservant nor a groom, for his business was personal. It would, Arthur knew, be useless to approach Sarah's brother for he would merely repeat his lie if it was one. First, Arthur must visit Sarah's grave; he should have done it years ago but something had held him back – grief or pride, he could not be sure now why he had left after that fight with her brother.

He had given much thought to what he might learn since he saw that trinket in Ruth's hands. What fate had caused her to find and keep it for Eliza all this time? Many another would have sold the mount long before this – certainly it would have disappeared had it fallen into Miss Simpkins' hands. Arthur could not but think that he was meant to see it, and yet nothing was certain. Perhaps he was snatching at straws in the wind, because he wanted it to be true. He wanted that trinket to be a message from the woman he'd wronged.

His mouth settled in a grim line for hope had lit a flame in him and if it were to be extinguished, it would leave him emptier than before . . .

Arthur visited the churchyard and hunted for Sarah's grave. At last he found it, but it was badly neglected, and the simple wooden cross at its head had fallen sideways, the name Sarah hardly discernible now, and there was no surname. He felt angry as he saw how dreadful her brother had been, refusing to allow the use of the family name because she had shamed him so. Surely she deserved a decent stone and her resting place should be cared for by someone!

'Forgive me,' he said. She had been too young to die and he was responsible. 'If I could give you back your life I would . . .'

Laying the flowers he'd brought with him on her grave, Arthur said a prayer and made a vow that he would have a stone erected. Only the name Sarah was on the cross; he'd been almost certain of it and now he was sure: if her child had died with her, it had not been named or buried here. He felt bitter regret that he'd done nothing all these years.

Leaving the graveyard, Arthur decided to visit the village doctor and ask the questions he needed answering

– but first he must speak to the parson. If these men still lived and worked here, perhaps one of them would be prepared to tell him the truth.

As he walked from the graveyard, Arthur saw a woman entering. She looked at him, and it seemed for a moment as if she knew him and would speak, but then she went on. He looked back but saw nothing that made him think he might have known her.

The parson was in his study, composing his sermon for the coming Sunday service. He rose as his housekeeper announced Arthur and looked at him inquiringly. It was obvious that he did not know Arthur's name and wondered what his business might be.

'Good day, sir.' Arthur sat in the chair he was offered. 'I know you are busy and so will come straight to the point. I believe you took the service when Sarah York was buried almost fourteen years ago?'

'John York's sister?' The parson looked surprised. 'And you wish to know because . . .?'

'I cared for her.'

For a moment the parson hesitated, then inclined his head. 'That unfortunate young woman . . . Yes, I remember very well. Sarah died of a putrid fever, some twelve weeks or more after the birth of her child.' He shook his head sadly. 'I thought it such a waste of a young life . . .'

Sarah *had* given birth to his child! For a moment Arthur was too stunned to speak, and then he managed: 'Yes, it was, but women too often die in childbed.'

The parson shook his head. 'As I recall, she had recovered from the birth of the babe but was later struck

251

down with a rabid fever that affected several villagers. Her child was more than three months old when she died, a lusty babe that did not take the sickness.'

'Sarah did not die of a broken heart?' Arthur's throat was so tight he could barely force the words from frozen lips.

'It was her brother that broke her heart, for he put her from his house when he discovered her condition, and she was forced to beg a home from anyone who would have her. She was taken in by Mistress Burns, an elderly lady of good reputation but little money, and sadly dead these past seven years. She gave Miss Sarah a home, but expected her to work for her living as her servant – and I think it was Sarah's weakness after the birth, coupled with the hard work she had not been used to, that made her succumb to the fever. We lost several villagers that winter, but Sarah was the youngest.'

'And her child?' Arthur's heart raced. 'Tell me, sir – was the child a girl?'

The parson looked at him in silence for a long time, and then inclined his head. 'The child lived, but Mistress Burns would not keep her when Sarah died. She brought the babe to me and I arranged for her to be taken to the Sisters of Saint Catherine.' His gaze narrowed. 'Was that child yours, sir?'

Arthur met his gaze, which was surprisingly free of condemnation. 'Yes, Sarah's child was mine. She never told me she carried the child – nor that she needed help. Had I known . . .' Tears stung his eyes and he dashed them away angrily. 'Forgive me, I thought Sarah dead of the unhappiness I brought on her.'

'You were told that? John felt his sister had shamed

him and he was angry when he threw her out, but when she died he blamed himself . . .'

'He blamed me,' Arthur said. 'I deserved it, for I did not treat Sarah well. I seduced her and deserted her carelessly and so the blame for her death must lie with me.'

'Yet you would have helped her had she told you . . .' Something in the elderly churchman's eyes touched Arthur and he looked away. 'I think you have paid for your carelessness, sir. God does not demand that we should go on suffering for a past sin forever, Mr Stoneham.'

'Do you know what happened to my daughter, sir?' Arthur asked. 'I would find her if I could.'

'My maid Janet visited Sarah many times before she died, and it was she I entrusted the child to. She takes flowers from our garden to Sarah's grave every week – and I believe she has just returned from there. Shall I ask her to come in?'

'If you would be so kind – for I wish to know where the babe was taken.'

He managed to contain his urgency as the housekeeper was summoned and then the maid fetched. Arthur recognised the woman he'd seen entering the churchyard as he left earlier that morning but he did not speak as the parson explained his errand.

For a moment the woman stared at him, then she nodded. 'I took the child to the Sisters, as my master bade me, sir, but they said they could not keep her. I believe she was given to a woman who had no child, but she was not of this parish. She and her husband had travelled here from London to be blessed, for it is

253

said that if a childless woman makes a gift to Saint Catherine's shrine she may be blessed with a babe of her own.'

'And so the Sisters gave the child to this childless woman?' Arthur tried to read the woman's mind, but her eyes were dark and secretive and he suspected that she did not speak the truth. 'Do you know the woman's name?'

'No, sir, only that Sister Mary told me they would give the babe to a woman who had come to pray at the shrine.'

Arthur thanked her and gave her a gold sovereign, which she slipped into her pocket hastily before being dismissed. Arthur thanked the parson for his help, offered a donation of several guineas for his church restoration, and left. He had decided that he would go to the Sisters of St Catherine's and ask them for the truth. If Eliza was his daughter, and she'd been given to a woman who longed for a child, why had the childless woman given the babe away?

As he mounted his horse, he was aware of someone looking at him from the windows upstairs and when he turned to look saw the pale face of the maid who he felt instinctively had lied to him – perhaps because she had been afraid to tell the truth in front of her master.

CHAPTER 21

'A child brought to us by Janet, who is maid to Parson Strong?' the nun asked and frowned as she looked through the well-worn register. 'I can see no record of it, sir. We cannot care for new-born babies here, though we take in orphans of the parish for a short time before sending them on to a workhouse that will accept them. The child would have been registered here had we received it.'

'Would you have given a babe of three months to a woman who had none of her own? A woman who had come to the shrine to pray?' Arthur asked her, and she looked at him solemnly.

'We abide by the law in this house, sir. We do not have the right to give away children brought to us. Our rules are that orphans with no surviving relative, must be given into the care of the guardians of a workhouse, and if such a child was brought to us that is what would have happened to it – but we have no record of such a child being brought here in the year you mentioned.'

'Thank you for your help, Sister.'

Arthur questioned her no further. He had suspected

the parson's maid of lying and now he was certain. For some reason she had not obeyed her master but she had not wanted to confess it in front of him – perhaps because she feared dismissal from his service. She was a woman of thirty-odd years, plain and poorly educated. It would not be easy for her to find another job without a reference from her master and he was unlikely to give her one if he discovered that she had deceived him.

Arthur must return to the village and speak to the maid alone this time – and he thought that the best place would be in the churchyard when she visited Sarah's grave the next day as he suspected she might.

And Arthur indeed found the maid visiting Sarah's grave the next morning. She saw him but made no attempt to flee, simply waited for him to come to her.

'I thought you would come back,' she told him. 'Sarah was too proud to ask for your help, though I begged her to. She was never meant for a servant's work and her mistress drove her hard. There was no true charity in Mistress Burns and she gave Sarah and her child a home only because she did not have to pay her for her work.'

Arthur nodded grimly; her words made him wish that he had come years ago for Sarah's sake, but it was all too late. 'You saw Sarah often before she died. Did she hate me for what I did to her?'

Janet smiled oddly. 'Did you never know how much she loved you, sir? Sarah loved your child and she forgave you for deserting her – as she forgave her brother for turning her out. When she died she gave me something she found of yours when walking in the woods.

256

It was a lucky token – a halfpenny set in gold with a diamond clasp that once fastened to your watch chain.'

'I threw it away after I fought her brother . . .' He frowned. 'But I thought Sarah already dead then. Her brother told me so.'

'No, sir, she was not,' Janet said. 'Her brother lied to you – the grave you were standing by yesterday was that of a beggar who shared Miss Sarah's name and who died within our parish. If you had searched further, you would have found Miss Sarah's grave.'

For a moment Arthur closed his eyes as anger fought the grief. 'So Sarah lived when I came here, when I fought with her brother?'

'Yes, sir. Had you walked into the village then you might have found her and saved her from her fate.'

'Then where is her grave?'

'She lies in a secluded spot which I tend. I waited here today for I suspected you'd thought that this poor place was her grave because of the name. Come, follow me, and I will show you where she lies. I took your flowers to her, for I knew that she would like them.'

Arthur shook his head in disbelief: Sarah's brother had tricked him, lied to him and prevented him from finding Sarah and making amends. Anger raged and he wanted to kill the man who had hurt her to spite him. However, when he saw the well-tended grave with a small headstone in a quiet corner of the graveyard, he felt tears sting his eyes and his rage became sorrow.

'Did you do this?'

'Some of Sarah's friends provided money for the stone and I have always tended it. I loved her, for she was kind to me . . .'

'You say she gave you the lucky halfpenny she found in the woods. What did you do with it? Please tell me the truth, for it is important.'

'I fastened it to the inside of the babe's shawl, and I gave the child to a woman who came to worship at the shrine of St Catherine. I saw her weeping because she had no child – and she saw the babe I was meant to give to the Sisters. She asked if I would give her the child and looked at the babe so tenderly that I thought it was what Sarah would want.'

'That trinket was found fastened to the shawl of a babe given to the mistress of the workhouse in Spitalfields. If your story is true, why would a woman who wanted a child give away a babe that had been given to her?'

'I do not know, sir. She begged me to let her have the babe and I did so, because I knew that the Sisters would not keep the child – they would have sent it to the workhouse.' Janet hung her head. 'I lied to you yesterday because my master would've been angry that I disobeyed him.'

'Yes, I understand that,' Arthur said. He could not find it in him to be angry with her. Janet had told him the truth. It was Sarah's brother who had lied to him – he who had destroyed the chance his sister had to make a better life, because had Arthur known the truth he would have asked her to be his wife. Bitter regret swept through him, and then anger because his child had been denied both her mother and her father. 'Tell me, do you know the name of the woman to whom you gave Sarah's daughter?'

'She said her name was Flora Miller and she and her husband came from London.'

'Did she pay you for the child?'

'No, sir! I swear it,' Janet said. 'I did what I thought was right for Sarah's child and the grieving woman.'

'I think her tears were false and meant to deceive you.' Arthur was angry now. 'That child was taken to a workhouse and given to the mistress who treated her ill.'

'I would swear on my dear Sarah's grave that it was not so, sir. Had you seen the woman's face when I placed the babe in her arms, you would have believed, as I did, that she would always love and cherish the child.'

'It is a mystery,' Arthur said, because the riddle of that lucky token in Eliza's shawl had deepened. 'If you have told me the truth then I must accept it, but I am no further forward in my quest to discover my daughter.'

'Forgive me, sir. Had I believed you cared, I would have brought the child to you in London . . .' Janet met his eyes. 'Sarah hoped you would come and find her. Even to the end she believed in you, and that's why she gave me the token to show you if you came looking . . .'

'And I did come, but her brother lied to me. He told me she was dead some three months before she left this life. I saw the pauper's grave and believed it hers.' Arthur felt the bitterness of that deception, and yet with it came a lightening of the load of grief and guilt he carried. John York had played a large part in his sister's demise. 'Thank you for telling me the truth, Janet . . . I should like to reward you.' He took a pouch of gold coins from his greatcoat pocket and counted out twenty, offering them to her, but she shook her head.

'I do not deserve it, sir. I should have brought the babe to you in London, but . . .' She sighed, for it was too late for regrets.

Arthur pressed the coins into the maid's hand and walked away. It was time that he returned to London. His search for the truth of Eliza's birth went on. If she was his daughter, as he now believed, he would protect her, but he would not force her to leave Miss Edith unless she wished it.

His mind was filled with thoughts of regret as he turned his horse toward the London road. If Janet had entrusted his daughter to a woman who truly wanted a babe, why would she give it to Mistress Joan Simpkins? He would have to find a way to force the truth from her even though it went against the grain to bargain with that witch . . .

Returning from her nightly walk about the workhouse, Joan was startled to see Sadie standing outside in the corridor and a light on in her sitting room.

'What is the matter now?' she asked crossly. 'If someone is ill they may wait for the morning, for I will not call the doctor out at this hour.'

'It ain't nothin' like that, mistress,' Sadie said and her eyes gleamed. 'I reckon there's someone wants ter see yer – waitin' in yer room.'

'And who let this person in?'

'He come to the side gate and used the key what that other one used ter use,' Sadie said, her eyes narrowed in gleeful malice. Joan frowned, because she had not thought anyone knew of her schemes or the way Drake came secretly to her at night when he had some business for her. 'Don't worry, mistress. Sadie don't never tell – but it helps if yer make me a supervisor.'

'You want extra rations, is that it?' Joan glared at her. 'Very well, you may wear the yellow badge and oversee the basket making; it is an easy job and pays one shilling a week.'

Sadie grinned toothlessly. 'He be the one that come the other day wiv the man from the Board.' She went off, cackling to herself, leaving Joan uncertain as she went into her office. How could Mr Stoneham have discovered where the key to the side gate was hidden?

Seeing the large, red-cheeked man who stood looking out of her window at the courtyard, Joan checked. Not Mr Stoneham or his friend then – but the man who had sided with her against them. She assumed a sweet smile as she addressed him. 'Good evening, major. What may I do for you, sir?'

'Well, I think we may be able to help each other, dear lady,' the major said and the look in his eyes held Joan mesmerised. What was he suggesting? 'I believe a mutual friend spoke to you of some special merchandise . . .'

Joan held back the exclamation of surprise. It was all clear to her now. She would never in a thousand years have suspected it, because to all intents and purposes this man was respectable, upright and honest, a pillar of the community. Arthur Stoneham had picked him to help him expose her and instead of that . . . a gurgle of wild laughter started up inside her but she reined it back. This man was taking a chance in coming out of the shadows. She suspected that only Drake's stubborn refusal to have any more to do with the trade in young girls had forced him to speak to her – but he had recognised a kindred spirit in her and known that she would do anything he asked for a price.

'You know what I want,' he said. 'The younger the better. Those other girls were too old . . .'

Joan nodded, understanding that to satisfy his filthy lusts he was willing to pay. 'I have none for the moment, but I'll find you a girl as soon as the chance arises. Where can I contact you?'

He reached into his pocket and took out a small scrap of paper. 'Memorise this and then destroy it. You may leave me a message there and I'll pay once you bring the girl.'

'How much. It's dangerous for me to bring her – you must make it worth my while . . .'

'A hundred and fifty guineas,' he said. 'I'll give you fifty guineas now and the rest when you deliver – and the younger they are the more I will pay.'

Joan smiled and nodded, her delight almost too much to hide. She could see that the next few months could be very profitable for her. 'I shall be delighted to do business with you, sir.'

He took a small purse from his pocket and gave it to her. 'The bargain is sealed. I believe that we shall work well together, Miss Simpkins.'

Joan took the money, inclined her head and waited until he'd left to count the money. Fifty golden guineas, as much as Drake would have paid her for the three girls he wanted. The prospect of another hundred guineas the next day made her eyes gleam. She could amass a fortune in a few months, because the very young girls never lasted long. The major and his friends would use them and then get rid of them, always wanting fresh goods – which meant that Joan only had to find enough girls of the right age and in this bitter weather their parents were bringing them in every day, whole families on the brink of starvation. Sooner or later she would find a way of passing the right ones on to her new friend.

CHAPTER 22

Eliza looked at the feast Joe had got for them on Christmas Day. He'd carried an old wooden crate up to their little haven in the loft, spreading it with a red cloth that he'd bought from one of the travelling folk at the fair they'd visited on Christmas Eve. He'd bargained it for some wicker baskets he'd woven when his work was finished for the day, and now it covered their special table. On the cloth was a large pork pie, mince pies that the ostler's wife had given them, a jar of home-made pickles bought from the market from a friendly woman, who had given Eliza a small jar of potted chicken as a goodwill gift. Joe had bought bread made fresh the previous day and carefully stored to keep it soft, two toffee apples from the fair, a handful of nuts and a little bag of sugared almonds. To wash this feast down they had a jug of lemon barley the ostler's wife had made them, and another jug of milk that Joe had bought from the dairy along with some eggs for their breakfast.

That morning they'd built a fire in a field a few minutes' walk from their home and cooked their eggs in a blackened pot that Joe said he took everywhere with him, boiling the eggs until they were hard and eating them with a sprinkling of salt. They'd washed the food down with a billycan of tea, drinking from battered enamel mugs.

'This is what it will be like when we travel the roads,' Joe told her as she bit the top off her egg and ate hungrily, the cold air sharpening her appetite. 'When we camp, Bathsheba and my mother build a fire and they cook our meals in a big black pot hung from a tripod. Sometimes we roast a chicken on a spit over the fire, but often the women make stews in the pot – 'tis good filling food for when you've worked hard in the fields.'

'What sort of work would I do?' Eliza asked, nibbling an apple that was crisp and nutty. She recalled Edith speaking of a gypsy woman who sold her herbs.

'When it is harvesting time you might help to gather the wheat and barley into stooks,' Joe said. 'We tie them with thin twine and stack them together in the fields until they are dry and then they are piled on to the farmer's cart and taken to his yard – unless he does the threshing in the field. Sometimes, it saves losing too much wheat, for else overripe kernels fall out and the birds eat them – and when 'tis time for the potato harvesting, we each take a section and bend over the rows, picking with both hands as we go and filling our baskets. The children work in twos, because the baskets are too heavy and we carry them between us – but I am strong enough to carry my basket alone now. If we worked together, you would help me fill it. We should get down our piece quicker then, and that pleases the farmer because he can have a sharp turnaround. We're always battling the weather, especially on the heavy ground.' For a moment he seemed to be far away from her, as if remembering. 'Even Bathsheba helps with the harvesting, though she is our wise woman and spends much of her time making cures and gathering wild plants.'

So Bathsheba was one of Joe's family. Eliza remembered now the woman who had sold her lavender on the market and told her fortune – was she Bathsheba?

'It sounds a good life.'

Eliza listened to Joe's stories. She enjoyed being here in this field with him, which was where the fair came at midsummer and on Christmas Eve, and cooking food in the open air. Some of the fair people were still here but they stayed in their own camp and did not disturb them. It was companionable and fun, but sometimes she missed the comfort of Miss Edith's bed and she wished she was there to help with making the medicines. It was so much for her employer to do alone and she would get very tired.

'What are you thinking?' Joe asked as Eliza munched a slice of the delicious pie with some pickles that evening. Joe had worked most of the day as usual, for the horses needed to be cared for even though it was a holiday and the shops were closed.

'I was thinking of our breakfast,' she answered truthfully. 'It will be fun travelling with your people, Joe – but I am not one of you. Do you think your folk will accept me?'

'You're more like my mother than you know,' Joe said. 'Her hair is fair, though darker than yours when yours is washed fresh, but she speaks a bit like you. She was not one of us until my pa found her and made her his wife.'

'What do you mean "found" her?' Eliza asked.

'I think she was ill.' Joe shook his head. 'I hardly know, Eliza, for they do not speak of it – Bathsheba explained why Ma speaks differently, but it is not so different these days as I remember it was once. I think she has forgotten the life she knew.'

'I never knew my family – except for Ruth. I suppose she was truly my mother,' Eliza said. 'She did not give me birth, but she cared for me all my life – and I wish I could see her again before we leave London.'

'We must look for her,' Joe said. 'You do not know where she might be?'

'Molly said she'd gone to work for Mr Stoneham. Mr Arthur Stoneham is one of the governors at the workhouse.' She sighed. 'I know nothing more than that.'

'We could ask people,' Joe said. 'Ostler's wife be friendly. She might 'ave 'eard of Arthur Stoneham. We've a while yet afore my pa be free.'

Eliza nodded and smiled. She loved Joe and sharing his life, but there was a part of her that still hankered for the life she'd known at Miss Edith's – and she knew she always would.

Eating her lonely Christmas meal of roast chicken, Edith thought with regret of the girl she'd driven away in her distress. Lying on Eliza's bed was the new dress she'd bought for her, though she would probably never wear it. And that was Edith's fault. She wished that she had cut out her tongue before she said those cruel things to Eliza, for she'd known almost as soon as she spoke that it could not be she that was the thief. Eliza's face had been so white, so stricken . . . and Edith ought to have known who the viper in the nest was as soon as she'd discovered the theft. In her heart she'd known he was stealing from the shop takings long before Eliza arrived.

Malcolm's mother had been to the shop to plead for her son. She refused to believe that he had stolen so much money and in the end lost her temper and said that it was Edith's own fault for paying him such mean wages. Her accusation had cut Edith to the quick, because she'd given the boy as much as she could afford and more than he was worth, but of course his mother did not believe that and they parted on bad terms.

So now Edith was trying to manage both the shop and the cures by herself and it meant that she had to work all hours. She never went to bed before eleven at night and was up again by five in the morning; she was tired and lonely, and her health was suffering. She had no one to share her Christmas with and the surprises she had prepared for Eliza lay on her bed unopened. Edith kept hoping that the girl would return and she could apologise for her harsh words, but with each day that passed, her hopes faded.

She might have to go to the workhouse and take another girl – and yet she knew that she could never find another Eliza. The child was quick, bright and intelligent and once taught she had gentle manners and was learning to speak well. Edith had known she was the perfect person to share her life with and to pass on her knowledge to so that she could continue Papa's work.

A tear slid down her cheek and she brushed it away impatiently. Feeling sorry for herself would do no good. She must soon decide whether to return to the workhouse and take another girl or ask if one of Ruth's ladies would like to work with her. It would not be the same – nothing could ever be the same – but she needed help or she would be ill herself.

Sighing, she pushed away her plate, the food halfeaten. For years after her father died she had managed alone, but that was before she'd known the pleasure of working and living with her dearest Eliza.

'Oh, Eliza, come back to me,' she said and bent her head and sobbed, giving into the wealth of feeling that overcame her.

As she wiped her tears, Edith made up her mind that she would make a will now. She did not know if she could ever find Eliza and make her her heir, as she'd planned, but she was determined that her greedy aunt and cousin would never get their hands on her home or the shop. She would much rather that it went to a charitable trust for children like her Eliza, to provide a home that was kinder than the workhouse.

Arthur had spent Christmas morning with Ruth at his and Katharine's home for unfortunate women, and then dined at four with Toby at their club. Afterwards, Toby had gone home to spend the evening with his father and a few friends, but despite his friend's urging, Arthur had returned to his own home to sit with a book, a bottle of good brandy and some of his favourite cigars by the fire. He wanted to think about the future. His agents were already searching for Eliza but he was uncertain what to do for the best when he found her. Arthur believed that Eliza was his daughter, though unless he could trace the woman who had taken her to the workhouse he would never have proof. Would Eliza accept his word – would she even wish to know that she was his child and that her mother's name was Sarah York?

Grief twisted inside him. He wanted to make up to that child for all that she had suffered at the hands of others but knew that he could not just lay claim to her. He would find her and he would punish those who had hurt her – but Ruth had told him that Miss Edith loved Eliza.

'She had Christmas gifts for the child,' Ruth told him on his return from the country, her eyes red with weeping. 'It was a misunderstanding, but I believe she cares for Eliza.'

Arthur had accepted her word. He wished that he could have rested, knowing she was safe with the woman who had taken her from the workhouse and that he might give her a Christmas gift. If he'd only realised sooner . . . and yet he'd known that woman Mistress Simpkins was mistreating her. Why had he not taken her away himself?

He felt ill at ease surrounded by the comforts of his home and the gifts he himself had been given. Some fine cigars had been Toby's gift and the book was a book of Tennyson's poetry, which had been Miss Katharine Ross's gift to him.

She had signed it: *To my dearest friend Arthur, with sincere affection from Katharine.*

The penmanship was beautiful and Arthur held it to his nose because it smelled of her own special scent. He could not fail to know that Katharine liked him, perhaps too much for her peace of mind, and he felt more deeply for her than he could say – but to take her sweet affection would surely be to betray her. Yet it was in his mind to see her and confess his feelings and his unworthiness to offer her marriage. Would she find it in her heart to forgive him? He could not hope for more but perhaps she might be his friend.

Arthur had thought long and hard before choosing a Christmas gift for Katharine. His preference would have been to give her sapphires and diamonds to match the sparkle of her eyes, but such a gift would not be acceptable to a respectable lady – unless it was accompanied by a proposal of marriage. In the end he had settled on a rather lovely gold cameo brooch.

Pushing his fears for Eliza to the back of his mind, he opened the book of poems and began to read. How could Katharine have known that these were some of his favourites? It seemed that they had so much more in common than their desire to help others . . .

CHAPTER 23

'I need a girl.' The major looked at Joan and she felt sickened as she saw the gleam in his eyes. 'You promised to find me one, but you have not sent word.'

'It is not always easy to get them so young,' she prevaricated. 'At the moment I do not have any girls under twelve'

'If the girl is pretty and slight she will do . . .'

'I will do what I can – wait until you hear from me.'

'I will pay more for the right one,' the major said, and Joan watched in dreadful fascination as a dribble of saliva trickled down his chin. 'Two hundred guineas if she looks young and has pale hair . . .'

'I will do my best for you, but the only girl of that age I have at the moment is deformed and drags her leg.' He shook his head impatiently, dismissing the offering. 'As soon as a girl comes in that I think would suit you, I will come myself and tell you.'

'Very well,' he said, annoyed, 'but if you let me down I shall have to look elsewhere. There are mothers willing to sell their daughters for half what I pay you.'

As he took his leave Joan was tempted to ask him

why he bothered with her if this was the case, though she knew the answer. The children he spoke of were ill-nourished and often diseased, whereas the children Joan oversaw were reasonably well fed and clean. Any illness was treated by the doctor and she knew better than to send the major an ugly child, because it was the fragile beauty of an innocent that appealed to these wretched men.

Once she was sure her visitor would not return, Joan took her savings box from her desk drawer and counted the money. She had nearly five hundred pounds. It was a small fortune and would set her up with a house and a business of her choice, and she could live at her ease. One sale to the major and she could vastly increase her haul of blood money – for that was what it was.

Men were all the same, Joan thought, her mouth tight with disgust. She vowed that she would find one last girl for Major Cartwright and his perverted friends, and then she would leave this place – but where to find a girl that would suit his purposes. All the girls were dark and that little bit older . . . For a moment the picture of a girl's face came to mind and she regretted that she had sold Eliza for ten guineas to that interfering woman. Had she refused, she might have had two hundred for the girl – and she would have gladly given that particular trouble-maker to the major. However, Eliza had gone beyond her reach . . . unless she could steal her back from Edith Richards.

Joan racked her brains to think of a way to deceive both Miss Richards and Eliza, and then the idea came to her. If she were to tell them that Eliza's mother had come looking for her, the girl would come willingly – and Miss Richards would think it a kindness to let her.

Yes, it was worth a try, Joan thought and decided to visit the apothecary the next day. If she gave the major Eliza, she would keep him occupied for a few weeks at least and by that time Joan would already have made good her escape from London.

'So, you have returned from the country,' Katharine Ross said that morning when they met at the home in which they shared a charitable interest. 'I trust your time was well spent – and that you enjoyed Christmas Day?'

'I lunched with Toby,' Arthur said and smiled, for she was wearing his brooch at the neck of her gown. 'I wished that I might call on you, Miss Ross, but I thought you might have guests.'

'My aunt had friends to lunch, but we spent the evening alone,' Katharine said and sighed. 'I should have been very happy to see you, my dear friend . . .'

'Will you walk with me?' Arthur asked. 'I know it is cold, but I would be private with you.'

'I have my carriage, could we not drive in the park?'

'Even better,' he agreed and offered his arm. 'I wish to talk to you, Miss Ross – Katharine – and I do not wish to be overheard.'

Katharine looked at him and a dimple appeared in her cheek. She looked so lovely that Arthur felt his heart contract for love of her and his courage almost failed.

'What is it that you wish to say to me?' she asked as they settled into the comfortable squabs in her carriage, and her driver set the horses in motion.

'I have a confession to make,' Arthur said and saw her lips curve. 'I daresay it would not come as a surprise if I told you I admire you a great deal, Miss Ross?'

'A mutual admiration, I daresay,' she said and gave him a roguish look.

'If that were all I had to tell you I should be a happy man.' Arthur hesitated, then, 'I would wish to ask formally for your hand, Katharine – but I am not worthy of you. No . . .' He held up his hand to prevent her as she would have spoken. 'Please hear me out for I think I may lose your good opinion once you know me for what I am.'

Katharine's smile was lost as she saw how serious he was, and Arthur felt his throat contract. He found it difficult to speak the words but knew he must.

'I believe the child Eliza – whom you know of – may possibly be my daughter. I deserted her mother after seducing her, for though she was a girl of gentle birth she had no fortune and I, a foolish young man, thought an uncle's wealth more important than the sweet girl who loved me, for my uncle told me I must marry a girl of his choosing and it was not she.'

Katharine stared at him in shock, all colour gone from her face, and Arthur felt as if a knife had plunged into his heart. She did not speak and he explained further, telling her that he had regretted his cruel desertion, informed his uncle he loved another, and tried to contact Sarah – but had been given to understand that she had died of a broken heart.

'It is only recently that I have learned that Sarah bore my child – a daughter,' Arthur said, and explained that the babe had been given to a childless woman and yet later brought to the workhouse in Whitechapel: something he'd discovered only after seeing the trinket Ruth had kept all these years.

'So you have only the trinket to guide you,' Katharine said, finding her voice at last.

'And an instinct that told me the child meant something to me.'

'And now she is lost . . . oh, how difficult this is for you.' Tears of sympathy hovered in Katharine's eyes.

'I am torn between the need to find Eliza and the urge to force that witch at the workhouse to tell me the truth of why she was taken there.'

'Perhaps I might speak to Miss Simpkins for you?' Katharine suggested. 'I might pretend to come from Eliza's mother – to be her aunt. I could offer her money for the truth.'

'You would do that for me?' Arthur asked in wonder. 'Do you not turn from me in disgust now that you know what kind of man I am?'

Katharine smiled and touched his cheek with her gloved hand. 'I have always known what kind of man you are,' she said gently. 'A man who might make a mistake and be sorry for it – a man of great kindness and generosity.'

'Katherine!' Arthur seized her hand and kissed the fingertips. 'Do you really not hate me?'

'I really do not hate you . . .'

'Then, dare I hope? But no, I ask too much . . .'

Katharine seemed to hesitate, then: 'I suggest that you come to luncheon and meet my aunt,' she said, 'for I may have feelings for you that are quite the opposite of what you feared . . .' Her lovely eyes twinkled with mischief. 'Yet I shall not admit them until I have been courted for at least three months – my poor aunt would be horrified if I announced my betrothal to a man she does not know.'

'Bless you, sweet Katharine!' His eyes answered hers with an unspoken challenge and she nodded.

'I will help you discover the truth about the child, Arthur,' Katharine said, 'and I pray to God that we shall find Eliza very soon.'

CHAPTER 24

'What will you do today?' Joe asked as they ate their breakfast of bread and cheese, washed down by half a cup of milk each. 'I plan to visit my father this morning, as I told you, and it's best you don't hang around here alone, Eliza. Some of the men who stable their horses here are not good men. It's all right when I'm here to protect you, but you should go up to the house and ask the ostler's wife to give you a job.'

'Yes, Joe, I will,' Eliza promised, because she knew he worried about her since one of the customers had tried to grab her a few days earlier. 'I won't stay here alone.'

'I shall be back by the time the clock strikes four this afternoon,' Joe told her. 'Pa will be out of prison in another week or so, Eliza. We'll be orf then and it will be better. You'll be safe with me ma and Bathsheba and my brother. John be younger than me, but he's a good lad.'

'Bathsheba will teach me to make peg dolls and baskets to sell at the fairs,' Eliza said, repeating what Joe had told her so many times. 'I am looking forward to it – especially now 'tis not so cold.'

'The winter 'as been 'ard,' Joe admitted. 'You would never 'ave survived alone on the streets, Eliza. I know you had friends before and you managed, but the winter was too cold and if we'd not had our place 'ere you might have perished. We be lucky to have bided 'ere all this time.'

'I've been happy,' Eliza said and hugged his arm. 'I do love you, Joe, and I always shall . . .'

She did not tell him that she had other plans for her day. Before she left London with Joe and his family, she wanted to say goodbye to Miss Edith. Perhaps now that so much time had passed, her former employer would have stopped being angry and might listen to her – and she wanted to ask if Miss Edith would go to the work-house and speak to Mistress Simpkins. If she could discover where Mr Stoneham lived, she could write to Ruth and tell her that Eliza was travelling with Joe.

Perhaps when she had earned a few coppers of her own, Eliza might be able to write to Miss Edith and to send her a letter to pass on to Ruth – and perhaps one day she might find a way of letting them know where they could write to her. It all depended on whether Miss Edith still thought Eliza was a thief.

Eliza waited until Joe had left for the prison. He could not walk all the way there and back in a few hours and must take the omnibus or a hansom cab, but that would cost a whole shilling and so he would walk part of the way and save sixpence. So Eliza had plenty of time to walk to Miss Edith's house while he was gone, for it would take no more than an hour.

She heard the ostler's wife call to her as she left the stable yard, but merely waved a hand at her. Usually,

Eliza was happy to perform any tasks the kind woman asked of her, because she gave them food and milk, and her husband allowed them to sleep in the hayloft. On her return she would go up to the house and ask what Mrs Ostler wanted. They called her that, just as they called her husband Ostler, though they knew their names were Will and Jenny.

Walking slowly but steadily, Eliza retraced the way she had come with Joe all those weeks earlier. She had not been back to the market, because she had no money to spend. Joe gave her food and Ostler's wife had given her a blanket and a comb for her hair, also some soap to wash herself, but no one gave her money. She regretted it, because she would have liked to buy a gift for Joe – and something for Mrs Ostler before they left, but no one thought she needed money.

When she came to the market, Eliza's nose twitched at all the exotic smells. She was tempted to linger by the stalls, looking at things she would have liked to buy. She saw a penknife with several attachments and thought how Joe would love it, but when she tentatively asked the price the stallholder said it was five shillings. Eliza could never have afforded so much and she shook her head, walking away reluctantly. A little further on she saw a stall with pretty scarves fluttering in the breeze but did not bother to ask the price. The only thing she might have bartered was the tortoiseshell comb Mrs Ostler had given her but she did not think she could buy either the penknife or the scarf with the few pennies it might raise.

She was about to leave the market when she heard a commotion behind her and saw that some children were stealing from a stall selling bread and cakes – and in that instant she recognised Tucker. She froze as she heard the enraged cries from the owner of the stall and then a constable blew his whistle and all hell broke loose as men and women started shouting and chasing the children. Tucker was coming towards her. He saw her, gave a start of recognition, and thrust a loaf at her, telling her to run. Eliza just stood where she was, stunned and unable to think. She was not even aware that she was holding a stolen loaf until a large hand descended on her shoulder.

'Here's one of 'em, officer,' a man said. 'She's been hanging around all morning.'

Eliza tried to protest. She had only been there a short time and she'd done nothing but look, but she could see the look of satisfaction in the constable's eyes as he grabbed hold of her arm.

'She looks a bit different from some of the others,' he said with a slight frown, 'but the proof is in the pudding – and she's one of 'em all right. She's got one of your loaves, Bert, and I saw the leader give it to her and tell her to run.'

'I didn't take it. I was just standin' here,' Eliza protested.

'Aye, but you're one of them,' the baker said coming up to them. 'I recognise her, officer. She used to hang around with the gang and she's got the bread – what more proof do yer need?'

It seemed the constable did not need more proof. He brought out a pair of handcuffs and put one on Eliza's wrist and the other on his own belt, fastening hers so tightly that it cut into her flesh. She wanted to scream and protest her innocence, but the men and women were jeering and complaining.

'They be nothin' but a nuisance them kids. 'Tis time they was stopped. Make an example of her, officer. Hang her – that would give them somethin' to think about.'

Eliza looked at the man who had spoken and knew him. He was the man she'd asked about the penknife. No doubt he thought she'd been planning to steal from him. Her throat was tight with emotion and she wanted to weep but instead she stuck her head in the air and said nothing, her pride making her stubborn. Why did everyone think she was a thief? She'd only once taken some food and that was because no one would give her work.

'Keep yer head up, girl,' the constable said, and his tone was not unkind. 'We don't hang young 'uns fer stealin' a loaf of bread these days.'

'I didn't steal it – he pushed it into my arm,' Eliza said, and then wished she hadn't as she saw disbelief in the portly constable's eyes. 'I live at the stables at Friar's End with Joe and Mrs Ostler – Jenny.' He gave her a stern look. 'I help in the kitchen sometimes and Joe works with the horses.'

'So what were yer doin' loiterin' round the market?'

'I just wanted a present for Joe but I have no money . . .' Eliza faltered as she saw the look in his eyes. 'I was only lookin'!'

'Save it for the magistrate in the mornin',' he said. 'My job is just to bring yer in, girl. Likely, they'll give yer a month in prison to teach yer a lesson.'

Eliza shivered as she saw the hard set of his mouth. He thought her guilty, just as the magistrate would in the morning. She might find herself locked up in prison somewhere and she'd heard terrible tales of the punishments handed out in the past. Men and women in the workhouse had talked about prison fever and people dying in their cells of starvation or sickness and she did not know how much was true and how much invented to scare the children into being good.

Eliza wished that she had never ventured near the market. She should have gone straight to Miss Edith's house. Miss Edith might think her a thief but she didn't believe her old mistress would have sent for the constable. Tears burned behind her eyes but she held them back. Crying was a sign of weakness and she had to stay strong. Whatever her punishment, she must take it and hold her head high. In the past, Eliza had been beaten and she'd gone hungry and she'd known bitter despair, but then she'd found happiness and that thought would sustain her throughout the ordeal to come . . .

'You wanted to see me?' Joan Simpkins asked in a belligerent tone. The elegant woman who had been shown into her office was exactly the kind of woman she disliked most. 'If you're looking for a baby I've none to sell at the moment. Give me your name and I'll be in touch when one is available.'

'No, I come in search of an older girl,' the woman replied in a soft voice. 'My aunt fell upon hard times some years ago and brought the babe to you – she asked you to care for her and hoped to return for the child but was unable to.'

Joan felt her stomach twist. It couldn't be – and yet this woman's hair was similar in colour to the child's.

'How long ago?' she demanded. 'Many children are brought in.'

'My aunt's name was Flora Miller,' Katharine said. 'I believe she called her child Eliza?'

For a moment Joan was too shocked to answer. She took a deep breath.

'There was such a girl here,' she said reluctantly. 'Her mother told me that her husband had been killed in a terrible accident and she was left next to penniless. She begged me to care for her child and I did.'

'Then the girl is still here?'

'No one came for her,' Joan said defensively. 'I allowed her to go to a mistress . . . a good woman.'

'You can tell me where she is?'

Joan thought quickly. She could never permit this young woman to discover the truth of how she had treated Eliza. 'I am not sure,' she prevaricated. 'I shall check my register. Please leave me your address and I will contact you.'

'Very well.' The elegant lady rose and placed two gold sovereigns on the table. 'There will be more if you can tell me where to find Eliza.'

Joan nodded and promised to do her best, but as she closed the door after her visitor a determined look came to her face. She must get Eliza back and make sure she couldn't tell her tale – and the best way to do that was to sell her to the major!

CHAPTER 25

'She ran away from you?' Joan looked at the other woman in disbelief. 'How could you have given her so much freedom? What did she steal from you?'

'Nothing,' Miss Edith said, and the look in her eyes showed Joan that the other woman despised her. 'We had a misunderstanding and she ran away before Christmas. I was going to come and ask you whether she had found her way back to the workhouse.'

'I have seen nothing of her. I should naturally have asked you if you wanted her back,' Joan lied and then frowned. 'After this bitter weather I very much doubt she is still alive. I do not see how a child of that age could survive alone on the streets.' Eliza was either dead of cold or starvation, or someone like the major had snatched her from the streets, in which case she might well be dead anyway.

'Oh, do not say so,' Miss Edith said and looked as if she might burst into tears. 'I have prayed that she was safe and well – perhaps someone else gave her work, for she is a good girl and intelligent.'

'Well, there is nothing more to be said.' Joan nodded

sharply and took her leave. She wanted no sentimentality, especially when she had been thwarted again. Eliza was worth a small fortune to Joan, but this stupid woman had let her slip through her fingers.

Leaving the apothecary's shop, Joan was thoughtful. She had to be careful these days, because her brother had begun taking an interest in her side of the workhouse. He'd warned her not to do anything foolish, told her that he would be very angry if she did something that attracted the attention of the governors, and that meant she dared not sell one of the children who had parents who would complain to the master.

It was as she approached the market that she saw some children being chased and the charge of theft was on several tongues. Stopping in her tracks, Joan realised that here was another source of merchandise that she had not considered. Children removed from the streets for petty theft or vagrancy were sometimes taken before the magistrate but more often than not the authorities simply sent them to one of the workhouses in the city. London was a large sprawling city and Joan received only some of those found on the streets in her area, but there must be many more. If she went down to the magistrates' court, where these children were often held overnight, she might see a suitable girl. She could offer her a place in the workhouse, say that she had work for several girls and see what they gave her. She might have to grease a few palms, but it would be worth it if she found something she could sell – a piece of high-quality merchandise.

Joan had decided to think of the children she sold in this way. It was foolish to consider what might happen to them afterwards; that was not her concern. She needed to please Major Cartwright and then she could retire and forget all this . . . unpleasantness.

Eliza sat in the corner in the magistrates' holding cell with several women and children. Most of them had been brought in because they were vagrants and were dressed in rags, their hands, hair and faces filthy, several of them so thin that their eyes were sunken and their skin hung loosely on their bodies.

One of the children came up to Eliza; she was sucking her thumb and her face was dirty, dried snot about her nostrils, and her eyes stuck with pus that she kept rubbing at. Great scabs covered half of her face and her hands and she was crying.

'Has yer got anythin' ter eat?' she asked and Eliza shook her head, but then remembered that she was still clutching the stolen loaf of bread. The constable had not bothered to take it away from her.

'Yes, have this,' she said, and pulled it out from beneath her shawl, where it had lodged. The child snatched at it and ran off into a corner but she was immediately surrounded by women and children, all grabbing at the loaf and trying to take it from her, punching, kicking and screaming until all the bread had been thrust into hungry mouths.

Eliza watched in horror. She'd known hardship and hunger in the workhouse and on the streets but she'd never experienced the kind of starvation that would make women steal bread from a child that needed it so badly. Turning away from the sight that made her want to weep, Eliza tried to shut out the sounds of fighting and screaming. If she'd known what would happen, she would have broken the bread into small pieces and distributed it, but she could never have known what wretches like these were capable of.

She hugged herself and thought about Joe. He would be so worried when he got back to the stables and found her gone. Would he think that she'd run off and deserted him, or would he realise that something like this had happened? Would he come looking for her? Hope flared in her, but she knew that Joe could not help her. Even if he came to the prison and told them that she was living with him, and innocent, they would not believe him. She'd been branded a thief and no one would listen . . .

Eliza had not realised how bad prison could be; the stench of unwashed bodies, the mould of ages encrusted on thick stone walls, and human waste created a thick miasma that polluted the air and choked her nostrils. If she was shut up with people like this for months she thought that she would either die or lose her senses.

'You say she did not come when you called to her?' Joe looked at Ostler's wife and frowned. 'Eliza promised she would come up to the house and help you today. I can't understand it. She knows I'll be back by now and I wanted to tell her my news. Pa is coming out this weekend and we're goin' orf to Ireland straight away.'

'My husband shall miss 'e, Joe,' Mrs Ostler said and shook her head. 'And I be sorry you'm be goin' – but you'll be glad to be with yer family.'

'Eliza was to come with us. Pa said he would take her and she'd be one of us – be my woman when she be full grown.'

'Well, maybe she didn't want that,' Ostler's wife said with a little shrug. 'Else she wouldn't 'ave run orf the way she 'ave.'

Joe shook his head impatiently. 'You don't understand. There's a bond between us and she do love me – and we be 'appy together. I reckon she'm be gone ter see a friend of hers. She'll be back soon enough.'

'Aye, she'll be back fer 'er her supper,' Mrs Ostler said shaking her head as Joe walked off to do his chores for the night. She reckoned the girl had gone off for reasons of her own and Joe would see no more of her.

Joe was uneasy as he worked steadily until the light was gone, feeding, watering and grooming the horses, and his heart was heavy when he stopped to wash in the water butt and eat the supper of cold meat, pickles and bread he'd brought for them. Where was Eliza? He was certain she would not stay out this long without some reason – someone had caught her, but who?

Was it that witch from the workhouse or the butcher or . . . no, it would not be that Miss Edith, because Eliza loved her and she could not love a wicked person.

Joe made up his mind that in the morning he would do his work and then go to look for her. He had only a few days before his father was released and Jez couldn't wait to shake the dust of London from his feet. He would not want to wait to look for a girl who was not of their people.

Joe had to find her before it was too late . . .

'I am looking for a girl,' Joan said when asked her business. 'I am Mistress Simpkins, and I have the care of all the females at the workhouse in Farthing Lane. One of my girls ran away from her mistress and she has asked me to look for her.' She gave the jailer a simpering smile. 'The girl I am looking for has pale hair and is thirteen years old.'

The man looked at her through narrowed eyes, chewed and then spat tobacco juice at her feet. 'Ain't no girls like that 'ere,' he said. 'Be orf wiv yer. Jed knows your sort – you're after a girl fer yer whorehouse.'

Joan bristled indignantly. 'How dare you? I am a respectable woman and I am looking for a girl who has run away from her mistress.'

The man stared at her in disbelief and spat again; this time his spittle landed on her shoe and she stared at him in disgust. About to turn away, she heard a noise and saw a door open and several bedraggled women and children were thrust through it. Joan watched in frustration as they were shepherded down the corridor towards a door marked courtroom 2.

Suddenly, one of the girls turned her head and looked back and Joan's heart jerked and raced with excitement. It was Eliza! She looked different, taller, her face brown as if she had spent time in the open air and much healthier than when Joan had last seen her, but it was her. Of course she must be nearly fourteen now but she was still slight for her age and dressed in rags might look younger – besides, her hair looked like a golden halo, even though it was tangled and windblown. Major Cartwright and his friends would pay well for such a beauty.

Instinct made her follow the little convoy into the large courtroom. Three magistrates had taken their places at the bench and a hush fell before the trials began. Women were brought before the justices and accused of soliciting for vile acts of prostitution, of vagrancy and of theft. The first four were condemned to three years in prison and were sent down, wailing and protesting their innocence. Then three children were pushed forward and accused of begging and vagrancy, and the magistrate said that they would be dealt with leniently.

'These children will be sent to the workhouse in Shoreditch,' he said, and they were taken away, no doubt to be collected by the master of that institution.

Joan cursed, because two of the children were girls and would have been worth a few pounds to her, but the girl she was most interested in had now been brought forward. She was the last and the magistrate had taken out his watch, clearly bored with the proceedings.

'What is the charge against this girl?' he asked.

'She stole a loaf of bread,' the constable said.

'No, I didn't!' Eliza spoke up, shocking everyone. 'I was on my way to visit a friend when I saw the riot. A loaf was thrust at me but I did not steal it. I work at the stables at Friars Court—'

'Silence!' the magistrate roared. 'You were not asked to speak.'

'But I am innocent,' Eliza protested. 'They say I'm a thief, but I have no need to steal—'

'Silence that child,' the magistrate roared, and the constable gripped Eliza's arm and hissed at her. She looked at him angrily, but her face was white and she said nothing.

'Is there anyone here to speak for this child?' the magistrate asked and looked about him.

It was Joan Simpkins' chance. She leapt to her feet and raised her hand. 'May I have permission to speak, sir?'

'Are you the mother of this disgraceful girl?'

'No, sir; I'm Mistress Joan Simpkins and I am warden of the workhouse in Farthing Lane, Whitechapel. This girl is Eliza Jones and I raised her from a babe. Last year I placed her with a mistress but she ran away from her. I believe her mistress would take her back and if your lordship would place the girl in my care, I will guarantee that she will not be brought before these courts again.'

'Have you proof of your identity, madam?' The magistrate looked at her intently.

'Not with me, sir, but I can bring proof in to you later today.'

'Then I sentence the girl to a month's hard labour – unless you return to collect her by three this afternoon.'

'No, I have work at the stables,' Eliza protested, but the constable tightened his grip on her arm.

The magistrate looked down his long nose at Eliza. 'You may think yourself fortunate that Mistress Simpkins was here to speak for you, girl. Had that not been the case I should not have hesitated to sentence you to six months in prison.'

Joan cursed beneath her breath but there was nothing more she could do. And unless she could prove her identity in time, the major would have to wait another month for the girl, but it could not be helped. She watched as Eliza was taken away, still protesting and trying to break away from the man who held her.

Eliza sat in the dark cell into which the only light came from a tiny barred window high above and tried not to weep. She had already been told that she would be transported to prison that afternoon at three and that the work would be truly hard.

'You'll be set to it as soon as you arrive,' one of the other women convicted that day told her. 'It's scrubbin' floors in the mornin' and sewin' sacks or canvas sails all afternoon. They give us gruel and bread twice a day, but if the bastards take a dislike ter yer they miss yer out on purpose, and they hit you with short sticks if they feel like it. I swore I'd never go back inside.'

'Then why have you?' Eliza asked.

'It weren't my choosin',' the woman said. 'My old man forced me to rob the punter what paid fer me. He told me ter wait till he slept and then steal 'is purse, so I did – only the so and so weren't asleep and he roused the watch.'

Eliza nodded, understanding what had not been said. The woman had a black eye and would have been mistreated by the man she called her husband.

'I'm Clara,' she told Eliza. 'You'll be fresh meat fer them inside – best stick close to me and I'll look out fer yer – but yer'll 'ave ter pay me. Give some of yer food . . .'

Eliza nodded, feeling miserable. The threat of prison was like a black cloud and she was close to tears when her name was called and a warder beckoned to her. She rose and walked towards him, shivering as he caught her arm.

'Yer wanted,' he said in answer to her look of inquiry, but Eliza couldn't answer him.

When she saw Joan Simpkins waiting for her, a smile of triumph in her eyes, Eliza felt no relief. She thought that prison might even have been better than being returned to the care of this woman.

Eliza was pushed towards her and Joan Simpkins took a length of twine from her bag, tied one end around Eliza's wrist and the other to her belt and nodded her satisfaction.

'Come along, Eliza,' she said. 'I shall return you to Miss Edith . . .'

Eliza stared at her in silence as she pushed her ahead of her. She remained silent until they had left the court, thinking over what the magistrate had said to her.

'Will Miss Edith really take me back?' she asked at last.

Joan Simpkins looked at her, an unpleasant smile on her face. 'We shall just have to see, shan't we? You are a difficult girl, Eliza. You have caused me more trouble than most. I have never been quite sure what to do with you.'

'You sold me to that butcher and you knew what kind of a man he was,' Eliza said resentfully. 'I think you sell all the children in your care if someone will buy them.'

'I see that your time away from my care has not improved your manners or your tongue,' Joan Simpkins said. 'I am still your mistress, Eliza, and if I choose to discipline you, there is no one to stop me.'

Eliza stopped walking and looked at her proudly. 'You're a hateful, wicked woman, that's what you are – and there's no justice for people like us. It's a crime to be poor. You can go to prison for stealing a loaf – but no one will give you work so what else can you do if you're hungry but steal? All of those women and children were condemned with no thought for the reason for what had brought them so low.'

Joan looked at her through narrowed eyes, surprised at her spirited response. Few women in her care would or could have spoken to her in such a reasoned manner. 'That is what the workhouse is there for – to provide a place for those too lazy or idle to work. We discipline those who would prey on the good nature of others, teach them to be good citizens and then, if they pass the test, we give them the chance to leave and work for their living.'

'You and your kind don't care about anyone,' Eliza said. 'Miss Edith is better than you and I'm sorry I ran away from her, but I thought . . .' She faltered, as if she were hiding something, Joan Simpkins thought.

'Ah yes, why *did* you run away, Eliza? Miss Richards would not tell me – but she is a foolish woman and soft. I see that I did wrong in giving you the chance of a better life. She deserves better than an insolent wretch like you. No, I must think of something else for you, Eliza.'

'Where are we going?' Eliza realised that they were not headed towards Miss Edith's shop. 'I won't go back to the workhouse – I won't!' She tugged at the twine binding her to Joan, but it was strong and she could not break it.

'Do not worry.' Joan smiled in triumph. 'You will not be long beneath my roof – I have other plans for you. This time you will go to a master who will not let you run away. This time you will learn to do as you're told . . .'

CHAPTER 26

'Thank you, Mr Brand, you have done well,' Arthur said to the man standing opposite him in his library. The candles were flickering and the fire had burned low. Outside, the wind was howling and he thought it had begun to rain. 'My own inquiries had come to naught. You are certain that Eliza has been taken to the workhouse?'

'Yes, sir, I followed them to be certain. I had traced them to a stable yard in Friar's Court – the gypsy boy and the girl you wish to find. They have been working there; the boy is good with horses and the girl helps the ostler's wife and sometimes sweeps out the stable.'

'She was arrested for theft, you say?' Arthur arched his brows. 'Did you see what happened?'

'I arrived at the market as she was being taken off by the constable. From what I heard she was accused of stealing a loaf from a baker's stall. She denied it when she was brought before the magistrate and said she had work at the stables, which I knew to be true. I was about to speak out when this woman leapt up said the girl had run away from her mistress and claimed her.'

'You did not speak out in the girl's defence?' Arthur frowned.

'No, sir, forgive me, I did not. My calling being what it is, I am not popular with officers of the law, who consider me a nuisance because I interfere with their work – so I thought it best to follow and see what happened and then tell you.'

'Very well,' Arthur said and tossed him a purse. 'You have done your job – keep yourself in readiness as I may have other work for you. There is a woman I need you to find – if she is living . . .'

'Whatever you wish, sir. I am always at your service.'

Arthur smiled, saving his curses for when he was alone. The man might have saved him a deal of work had he spoken up for Eliza at the magistrates' court, but he supposed his excuse for not speaking out was valid.

He took the gold pocket watch from his waistcoat and glanced at the time; it was late, past midnight, for his agent had been waiting hours to speak with him as Arthur had only recently returned from dining with Katharine and her aunt. From what Katharine had been able to tell him, Arthur was fully convinced that Eliza was his daughter and he intended to take care of her – and to see that Joan Simpkins was punished for her treatment of the girl. However, it would cause too much of a stir to arrive at the workhouse and demand to speak to Eliza at this hour. He would go first thing in the morning.

Eliza was not put in with the other women and children. Mistress Simpkins locked her into a tiny room with just a mattress and a chair to sit on. She went away and left Eliza alone for what seemed like hours, before returning with a cup of milk and some bread in the middle of the night.

'It would not suit me to starve you,' she said. 'Behave yourself and I shall not beat you, Eliza. Remember that I could take you back where I found you. You know your fate then, I think?'

Eliza nodded. She was angry, but common sense told her to drink and eat, because stubbornness would not win her freedom. She was determined to be free again. Eliza had run away before and she did not see why she could not do it again.

'Good. I see you have decided to be sensible, Eliza. When you've eaten, I shall take you to the bath house and you will wash yourself and your hair. You will put on the clothes I give you, and use the oil I shall provide on your skin. It smells pleasant – and I daresay you would like to be rid of the stink of the prison, wouldn't you, Eliza?'

Eliza stared at her, and then inclined her head. There was only one reason the mistress would be kind to her and it was not a good one. She intended to sell her again – and Eliza knew enough of the world now to guess her probable fate. Miss Edith had warned her not to talk to strange men in the market – and more than one man had tried to abuse her. She would be shut up in one of those houses where men took their pleasure of women who were unable to refuse them. Molly had lived in such a place for many years, though now she was free to come and go as she pleased, and that was because she pleased Master Simpkins.

Molly would help her if she knew, but Mistress Simpkins was being careful to keep her presence in the workhouse a secret. She must be afraid that someone would stop her – and that could only be her brother. Ruth had always spoken of the master as being better than his sister – but he could not help her even if he would, because his sister would make sure that he did not know Eliza was here beneath his roof.

Escape from the workhouse was rare. Joe had managed it and one or two others over the years, but Eliza was being guarded and Mistress Simpkins would catch her if she tried to slip away to the cellar. Joe had told her there was a way out, but she had to reach the cellar first.

As she washed and clothed herself in the worn-out child's dress she'd been given, Eliza's mind was too busy to wonder why she'd been given something that was too small for her. It was too difficult to escape from this place so she must wait until they were outside again – perhaps when they arrived at the house to which she was to be taken.

The perfumed oil provided for her was strong and Eliza used the merest drop; she thought it best to obey her mistress. Mistress Simpkins might decide to beat her into submission if she resisted.

It was only just light as they left the workhouse. Her mistress was taking no chances of being seen and having her plans thwarted. Once again, Eliza was bound by a thin twine, which she knew she could not break. So there was no possibility of escape on the journey to her new prison.

She made no attempt to pull away for there was no point in struggling when she was securely bound. She looked about her as they walked, seeking some way of escape but nothing presented itself – and then she saw him watching her. Joe had come looking for her! A surge of relief went through her, lifting her spirits. Eliza pointed to her waist, indicating the twine that bound her. She saw Joe nod and put a finger to his lips and inclined her head. Was Joe intending to try and free her or merely to follow? All she could do was stay alert and wait.

Joe saw them emerge from the workhouse side gate. He had been wondering whether to enter through the tunnel he'd dug to escape when he saw them leave and knew that the old witch had made Eliza her prisoner. His immediate desire was to rush at them, cut the cord that bound Eliza and run away, but it looked too strong to cut quickly and he thought it was too risky. Even as he decided he must try, someone caught his arm and he turned to find himself staring into the face of a woman he vaguely recognised from his brief stay in the workhouse.

'You're Molly,' he said after a moment. 'Mistress's got Eliza and she's takin' her somewhere – she'll sell her to a cruel master again.'

'Yes,' Molly agreed. 'She has made a bargain with someone – a man who wants to use Eliza for his evil purposes.'

'We have to stop her,' Joe said fiercely, prepared to attack the witch with his knife, to wound or kill her if necessary.

'No,' Molly warned. 'Eliza be her ward and we might both end up in prison and Eliza would still be sold. I know someone who can stop her – but I need you to follow and watch where they go, though I know where Mistress went last night. I must find Mr Stoneham and let him know what is happening. He will say what must be done.'

'How do you know all this?' Joe looked at her, not sure whether to believe her.

'I watch what mistress does and I reckon I know who she be about to sell Eliza to – and believe me, you don't want that to 'appen. I'll bring Mr Stoneham to the house she visited the last night, but if I am not there by ten o'clock at the latest, meet me by the market and tell me where Eliza has been taken.'

'But—' Joe wanted to protest, because he thought they could free Eliza together.

'If we stop her this time, she'll do it again,' Molly said. 'She must be caught in the act; so go on, follow them, or we may lose them.'

Joe nodded and set off in pursuit of Eliza. When she noticed him and pointed to the twine about her waist his heart nearly broke to see the look of appeal in her eyes. She was hoping he would rescue her and he was tempted to ignore Molly's warnings and attack the woman who had so ill-treated Eliza and others. Yet he knew that if he harmed her bodily there would be such a hue and cry. If they were caught they would both go to prison – or worse. Joe knew that his father needed him and he would soon be free. He was torn between his longing to free Eliza and his fear that it might end badly, so he put his finger to his lips and smiled at his friend, trying to tell her that all would be well. Eliza trusted him; she must know that he would find a way of helping her – and perhaps Molly was right. Only a man of standing could stop this evil woman from carrying out her evil trade; he must be patient and bide his time.

Eliza looked at him again and he nodded. She inclined her head and then very deliberately she winked.

Joe's heart swelled with pride and love. His Eliza was so brave. She understood that there was a plan to save her and she was not afraid. Joe followed, not close enough for the old witch to catch sight of him but near enough so that he would not lose them in the labyrinth of dirty lanes and ancient filthy courts that Mistress Simpkins led them through. It was obvious that she was not taking a direct route lest someone was following, yet she had not noticed him, Joe was sure.

At last they paused outside a large but neglected-looking house at the end of one of the ancient courts; this rookery of slums was the haunt of rogues and thieves and even the constables stayed clear of them. From what Joe could see, most of the other houses were abandoned, and one was boarded at the windows. Mistress Simpkins knocked at the door and waited. A man opened the door almost at once and nodded at her and she entered, pushing Eliza in front of her. Eliza turned and threw a desperate look in Joe's direction; he nodded to her and mouthed the words: 'Soon. We'll come soon . . .'

Joe was on thorns once the door was closed. Had he done the right thing? Should he have cut Eliza's cord and trusted to their speed of foot to outrun the mistress

302

of the workhouse? If anything happened to her in that house Joe thought that he would never forgive himself. For a moment he thought of pounding on the door and demanding to be let in, but what then? No he must simply wait and trust that Molly would bring help.

Eliza's courage had carried her thus far, but once the door closed behind them, a chill seized her and she started trembling, her teeth chattering as though she was cold. The large hall was dark and had bars on the only window she could see, and the air smelled strange, making her stomach clench with fear. What was that smell? It was rather like the scent in a church when the priest burned incense.

The man who had let them in had left immediately, disappearing up a flight of steep stairs, and for a few minutes she and Mistress Simpkins were alone. Eliza felt as if she were in a nightmare, as if this could not be real. Then she heard the sound of heavy feet and a large man entered the room. He was dressed in a long loose gown which was made of brightly coloured silk embossed with patterns of a mythical animal, and clung to his bulky body where it was tied loosely in the middle. He wore a turban around his head, strings of beads hung from his neck, and his feet were bare. He had long feet and the toes curled at the ends with yellowed nails. The strange scent Eliza had noticed was much stronger now and seemed to waft about him – and his eyes were staring at her hungrily. She felt the vomit rise in her throat; she knew what that look meant.

'She is just what we want,' he said and his fat body shook with laughter beneath the loose gown. Eliza felt a surge of revulsion and hatred for this creature. How dare he look at her that way! 'You have done well, dear lady. She is well worth what I promised you.'

He handed over a heavy purse. Mistress Simpkins opened it and tipped some of the coins into her hand. Eliza saw the gleam of gold and an answering gleam of avarice in the woman's eyes. How evil she was! Selling innocent children for her profit, uncaring of what happened to them. Eliza wished that something bad would happen to her. Joe had seemed to tell her that rescue was coming, but Eliza was very afraid. She thought the fat man was wearing nothing but his robe and the thought of what he meant to do to her made her feel ill. She turned suddenly and vomited on the dark red carpet.

'What have you given her?' the man accused angrily. 'Is she sick?'

'She was perfectly all right when we came in,' Mistress Simpkins said and frowned. 'It's that awful stink in here – what is it?'

'Opium,' the man said and laughed softly. 'She will grow used to it in time. Untie her and go – I will come to you when we need more merchandise.'

Mistress Simpkins hesitated for a moment and Eliza wondered at the odd expression in her eyes – but in a moment it had gone and she released Eliza from her bonds, turned, walked to the door, opened it and went out.

The door was not locked! Eliza's mind seized on the information even as her thoughts spun furiously. Only that door stood between her and freedom.

'Now, at last, we shall enjoy ourselves, my little one,'

the man said in a voice that resembled a cat's purring. Anger was stronger than fear now. He was evil and he had no right to own her as if she were a piece of furniture. Joe had told her no one had the right to own another or use them for their own ends.

Revolted by the sight and smell of him, Eliza knew that she could not just wait for help to come; she must escape now, before it was too late. Once the door was locked, she would be a prisoner and she sensed that there would be no escape then. This house was a fortress but for just this one moment it was vulnerable. She ran to the door and tugged, trying to pull it open and follow Mistress Simpkins out into the fresh air, but the man grabbed her from behind, holding her pressed against him. She could smell the sickly sweet odour of his body mixed with the other strange scent, and kicked out at his shins violently as she felt his hands on her. He grunted but held on to her, his hot wet mouth pressed against her neck. She shuddered with disgust, anger making her even more determined. He was horrible and she would not put up with this; she would rather die! Jerking backwards with her elbow, Eliza felt it make contact with his body and heard him cry in pain. For a moment his hold loosened; she leapt away from his grasp, searching for some way of escape. But he was between her and the door and the window was barred; there was no other way out. She had to reach that door before it was locked and the key removed. Her frantic gaze fell upon a heavy metal object that she vaguely recognised as a brass doorstop and she darted at it, seizing it and brandishing it.

'Fred, I need you!' the fat man shouted and Eliza

knew that once his servant arrived she would be overpowered. Driven by her fear and revulsion, she struck out at the man who stood between her and freedom, hitting his legs with the metal object with all her strength, and, as he buckled and went down on his knees, she struck at his head and saw the blood spurt. He pitched forwards, face down, moaning slightly.

Eliza was terrified. She knew she had killed him and it meant she would hang if she were caught. She ran round his body where it lay on the floor, the blood pooling. Breathlessly, she wrenched at the door and, as it fell back, darted through the opening. Eliza heard the servant shouting behind her in the house and feared that she would be recaptured and dragged back inside, but then, as she reached the pavement, Joe sprang at her and caught her hand.

'I was so afraid they would come too late and I was right!' Joe said. 'How did you escape? I saw that evil woman come out but . . .'

'I killed him,' Eliza said, shaking with terror. 'We have to run, Joe. If they catch us I'll hang.'

Joe saw Molly coming with a man he did not know, but he grabbed Eliza's hands and pulled her down one of the tiny alleyways that abounded in these ancient slums, tugging her with him as he ran for his life and hers. By helping her escape, Joe knew that he was a party to murder and if they were caught, both of them could hang.

He heard Molly call to him but did not look back. The man with her might be good but he could not trust to that; their only chance was to run. They must hide for two days and then they would leave London with his father. In Ireland they would be safe and it was the only way Joe knew to protect Eliza.

'Too late,' Arthur said as he saw the children disappear into the maze of ancient courts and alleyways. 'But at least she escaped the fate they planned for her. Most girls disappear never to be heard of again once they are taken.'

'Eliza be always stubborn and resourceful,' Molly said. 'And Joe escaped from the workhouse and everyone thought him dead. I think she be safe enough with him for the moment.'

'But for how long while men like that live?' Arthur was staring angrily at the house, from which a servant had emerged and was looking down the lane. 'I intend to see that this one ends up where he belongs.'

Molly watched as he crossed the road, spoke to the servant and then thrust him to one side and entered the house. He was in there a few moments and then the servant came out and went running off down the road. Arthur came to the door and beckoned to her. Entering uncertainly, she saw a man sitting on the floor holding a napkin to a wound at the side of his head. He had bled quite a lot and it had pooled on the carpet.

'He's in no fit state to cause you any bother,' Arthur told her, 'but just watch him while I take a look upstairs – in case any other girls are being held here against their will . . .'

'She was to be a servant,' the man sitting on the floor mumbled as Arthur made ready to leave. He sounded drunk or dazed and Molly thought, from the reek of him, that it was a combination of the drug he had taken and the blow to his head, which had stunned him long enough to help Eliza make her escape. In Molly's mind it was a pity the child hadn't struck a bit harder, but she'd obviously hit him with all the strength she could muster. 'Little hellcat . . . not like the others . . .'

'What others?' Arthur demanded, delaying his investigation. He grabbed hold of his victim, hauling him roughly to his feet. 'You'd best tell me, Major Cartwright. You have already ruined yourself, so you may as well make a clean breast of it – and then I'll decide whether you should live.'

'Not my fault if they get too rough with them,' the major mumbled, his words slurring. He was clearly not capable of rational thought because of the opium he had used. 'Never mind; get another one from Mistress Joan . . . dear lady . . .' He gave a foolish little giggle, as if it were funny.

Arthur let go of him and he slumped to the floor again, too drugged to really understand what had happened or what he'd just said.

'If he moves, hit him again,' Arthur said to Molly and ran up the stairs. He was soon down again and shaking his head. 'He's alone in the house. I sent his servant for the doctor, but I also warned him that his master would soon be arrested for his crimes and I think it likely he may not return.'

However, the servant was back, bringing a doctor with him, by the time Arthur had completed a full search of the house. He took a few items he thought might help to convince the magistrate of Major Cartwright's addiction to drugs, and then spoke to the doctor, telling him what had happened here. When asked for confirmation, the major's servant decided to make a full confession, and Arthur asked him if he would accompany him to the magistrate's house. He agreed after he was promised that he would not be accused of being complicit in his master's crimes.

'They've killed other girls,' he told Arthur as they walked. Molly followed, listening, willing to give her testimony if it was requested, which she eventually did at the magistrate's bidding. 'I don't mind their bad ways, but I don't hold with that, sir.'

Molly's story took a long time to relate and every word of it was written down. Arthur backed her up by relating how she had twice come to him with stories of Mistress Simpkins perfidy and how Major Cartwright had backed her the first time and been instrumental in her being allowed to continue her wicked practices.

'Where is the child who fought this vile creature off?' the magistrate asked.

'I believe I know where she might go,' Arthur said. 'But first we must confront that woman – and one of your officers should go at once to the house we told you of and arrest that vile creature. If he once recovers his senses and remembers, I daresay he may choose to disappear rather than face the consequences.'

'Yes, Mr Stoneham, of course.' The magistrate called for one of his officers and gave orders. 'It is rare that we have proof of wrongdoing such as this – though we know it is happening. The murder of a child is a serious offence and we shall bring the culprits to justice.'

'I pray you do,' Arthur said, satisfied that Major Cartwright would have many questions to answer, though whether the law would be able to hold him was another matter. Too many of his kind managed to escape justice because they had power and influence, and it was difficult to find proof of their guilt. 'I shall go myself to Mistress Simpkins. I want her out of that place and unable to harm another of its unfortunate inmates.'

Molly followed him from the magistrate's house. 'What should I do, sir? Master Simpkins knew little of this – I would swear to it. You will not pursue him because of his wicked sister?'

'If Master Simpkins is innocent then I have no cause to harm him, though he is not fit to be in charge of the workhouse,' Arthur said. 'You may tell him that he will be treated fairly but his sister will pay the price – and I must thank you once again for all you have done to help me bring her to justice.'

'I hated her,' Molly said simply. 'I didn't want her to do to others what she did to me.'

'Then I hope you have some satisfaction in her downfall,' Arthur said, and grunted with satisfaction as he saw the woman he was after hailing a hackney cab. He sprinted across the road, catching her arm as the cab drew into the kerb.

'The railway station,' Mistress Simpkins said to the driver, but Arthur swung her round.

'I think not, madam,' he said and saw the fear in her eyes as she saw him and then Molly.

'How dare you obstruct me?' she demanded. 'I shall call for an officer of the law . . .'

'Then I shall be delighted to hand you over to him, Miss Simpkins. From what I know of the law you – and perhaps your brother – will be spending the rest of your lives in prison. At the very least he will leave his positon here, for we know this place is badly run. And we have the major in custody and we know you gave him Eliza – and you have sold others.'

'No – just her,' she said but the spark of defiance had gone. 'I was a fool because I knew what he was, but he offered me so much money and I wanted to leave this place . . .'

'And your brother – what did he get out of it?'

'My brother had nothing to do with it,' she said, and he saw defeat in her eyes. 'Robbie is weak and he has his vices but the rest was down to me . . .'

'Then I shall see he receives justice,' Arthur said. 'As for you, madam – I hope they hang you, though I daresay you will be confined to prison for the rest of your life.'

CHAPTER 27

'Good morrow, sir,' Jenny Ostler said when she answered her kitchen door next morning. 'If you have a horse to stable, my husband is in the yard . . .'

'I have a request to make of you, madam,' Arthur said and gave her a smile that was meant to put her at ease. 'I believe you may have a young girl living here and I should like to speak to her.'

'What be you wanting with Eliza, sir?' She was an honest woman and made no pretence of not understanding. 'She's in the stables with Joe and his father I reckon, for they're about to leave. I shall be sorry to see them go, for the girl has been a big help to me – and Joe has a way with horses like no other.'

'I mean no harm to either of them,' Arthur said. 'If I may, I shall walk down to the stable now and speak with them.'

Arthur nodded to her, turned and began to walk across the large yard towards the blocks of stables. It was a cobbled yard, strewn with straw and horse dung, and he could see the ostler talking to a customer and discussing a great black horse, which was stamping its feet, clearly uneasy in new surroundings.

'I'll be with yer in a moment, sir,' the ostler said.

Arthur smiled and walked on. There were two blocks of stables and he was not sure exactly where Eliza and Joe would be. He did not want to frighten them, because the last thing he wanted was for Eliza to run away again. Arthur hoped to persuade her that she should live with Ruth – or, if she preferred, with Miss Edith Richards.

Catching sight of a girl with fair hair standing outside one of the stables, he paused. She had grown since he'd last seen her and he was uncertain whether it could be the same girl. No, it must be her! Arthur's pulses raced. He now truly believed that Eliza was his daughter, his blood, even if there was no written proof. She was Sarah's child and he wanted to protect her, to make up for all that she had suffered, yet he did not wish to startle or frighten her. As he paused to watch for a moment, she went into the stable through the open door.

'Joe, you be foolish lad.' Joe's father was speaking as Eliza paused outside the stable. 'We can't take her with us. She will be hunted, and if they find her with us, we'll all be taken as murderers. They will hang me, for I am branded a troublemaker, and you'll go to prison.'

'I won't leave her here,' Joe said stubbornly. 'Eliza is my friend and I promised her she could come with us.'

'If she had not killed that man I would have taken her – though we might still have been in trouble. She is a child and folk do blame us for stealin' children. She would always be a danger to us – and I'll not risk all our lives for her sake.'

'Then you must go alone,' Joe said, and his mouth set stubbornly. 'I will not come with you to Ireland unless Eliza comes too.'

'You will do as I bid you,' his father said and took hold of his shoulder roughly. 'I am not a violent man, Joe, but if you defy me, I will thrash you!'

'I don't care, I'm not coming with you,' Joe said and glared at him.

'You must go with your pa,' Eliza said softly and they both whirled round to look at her for neither had heard her enter. 'He is right – I should mean trouble for you. I am wanted for murder and when they catch me I shall hang.'

'No! I will not let them take you.' Joe looked angrily at his father. 'We will go away somewhere together, Eliza. In Ireland you would be safe.' He looked at his father with a mixture of appeal and stubbornness. 'I can't leave her here, Pa. Either she comes, or I stay.'

'Joe lad,' his father said and shook his head. 'If it were not for the murder I would risk it – but don't you see? There will be a hue and cry out for her and if we're discovered . . .'

'We could colour her hair black and rub dirt on her face and no one will know her,' Joe said and now he was pleading. 'If you do not help us I shall never forgive you.'

'No, Joe,' Eliza said softly and touched his arm. 'Your pa is right. I should only bring trouble on you. You must go to Ireland with him – and one day perhaps you will come back and find me.'

'But what will you do?' Joe asked. 'How can you live alone? I want to look after you, to take you with me . . .'

'Eliza will not be alone. She has friends who care for her . . .' Another man's voice startled them all. Joe sprang in front of Eliza, his fists up like a prizefighter, ready to defend her with his last breath.

'I won't let you take her! I won't let her be hung or left to rot in prison.'

'Eliza didn't kill that man,' Arthur said and smiled at Joe. 'Some of us might wish she had rid the world of a foul creature who is not fit to live – but she will not go to prison, nor will she be hung. It is he who will face trial and, if there is any justice, face imprisonment though I fear he will escape the rope for lack of proof.'

Joe frowned, his brow wrinkling, then, 'You're the man Molly brought yesterday . . .'

'We intended to rescue Eliza but the clever girl rescued herself,' Arthur said. His gaze moved to Eliza's face, seeing her apprehension and doubt. Obviously, she did not trust him, and who could blame her? He played his only card. 'Ruth wants to see you, Eliza, and so does Miss Edith – they both love you, and you would be welcome to live with either of them . . .'

'Miss Edith is not angry with me?' Eliza said, her heart beating a little wildly now, but the fear had gone. She looked at him uncertainly. 'Are you Mr Stoneham, sir?'

'Yes, Eliza, I am – and I must humbly beg your pardon.' She looked puzzled and he reached out his hand to her. 'I knew something was amiss that day I saw you being tended by Ruth in the workhouse infirmary. I should have taken you away then and found you a good home. Had I done so, you would have avoided much suffering. Can you forgive me for leaving you there, Eliza?'

Eliza's eyes stung with tears, but she blinked them away. 'Will you take me to Ruth, please?' she said.

'Eliza – you must come with us,' Joe said and caught her arm. 'Do not trust him; he might take you back to that evil woman.'

'Miss Simpkins is no longer employed at the workhouse,' Arthur said. 'Indeed, she is awaiting trial for her crimes. Her brother is abjectly apologetic for what she did and may escape with a reprimand. I think he has learned a hard lesson. However, Eliza will never be forced to live in such a place again. The choice of where she lives is hers.'

'I shall go to visit Ruth and then I must see Miss Edith,' Eliza said and threw herself at Joe and hugged him. 'I might have died this winter had you not cared for me and helped me, but I do not want to cause trouble for your family. You must go with your father – but one day, if you still want us to be together, return to London and we shall talk then.'

'If you go with him I will come with you to make sure you are safe,' Joe said and glared at Arthur and then turned to his father. 'I shall return, but only if Eliza is safe and happy.'

'Joe, perhaps now we might risk it,' his father said but Eliza shook her head.

'No, you would not help her when I asked,' Joe said

316

and the look he gave his father was cold. 'You are my father and I must obey you – but I shall not forgive you.'

Eliza looked at Jez's face and saw the pain in his eyes. 'You must learn to forgive,' she whispered as she took Joe's hand. 'If I can forgive, so can you.'

Joe shook his head stubbornly, holding her hand tight as they followed Arthur from the stable. Outside the stable yard there was a gig waiting and a lad not much older than Joe stood holding the reins of the impatient horse, which was pawing at the ground and clearly not happy at being kept standing.

Joe went to the horse's head and put his mouth close to the horse's nose, breathing gently and whispering soothing words. It quietened at once and he looked at the lad scornfully.

'You should 'ave walked it,' he said, and then climbed up beside Arthur and Eliza.

Arthur tossed the crestfallen lad a coin, took the reins and the lad stood back releasing the horse. 'Where did you learn that?' Arthur asked of Joe as they moved away.

'My father breaks horses for his living. But I knew it from the moment I saw my first horse and rode on its back. Horses either trust you or they don't.'

'You have a wise head on you, Joe.' Arthur nodded to him. 'One day, when you are older and can make your own choices, you may come to me for a job in my stables.'

'I could work for yer now,' Joe said.

'You could, and if you had no family, I would take you gladly,' Arthur told him. 'But Eliza was right, Joe.

317

You owe duty to your father and I should be a rogue if I took you from him. I am not that rogue, Joe – though it is my loss, for a talent such as yours is not easily met with. I shall hope that one day you will choose to return.'

Eliza saw that Arthur Stoneham's words had soothed the anger in her friend. She smiled and sat closer to Joe, because she knew that soon he would be forced to leave her and go to Ireland with his father. It was the right thing for him for now, because although they belonged together they were both children and Eliza was wise enough to know that their time was not yet. It would come one day, but she wanted time to become a woman and to learn all she could of life first.

'Mr Stoneham is right,' she whispered. 'One day we shall be together, Joe – and then nothing shall part us.'

'You promise on your heart?' Joe placed his arm across his chest and Eliza did the same.

'I promise,' she said. 'One day we shall travel wherever we please, Joe, but we are too young to go alone. People would always try to part us and lock us up in schools or the workhouse. When we are older they will not be able to part us.'

'As long as you are safe and happy, I shall go to Ireland,' Joe said, 'but I shall not forgive him, Eliza . . .'

Eliza shook her head but said no more. Joe was angry because his father had broken his word. He'd told Joe that she could go with them, but then he'd changed his mind because he feared she might bring trouble on them. Eliza knew that Jez had some right on his side. There was something about her that attracted trouble and she did not wish to cause a breach with Joe's family. If he

318

came back for her, they would have their time – but that time was not yet.

'Eliza, my love, my girl – you be grown so!' Ruth cried as she saw her enter the house. She rushed at her and hugged her to her ample bosom, tears running down her cheeks.

'Ruth, I'm so glad to see you,' Eliza said. 'I wanted to visit you but I did not know where you lived – and you are only a few streets from the market where I shopped for Miss Edith. All this time I have needed you, and I could've visited you!' She felt tears on her cheeks and wiped them away.

'Oh, sir, how can I thank you for bringing her back to us?' Ruth said. 'I have feared for her day and night – at the mercy of that evil woman.'

'Mistress Simpkins was not the worst of them,' Eliza said and gave a giggle of sheer relief. She was safe at last, and she had Mr Stoneham to thank for it. 'But you are right, Ruth; I must thank you, sir, for bringing me here.'

He nodded, looking at her oddly, a faint wistfulness in his eyes as if he wanted to say something to her and could not find the words.

'Have you eaten?' Ruth said and looked at Joe curiously. 'You're not dead then, lad. We all thought mistress buried you in the cellar, for the men heard noises coming from there.'

'That was me digging my way out,' Joe said and grinned at her.

'Well, I've some good stew if either of you is hungry.'

'I am,' Joe said and looked at Eliza. 'We had bread

and a cup of milk this mornin' – and that stew smells good.'

'Will you stay too, sir?' Ruth looked past Eliza at her employer who had picked up his hat and gloves.

'No, thank you, Ruth, not this time. I have other business. Eliza is safe now and I shall return later to speak to you.' He nodded to Joe. 'Remember what I said, lad. When you're older there will always be a job in my stables.'

'Thank you, sir. I'll not forget.'

'Thank you, sir,' Eliza said and looked at him. 'I shall see you again?'

'Oh yes, be sure that I shall not forget you,' he said, looked at her for a moment and tipped his hat to her before he left.

'He is such a good master,' Ruth said after he had gone. 'Now, you two, come to the kitchen. Cook has been waiting to see you, Eliza – and she'll be surprised to see you, Joe.'

'Ruth, will you come with me to Miss Edith's house after we've eaten?' Eliza asked. 'Mr Stoneham said she had forgiven me – but I would rather not go alone.'

'You know you can bide 'ere with us, love?' Ruth said, a little surprised.

'Yes, I know, and I shall come often to visit,' Eliza told her, 'but I want to learn all the things Miss Edith can teach me for I should like to be an apothecary one day, if she will take me back. She helps so many, Ruth, and I should like to do the same.'

Ruth frowned. 'She has not been well of late, Eliza. I daresay she needs a little help with her work.'

'Then may we go after we have eaten?'

'Of course we shall,' Ruth said, 'for I know she has been anxious for your safety.'

Miss Edith had just finished serving a customer when they entered the shop and had her back to them as she tided something into a drawer.

'I shall not keep you a moment . . .' The words died on her lips as she turned and saw Eliza. Immediately, the colour left her cheeks and she swayed, and then the silent tears started to trickle down her face. 'God be praised! Eliza, my love. Forgive me. I beg you will forgive me for the wicked things I said to you.'

Eliza dodged round the counter and threw her arms about her, hugging her, her face against her thin body, feeling the bones so prominent now. Miss Edith had lost weight and seemed more fragile. Tears were on Eliza's face as she looked up at the woman she both admired and loved, understanding that in many ways their roles had been reversed. In the years ahead, it would be Eliza who cared for this woman, nursing her through the long illness that had just begun to show its ugly head.

'You are too thin,' she scolded. 'I see that I have not returned a moment too soon. I think you have not been eating properly, Miss Edith.'

'The food choked me when I thought of you starving on the streets.'

'I have not starved – or only a few times,' Eliza said. 'This is my good friend Joe. He took care of me and I would have gone to Ireland with him but then Mr Stoneham found me and told me I was not a murderer – and so I came back to you. Will you have me back, ma'am? Mr Stoneham says I'm in no trouble, even though I hit the man who grabbed me and made his head bleed.'

'If he sought to harm you, he deserved it,' Miss Edith said and smiled through her tears. 'My dear girl . . .'

'He was a bad man and Mr Stoneham says he should hang if there was any justice, but I care only that he should not harm other children.'

'You are so grown-up,' Miss Edith said, looking at her in wonder. Eliza had grown in inches but also in her manner of speaking and thinking. When she had run away she had been a child, but now she was a young woman, though still only thirteen years. Yet she had a maturity that made her seem older and it could only be because of the way she had lived; it had made her stronger, wiser and more caring, although she had always been able to give love. 'Oh yes, Eliza, if you can forgive me, I should be happy to have you live with me.'

'You will teach me all you know of herbs,' Eliza said, 'and I shall look after you . . .'

Eliza heard the shop door close behind her and when she turned round she saw that Joe had gone without saying goodbye. Her first thought was to run after him, but then she realised that he had taken the only way he knew how to part, for any other would be too painful. It had been settled between them. He must do his duty, which was to go with his father, and hers was to look after the woman who had been such a good friend to her, because she knew that Miss Edith was ill. She looked frail and was clearly in need of loving tender care – which Eliza would give her.

'Thank you for bringing her back to me,' Miss Edith said, looking at Ruth.

'You must thank Mr Stoneham for that,' Ruth said. 'Eliza asked me to come here with her, but it was he who brought her to us – and I shall remember him in my prayers every night for it.'

Miss Edith made a little sign of the cross over her breast. 'I shall do the same. Ruth, you will take tea with us whenever you have the time to spare? You are always welcome here, for it was you that cared for my dear Eliza like a mother all those years she was shut up in that terrible place.'

Ruth's face lit up with pleasure. 'I thank you for the invitation and you are both welcome to call on us. I shall leave you now, Eliza, for I believe that you are safe here.'

Eliza ran to her and hugged her. 'I love you, Ruth,' she whispered, 'but this is where I must live – do you understand?'

'Yes, I understand,' Ruth said and kissed the top of her head. 'Take care of her, my Eliza. She needs you very much just now.'

Eliza stood back as her friend left and then returned to Miss Edith. 'Why don't you go and rest with a nice pot of tea? I can serve the customers and anything I don't know, I'll come and ask.'

'No, put the closed sign on the door,' Edith said. 'We have so much to talk about, Eliza, and it's time I had a little holiday . . .'

Outside, in the street, Ruth paused for a moment and fingered the trinket in her pocket, the diamonds sharp beneath her finger. She had meant to give it to Eliza

323

but this was not the time. This was a happy reunion for the girl and it might cause her unhappiness to think of the woman who had placed that trinket inside her shawl. The identity of her mother was still a mystery to Ruth and there was no way of solving it that she knew. Pray God, Eliza would come to no more harm and there would be plenty of time to give her the half-penny set in gold and clasped by diamonds.

Ruth was observant and she'd noticed how struck Arthur Stoneham had been when he saw the trinket she'd taken from Eliza's shawl. Her instinct told her that he knew more than he'd revealed to her. Perhaps there was some connection between him and Eliza. Ruth could not know but she believed that her employer would watch over the girl she loved and for the moment she was content with that. Eliza had been found and she was happy and perhaps that was all that truly mattered.

CHAPTER 28

Arthur stood looking into his dressing mirror. He was wearing riding dress and about to set out on a jaunt into the country. Katharine had told him much of her own story since that afternoon they had talked in her carriage. She had wept as she described the grief that had ruined her life and almost killed her poor father.

'Marianne was his darling, for she looked just like my mother,' Katharine had explained. 'I loved her, and she cared for me. She would never have left without saying goodbye to me. Folk said that she had run away with a lover, but I know it was not true. She had been to visit friends that afternoon and it was summer, so we did not worry until it grew dusk . . .'

'You have never heard from her?' Arthur asked, and she shook her head.

'No, nor found anything but one shoe in the woods . . .'

'A shoe was found?' Katharine nodded, and it brought a frown to his face. 'Some folk thought she must be dead – but I feel that she is still alive, and yet she would surely let me know she lives – if she could.'

'Many years have passed,' Arthur said, 'but we can begin a search for her though it may bring no news.'

'We searched and searched and our friends did all they could,' Katharine said, sighing. 'I fear she is lost to us . . .'

'Yet I shall do what I can to find her for you, my dearest love.'

Katharine smiled and thanked him. 'I do not expect it, but it would mean so much to me.'

'Tell me everything you remember,' he said gently, 'and I will return to your old home and see if there is any clue that might lead us to her.'

'Yes, and if there is not, then – then I must accept that she is truly lost.'

'I found Eliza against all the odds,' he told her, 'and I believe she is my child, though there is no final proof and never can be. I shall not tell her yet, but I shall watch over her and keep her safe. If I find your sister, my love, it may be that we shall have to do the same for her.'

'You mean that she may have suffered too much to ever come back to us?'

'If she has been lost more than twelve years it is unlikely that she is the girl you knew,' he said and held her hand. 'Finding her does not mean she will be happy to be found.'

'Yet, I would know the truth . . .'

'Then I shall set my agents to finding her,' he promised.

Arthur picked up the bag his manservant had packed for him. There was but one way to discover the truth and he could only hope that if he found Katharine's sister it would not grieve her too much.

As he took leave of his household and went out to where his groom stood waiting, his thoughts were tortured by concern for the woman he loved. It was possible that if he ever discovered what had happened to Marianne Ross it would cause Katharine more pain. He mounted his horse, nodded to his groom to follow and set his mind to the task ahead. And then a smile of content touched his mouth. At least his daughter was safe and happy with a woman who loved her. For the moment he was pleased to have it so. One day he might tell her his story, but he must get to know Eliza and give her reason to trust him before he claimed her as his own. He would make certain her future was secure and, who knows, perhaps he could do as much for Katharine's sister.

Eliza looked around her bedroom and felt the comfort and pleasure it brought her to be home. This *was* her home, for some years to come at least, and she knew that it was where she needed to be while she grew and learned. Miss Edith was her mentor and her friend and she loved her. Ruth had been the only mother she'd ever known, and she would always love her. Two women in her life and both dear to her – and yet there was a third.

Somewhere there was a woman who had given her birth. Would Eliza ever know her? She realised it was almost impossible, because of all the years that had passed. No one had ever visited her or sent word or even asked . . . There were many reasons why a woman might abandon her baby, but if her mother had loved Eliza, surely she would have kept her, however hard her life was?

Eliza shook her head as she removed her clothes. She had bathed earlier and Miss Edith had found her some new clothes. She pulled back the clean sheets, which smelled of lavender, and slipped into bed, leaning over to turn down the oil lamp. It no longer mattered who was her birth mother. She was safe here and she had people who loved and cared for her. Why waste her time thinking of the past when she had a wonderful future ahead of her?

Eliza knew that Miss Edith's cures helped sick people and what better way was there to live than making life a little easier for others? Eliza would take care of Miss Edith and learn all she had to teach her, and she would do what she could to help those less fortunate than she. And one day perhaps Joe would come back, but that was for the future . . .

IF YOU ENJOYED THIS BOOK,
THEN DISCOVER SOME OF
CATHY'S OTHER GRIPPING NOVELS...

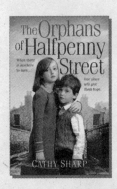

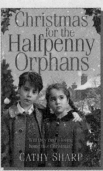

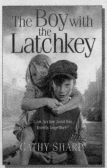

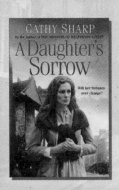

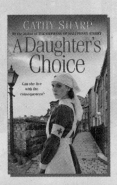